The Other Half of My Heart

♡

ALSO BY SUNDEE T. FRAZIER

Brendan Buckley's Universe and Everything in It

The Other Half of My Heart

☀ ♡ ☾

Sundee T. Frazier

DELACORTE PRESS

All rights reserved. Published in the United States by Delacorte Press, an imprint of Random House Children's Books, a division of Random House, Inc., New York.

Delacorte Press is a registered trademark and the colophon is a trademark of Random House, Inc.

Visit us on the Web! www.randomhouse.com/kids

Educators and librarians, for a variety of teaching tools, visit us at www.randomhouse.com/teachers

Library of Congress Cataloging-in-Publication Data
Frazier, Sundee Tucker.
The other half of my heart / Sundee T. Frazier.—1st ed.
p. cm.
Summary: Twin daughters of interracial parents, eleven-year-olds Keira and Minni have very different skin tones and personalities, but it is not until their African American grandmother enters them in the Miss Black Pearl Preteen competition in North Carolina that red-haired and pale-skinned Minni realizes what life in their small town in the Pacific Northwest has been like for her more outgoing, darker-skinned sister.

ISBN 978-0-385-73440-0 (alk. paper) — ISBN 978-0-385-90446-9 (lib. bdg.)
— ISBN 978-0-375-89663-7 (e-book)

[1. Racially mixed people—Fiction. 2. Twins—Fiction. 3. Sisters—Fiction.
4. Identity—Fiction. 5. African Americans—Fiction. 6. Prejudices—Fiction. 7. Beauty contests—Fiction. 8. Grandmothers—Fiction.] I. Title.
PZ7.F8715Ot 2010
[Fic]—dc22
2009013209

The text of this book is set in 12-point Goudy.

Book design by Trish Parcell Watts

Printed in the United States of America
10 9 8 7 6 5 4 3 2 1
First Edition

For my precious pearls,
Skye Lettiann and Umbria Mae

Chapter One

Minni's heart soared as the small plane's wheels lifted from the ground. She loved being up in the clouds with Keira, Mama and Daddy, looking down on the lush carpet of evergreens, the never-ending blue-gray ocean, and the rugged mountain peaks. Gliding, like a bird on the wind.

Keira sank her nails into Minni's arm. It hurt, but Minni didn't pull away. It wasn't often that *she* got to be the brave one.

People who didn't know Keira thought she wasn't afraid of anything. After all, she'd been the first person on the Jefferson County gymnastics team, boy or girl, to execute a double front flip without a trampoline.

But Minni knew her sister better than anyone, and after reading out loud in front of others, Keira's next greatest fear was of riding in the tiny single-engine plane. She only ever got into Daddy's Cessna 172 out of loyalty—because she prized being together as a family more than she feared falling from the sky. She had told Minni this when they were curled up in their giant zipped-together sleeping bags, lying under the stars on the back deck, listening to the ocean waves pound the rocks like the earth's heartbeat.

The engine's rumble filled Minni's head, and her chest vibrated along with its purring. The crowded space inside the four-seater smelled like gasoline. Daddy must have spilled some fuel on his pants or hands, which were covered in grease more often than not. Mama said the skin under Daddy's nails had been permanently turned black. "Just like half my heart," he would always reply.

The plane bumped over a rough patch of air, and Keira's nails dug in a little deeper. Mama's voice crackled through Minni's headset. "The Sisters are out today." She pointed to the Olympic range.

The two mountains were actually called the Brothers, but their family called them the Sisters. They stood side by side, connected at the hip. The taller one the family had dubbed Minni, and the shorter one was Keira. Minni gazed at the twin peaks, dusted with patches of snow even in late June.

"Just in time for our story," Daddy said. This was their tradition. Every year on June twenty-third, for as long as Minni could remember—first, pastrami and pickle sand-wiches at Jerry's, and then, a spin in Daddy's plane. Their destination was always the same: Forks, Washington. And along the way, they heard The Story.

2

"The day you were born," Daddy said, "you made news around the world."

Mama didn't much like talking about it, even though it had turned out to be the best day of her life, seeing that she'd gotten Minni and Keira in the end. To her it was a tragedy narrowly escaped, but to Daddy it was an escap*ade*, an adventure, the way Daddy saw everything in life.

After so many years, Mama must have decided it was okay. She didn't even say, "Oh, Gordon, do you have to?"

Daddy liked to say the crazy in him called out to the cautious in Mama, and the steady in Mama called out to the roller coaster in him, and that was how they got together. "The day you were born," Daddy continued, "the crazy won over the cautious."

Minni looked out at the mountains and listened to Daddy tell them again how she and her twin sister had come into the world, exactly eleven years ago.

It was a clear day, one of those days when the sky is so blue you wish the world would tip upside down so you could fall into the heavens and splash around. Those days were rare where they lived on the Olympic Peninsula—that part of Washington State that stuck out into the Pacific Ocean like a giant crab claw—which was why Daddy had wanted to take Mama flying in the first place. "Might be our last chance for a while," he said.

So Mama climbed into Daddy's plane even though the babies inside her were only six weeks from being due. Her stomach was too big to fit in the front seat, so she got in the back and Daddy flew her around like a chauffeur in the sky.

Mama had rubbed on her belly as if it were a magic lantern. Through the headphones, Daddy heard her telling her babies not to worry, that every little thing would be all right.

"It was the sun and moon told me," Mama said. "I knew things would work out because they were in the sky together that day—just like my babies were together inside me." It was good luck, she said, and was why Keira got named after the sun and Minni got the middle name Lunette, which meant "little moon."

When Mama's stomach started feeling funny, she didn't tell Daddy right away. She thought it was the pastrami and pickle she'd eaten before they took off. Or her body getting used to the lighter air thousands of feet above solid ground. Or the banked turn Daddy was making when she felt those first, hard squeezes.

But it wasn't the sandwich or the air or the turn.

"You were ready to come into the world," Daddy said. "Didn't matter to you that your mama was six thousand feet up."

"It was Keira," Minni said, elbowing her sister in the side. Keira had finally released her grip and held Minni's hand instead. "She was the one in a rush."

"I just wanted to give Daddy the chance to be a hero." Keira grinned and batted her eyelashes at Daddy.

"But you made sure not to come out first." Minni narrowed her eyes, even though she wasn't really mad at her sister about that.

When Mama finally faced the facts and told Daddy that it was time for the girls to be born, they were too far from Port Townsend to go back.

It had also turned gray, and Mama wasn't so sure anymore that every little thing would be all right. The sun and moon had disappeared and it was raining, and their plane bounced like a ball on the water, and Mama yelled at Daddy, "Get this thing down!" and Daddy said, "You don't have to yell," because they were wearing the headsets, and Mama yelled, "Yes I do!" and Daddy didn't say any more. He just got the plane down.

Daddy had to land them on the tiny airstrip in Forks, the rainiest town in the continental United States. One hundred and twenty inches of rain a year. Ten feet! Put that all together, and Minni and Keira could do their stunt where Keira stood on Minni's shoulders, and all you'd see would be Keira's tight black curls floating on the water.

The rest of the story was that Daddy got them down before they made their grand entrance, but just barely. He had sent an urgent message to Forks's air traffic control. The ambulance's flashing red lights cut through the gray air as the plane bumped to the ground. They were born in the backseat of Daddy's Cessna 172. Mama was too far along in the process, and nothing and nobody was going to make her get out.

In the end, it was a good thing Minni and Keira came when they did. Keira's cord was wrapped tightly around her neck. Mama joked Keira had been practicing her gymnastics in her belly and got tangled up in it. Minni's theory was that her sister had done a last-second backflip to avoid being born first and getting The Name. *Minerva*. After Grandmother Johnson, who had somehow gotten Mama to agree to the idea.

Mama always tried to make Minni feel better by reminding her that her name meant "goddess of wisdom." It never worked. If only their grandmother had been named Jacqueline or Samantha or Coretta . . .

Keira, which meant "sun" in Persian, was given the middle name Sol—"sun" in Spanish—so between her two names, she was one big fireball. Daddy also liked the name because it sounded like "soul" and they could tell the way she came out kicking and screaming—in spite of the cord— that she would have plenty of that.

Whatever the reason, Minni had come out first, staring with big blue eyes at a big new world, and then Keira, squalling as if she wanted her presence to be known for miles around.

The location of their birth got them on the evening news all across the country, but what got just as much attention, if not more, was something else.

Something they'd been told all their lives didn't really mean anything.

Same Mama and Daddy. Born seven minutes apart in the back of their daddy's plane.

But Keira, with her dark curly hair and cinnamon-brown skin, was black, like their mama, while Minni, with her reddish blond hair and milky pale skin, was white, like their daddy. At least that was what the articles on the Internet said.

One-in-a-million twins.

Daddy and Mama hardly ever mentioned it, but Minni knew from the Web that people had heard about them as far away as London, England. They weren't alone, either. She had seen pictures of other twins who came out looking as different from each other as she and Keira did. There were no pictures of her and Keira on the Internet, though. Mama would never allow that.

Some people said it couldn't be true. How could two babies, one black and one white, come from the same mama? Their story had even appeared on one of those Web sites that tell whether something is a hoax . . . which of course they weren't, and the Web site said so. Minni and Keira really existed, and they really were twins, although Minni sometimes wondered herself how it had happened.

She'd asked Mama once, "Am I just white? Or am I black, too?" because when she looked at her pale skin next to her sister's and Mama's rich brown, it sure was hard to see how she could be called black.

"Of course you are," Mama said, not really answering her question. Then she rested her hand on Minni's cheek. "Your blackness is just hidden a little deeper—like a vein of gold running deep within the soil of your soul."

Mama was always pointing out that of the millions of genes that made them all human, only seven or eight told their skin what color to be. A minuscule amount, she said. A very small difference.

So that was what Minni chose to believe, even though somewhere deep inside her brain, in a little drawer she rarely let herself open, lived the concern that the difference she'd

7

been assured didn't matter actually mattered a lot. That what she'd been told was small might be enormous. Not here, with her family in the sky. Never here. But somewhere. Maybe even everywhere except here.

A tingle ran down Minni's spine as Daddy dipped the right wing and circled over Forks. She squeezed her sister's hand and made an early birthday wish: *May nothing ever, ever come between Keira and me.* Nothing—*big* or *small*.

Chapter Two

Minni's mood plummeted as the plane touched down back home. As much as she loved life here in Port Townsend, it was always hard to leave the sky.

Daddy turned the Cessna toward the small airport. Minni's spirits sank even further when she saw the man with the rough red nose standing in the doorway of their shared hangar. He chewed on the end of his cigar. As usual, his eyes stuck to her family like magnets to metal.

"They both yours?" he'd asked once when Minni and Keira had come with Daddy to fly into Seattle for the day.

"Since the moment they were conceived!" Daddy replied.

"They got the same mama?"

Keira's hands flew to her hips. "You ever heard of twins coming from different mamas?"

The man's cigar had practically dropped from his mouth.

Daddy just smiled. Then he took them up into the air where they could be free.

As much as Minni didn't like the staring, she was used to it. Seemed like people stared at them everywhere they went. The locals all knew them, but Port Townsend was a major tourist destination on the Peninsula, and Minni had seen plenty of gawkers, as if their family was one of the small town's attractions.

Even in Seattle, where they went to visit the aquarium or ride the ferries and eat greasy fish and chips on the waterfront, people sometimes stared. Mama and Daddy would hold hands, and if there was room on the sidewalk, Minni would grab Mama's hand and Keira would grab Daddy's. They'd walk down the street looking like a chessboard row. The inseparable Kings.

Minni knew people were just trying to figure her family out—how they fit together—since they weren't all the same color like most families. But she still wished there weren't quite so much staring.

Today she ignored the man with the cigar, grasped her sister's hand, and swung it all the way to the parking lot.

Back in the car, zooming toward home, they belted out "Lean on Me" at the top of their lungs. Minni and Keira took turns leaning into each other—as far as they could with their seat belts on.

They passed the big wooden sign painted in red and light

blue: WELCOME TO PORT TOWNSEND — VICTORIAN SEAPORT AND ARTS COMMUNITY. They had lived here all their lives, in this little oceanside town, where it seemed as if half the people were artists and the other half wanted to be.

Mama was no wannabe. She was the real deal. Acrylics, watercolors, even fiber arts. She and twenty-some other artisans operated a collective shop in town called the Water Street Gallery.

"I need to make a quick stop at the food co-op," Mama said. "We're out of milk. And we can't have our birthday cake later tonight without milk!" She smiled over her shoulder.

Daddy pulled into the parking lot and Mama ran in. Her tightly twisted locks bounced with each step. Across the street stood the Family Veterinary Center, which also operated the local animal shelter. Minni had gone in this past week and asked if she could volunteer. She'd be helping feed and care for the animals three times a week once she got trained. She couldn't wait.

A few minutes later, Mama returned, carton in hand, and they headed for home.

In the kitchen, Minni ignored the blinking light on the answering machine and got herself two cookies from the cookie jar. She climbed into a chair at the kitchen island.

Keira ran straight in and pressed the message button. The recording played. "Lizette, it's your mother."

Keira's lips twisted in disappointment. "As if you wouldn't recognize *that* voice," she muttered, taking the milk from Mama and pouring a glass.

Grandmother Johnson's voice was pointed, like a newly sharpened pencil. "Call me immediately. It's urgent. And happy birthday to the girls. I assume they got my card." *Click*.

Mama sighed. "Now what? I swear, that woman should have gone into theater instead of education." Even after more than twenty years in the Pacific Northwest, Mama's lilting voice still hinted at the fact that she wasn't from around there. She sat kitty-corner from Minni and flipped through her new copy of *Art & Design* magazine.

Daddy pulled out the whole package of cookies from the jar and put them on the island. "Aren't you going to call? She said it was urgent."

"You know what that means," Mama said, not looking up from the page.

"Yeah, one of her prize flowers got bugs and she can't enter it in the biggest show of the century." Keira grabbed a cookie and dunked it in her milk.

Bugs *had* been the emergency once—as if Mama could do anything about it from four thousand miles away. Or would know what to do if she could. Another time it had been raccoons in the trash. Grandmother Johnson also seemed to have a lot of health issues. Last fall she'd gotten something called gout in her big toe, which had required minor surgery. More recently, it was some kind of intestinal trouble.

"I'll be in our bedroom, in case anyone *important* calls," Keira said, heading for the hallway with her milk and cookies.

"Hey, young lady, she's still your grandmother. Show some respect." Mama raised her eyes to meet Keira's.

"A-l-l-l right," Keira groaned. She disappeared down the hall.

"You're not exactly walking your talk," Daddy said.

Mama narrowed her eyes at him, but she didn't argue. "Little Moon, hand me the phone. Please."

Minni hopped down and grabbed the phone from its cradle. Mama pushed the buttons slowly, still reading her magazine.

Minni stayed to listen. As snooty as Grandmother Johnson could be, she had a certain mystique. She reminded Minni of Gigi's antique German clock. The one under the glass dome their other grandmother kept on her mantel. Minni could stand forever and watch that clock's wheels and sprockets spinning. She wanted to understand how it all fit together—literally, what made it tick—and how it kept time so precisely. If Grandmother Johnson was anything, she was complicated, just like that clock.

"Mother? What's wrong?"

Grandmother Johnson's voice pierced the air but Minni couldn't make out what she was saying.

"No, I suppose you didn't say something was wrong." Mama rolled her eyes at Daddy, pressed the phone between her ear and shoulder and went to the sink to fill her glass. "Okay, so what's urgent?"

Their grandmother was also extremely precise.

Mama put her drink on the counter and grasped the phone with her hand again. She stood silently, looking out

the window over the sink. When she turned, the skin between her eyebrows was wrinkled. She pinched the bridge of
her flat, triangular nose, the way she often did when talking
to her mom. "We've already discussed this. I agreed to let
them participate when they turn twelve. They just turned
eleven." Mama reached for a cookie. Normally, Mama didn't
eat junk food, but Grandmother Johnson, a large woman
who liked to throw her weight around, often drove her to do
things she wouldn't normally do.

"Black Pearls of America is a fine organization. I was a
part of it. Yes, I know the girls stand to gain by participat-
ing. But why—"

Keira came running down the hall in her socks and slid
into the kitchen. "Is she talking about the pageant?" she
asked Minni excitedly. She'd pulled her thick, tight curls
into two pompons, like Mickey Mouse ears. Afro puffs, they
called them in their house.

Minni shrugged. She hoped not. They'd been hearing
about Miss Black Pearl Preteen since they were six. From
Grandmother Johnson, of course—not Mama so much, although she had competed in Miss Black Pearl of America as
a teenager.

"Okay. All right. I'll think about it and get back to you
tomorrow morning. Would you like to talk to the girls?"

Keira and Minni shook their heads vigorously. Minni's
scraggly, wavy hair, which she tended to wear in two low
ponytails with wispy bangs, flickered at the corners of her
eyes like flames.

"Yes, they heard your message." Mama paused. "Don't

worry. *If* I agree to this, and that's a big if, I'll tell them all about it." Another pause. "Oh, they'll be prepared, all right. Believe me, if there were anything I'd want, it'd be for them to be prepared. Goodbye, Mother." She turned off the phone and handed it to Keira.

"Is it about the pageant?" Keira asked, handing the phone to Minni. Minni returned the phone to its place.

"Mother says the Black Pearl organization is struggling financially and they may not be able to continue the preteen division of the competition after this year. She wants you to come for this summer's program so you don't have to wait until you're thirteen."

Minni's heart sank.

Mama muttered to Daddy, "As if that would be the worst thing in the world."

In a flash, Keira was at Mama's side, pulling on the crook of her arm. "Can we please, Mom? Can we, can we?"

"I don't know if I buy it," Mama said, leaning against the sink. "Black Pearls of America is an institution in the black community. They've been going strong for over sixty years. They say they're not exclusive, but it's always been a club of rich, successful families—and social climbers, like Mother. They should be rolling in money. In fact, I seem to recall reading they bought a new headquarters building—some old plantation in Raleigh—just a few years ago."

"Maybe they overextended themselves," Daddy suggested.

"Who cares?" Keira cried. "Mom, we *have* to go!"

Minni stood on Mama's other side. "What about our

camping trip with the troop?" Keira might not have liked camping in general, but even she looked forward to their annual Girl Scout getaway because it meant another opportunity to earn a badge.

"That's not until August," Mama said. "The pageant is next month."

"But—the animal shelter! I'm volunteering there three days a week starting next month. Remember?"

"You'd only be gone ten days," Mama said. "I'm sure the shelter would let you start when you came back."

"But I don't *want* to start when I come back. I don't want to go anywhere!" Minni slumped against the counter. "Especially not to compete in a dumb pageant."

Keira rushed to Minni and grabbed her hand. "It's not just a pageant, Skinny! It's a *scholarship* program. I've looked it up online. You could win money for school!"

Minni's stomach churned at the thought of having to perform in front of hundreds of strangers. What in the world would she do for a talent? Somehow she didn't think dog impersonations would go over very well with a bunch of rich, successful people.

She looked at Keira. "You really want to stay with Grandmother Johnson for ten whole days?"

The last and only time they had visited North Carolina they had been six years old. Minni still remembered the sour taste of the buttermilk Grandmother Johnson made her drink when she complained of a stomachache. Minni had been sure their grandmother's awful cooking had made her sick in the first place, and she didn't understand in the least how drinking something even more awful was supposed to make her feel better.

"As long as we're there together—yes!" Keira lowered her voice. "Come on, Minni. We won't let her get to us." She hugged herself and twirled, shouting, "We get to be in a *pa*-geant! We get to be in a *pa*-geant!" She bounced around the kitchen. The Afro puffs bounced along with her.

Minni climbed into her chair and covered her ears.

"Slow down, missy. You seem to be forgetting that you had a previous commitment for this summer as well." Mama's hand was on her hip.

Keira's bounce went flat. Her forehead wrinkled.

"Tutoring?" Mama reminded her.

Keira frowned. A few months ago, she'd been diagnosed with severe dyslexia. If it hadn't been for Mama fighting with the school for its lack of intervention earlier, Keira might have been staying in fifth grade. Instead, Mama and the school had agreed on a summer tutoring plan to help her catch up and get prepared for next year.

"Maybe now would be a good time to tell your mother," Daddy said. "Didn't she help kids with reading challenges in her classroom?"

Mama crossed her arms. "It's hard to imagine her doing so with much tolerance or compassion."

Keira's face lit up. "I know! Minni can tutor me while we're there. We'll read together every night."

Minni looked at Mama and shook her head. Of course she wanted to help her sister however she could, but not by being her tutor. She already felt guilty that Keira struggled so hard with reading while she zipped through books.

"Come on, Skinny," Keira pleaded with puppy-dog eyes. She squeezed Minni's arm. "You tutor kids in reading all the time at school and at the library."

"That's different. They're not my sister."

Keira ignored her. "I'll help you get through the pageant, and you can help me with reading. I don't care *what* I have to do." She grabbed the slim Jefferson County phone book and thrust it into the air. "I'll read anything!"

Daddy chimed in again. "You know, it might not be such a bad thing for them to spend some time with your mom . . . without you."

Minni was starting to feel outnumbered.

Mama raised an eyebrow. She looked a lot like Grandmother Johnson when she did that, although Minni would never dare mention it. "What's that supposed to mean?"

"I just mean it might be a different atmosphere." He folded his arms and gripped his large biceps. "A little less . . . hostile." He looked at Mama sheepishly, then moved to squeeze her in his arms. "Who knows? Maybe they'd see sides of her that are harder for you to see, being her daughter and all."

Mama pulled away. "Shoot, I've known that woman since the day I was born. Believe me, I've seen all the sides."

Daddy grabbed her hand. His voice took on an edge of excitement. "It'd be *good* for them to learn more about your family, and I bet Minerva has some great stories in that steel-trap mind of hers. They've certainly heard plenty from my mom about their German-Irish roots."

Uh-oh. He was using the roots argument. Mama's weak spot. The last time Mama's best friend had visited from Atlanta, Minni had overheard Mama say she was worried her daughters weren't learning enough about their black roots, getting enough exposure to black people, but she had a hard time imagining leaving this community, where her art had actually grown a following. "I think about moving the girls, and then the summer comes around and it's like Port Townsend turns into New York City. That's how good the arts are here," she'd told Denise.

Denise told Mama to move them to Atlanta. "There's a whole lot more black people down there than in this Podunk town where there's approximately *two*. They'd buy your art." Denise saying two and not three had made Minni wonder about herself again, whether she was actually black, since there were at least Mama, Keira and her. But she never said anything because Mama was not a big supporter of listening in on conversations that were none of your business.

Daddy munched on another cookie. "Your mother may not be the first place you'd vote to send them, but at least you know she's not going to let them just do whatever they want," he said through a mouthful of crumbs.

That was the understatement of the year.

"Really, she's not that bad." *Munch-munch.*

Mama put her hand on her hip. "You seem to be

forgetting what she thinks about you—not 'good enough' for her daughter because you never went to college? Remember that?"

"They'll be having fun and making friends." *Crunch*.

Keira leaned into Daddy, looking up at him with an appreciative smile.

Daddy put his arm around Keira and returned the grin. "And—not that we would *ever* ship our kids off for our convenience—but you've been saying you need to get some concentrated time to work. You know that commission for the Seattle Public Library you were thinking about going after?"

Daddy was really making his case. If Minni didn't speak up soon . . .

Mama inhaled deeply. She looked back and forth between them, then blew out her breath. "I don't know. Maybe . . ."

Keira hollered with glee and grabbed Daddy around the middle, then scooted to Mama and hugged her, too. Minni's hands hung limply at her sides. Ten days of her summer— more like two whole weeks when you counted the preparation they'd have to do—*down the drain*. She had thought she had a whole year to figure out how to get out of this pageant thing. Keira was the performer—the one who loved the spotlight—not her.

"I can't!" Minni cried.

Mama, Daddy and Keira stared from the other side of the island.

"I can't get up in front of a bunch of strangers and talk

and dance and walk around in a silly, frilly, long dress." Her stomach quivered at the thought.

Mama put out her hand. "Come here, Little Moon."

Minni slid off her chair and walked over. She let Mama put her arm around her. "What do you always say is the best thing about your name?"

It was the *only* good thing about her name. MLK. "I share initials with one of the greatest people ever to live."

"That's right. Dr. Martin Luther King, Jr. And who do you say you want to be like when you grow up?"

"Dr. King."

"Dr. King spoke to hundreds of thousands of people, you know."

"Not in a silly, frilly, long dress, he didn't."

Mama and Daddy laughed.

Minni crossed her arms. "Anyway, that's not how I want to be like him. I just mean I want to make the world a better place for everyone to live." Which, of course, meant animals, too. "That's all."

"Oh, that's all, is it?" Mama smiled, revealing the gap between her two front teeth. Her widely spaced, round eyes were the color of root beer in a glass held up to sunlight. Tiny raised moles dotted her gingery brown cheeks. "That's enough, baby. But do you think maybe, just maybe, to accomplish your goal of a better world for all, you might need to speak up occasionally? I mean, in front of other people?"

Minni did not appreciate how Mama was taking her

dreams and aspirations and twisting them into the reason she needed to compete in a stupid pageant. She looked away.

Keira grabbed Minni's hand. "Come on, Skinny. It'll be fun."

"It will be for *you*. You're a natural." Minni's eyes stung. She was going to cry. "I'll be lucky if I don't trip over my own feet!" She pulled away and fled down the hall, brushing a hot tear from her cheek.

Chapter Three

In their bedroom, Minni's parakeet, Bessie Coleman, fluttered her wings and flew to the cage door. Minni fell on her bed, her back to the bird. She gazed at the mural of Mount Rainier Mama had painted on her wall. Daddy had climbed the mountain on his fortieth birthday. Minni planned to make it to the top long before she got that old.

The wooden floor creaked as someone stepped into the room. The bed dipped under Daddy's solid frame. Daddy was as tall and strong as a hundred-year-old pine tree. His arms were the branches to which Minni always escaped whenever she was afraid or unsure.

His heavy hand rested on her arm. "Where's my girl with the sense of adventure? The one who wants to climb Mount Rainier and learn to fly an airplane? The one who wants to roam the jungles of South America and observe animals in their natural habitats?"

"I still want to do all those things," Minni mumbled.

"But you're scared to be in a pageant where you have the opportunity to meet other girls and have some fun? Maybe even win some scholarship money?"

She turned her head to look at him. "I'm not scared—"

Daddy stroked his stubbly chin and nodded his strawberry blond head. "I see . . . ."

"Okay, maybe I am a little, but I just don't see the point in spending a bunch of time doing something that I'm not going to be any good at."

Daddy's eyes widened. "Whoa! Wait a minute. Did you really just say what I think you did?"

What had she said wrong? She was just being honest.

"Did you know you would be the school spelling bee champion before you competed?"

"Yes," Minni said. "Well, I thought I could be, anyway."

"Okay, did you know your poem would win a state honor before you wrote it?"

Minni rolled onto her back and crossed her arms. "I'm not going to win anything in a pageant. I'm sure of that."

"What if the point isn't to win anything? What if the point is to prove to yourself you can do it and learn something from the process?"

Bessie Coleman whistled. "Daddy's cool!" the bird said.

"Hey, whose side are you on?" Minni scowled. Daddy came into their room every day to reinforce that phrase, which Minni didn't mind—she wanted her parakeet to learn as many words as possible—but right now, her pet was just trying to get her father's attention, and *that* was annoying.

"You know, when I was a kid, I never won a thing. Not a spelling bee title or an award for a poem. Heck, I didn't get a single A my entire time in school, not even in metal shop."

"Not even in *gym?*"

"I missed too many days. I never liked school. When Keira was diagnosed with dyslexia, I realized why. Did you know I've never read an entire book?"

"In your whole life?"

"In my whole life."

Now that Minni thought about it, she'd never seen Daddy with a book in his hands. Not even a magazine. "But didn't you have to read to get your pilot's license?"

"I did like Keira and memorized the important words. Mostly I just listened to the instructors and the other guys in the program, and I watched carefully what they were doing. I learned by actually flying—first the simulators and then the real thing."

"Does Mama know?"

"She does now—since we found out what Keira's been dealing with. But I'd never told anyone before then. I was too embarrassed. Proud—and stubborn—like your sister. Your mom just figured I didn't like reading because I'm more of a hands-on kind of guy."

Minni considered Daddy's face—his sparkling sky-blue eyes under reddish blond eyebrows; his skin, pinkened from the sun and covered with so many freckles it looked as if he'd gone dune-buggy riding wearing goggles and everything except the circles around his eyes was dirt-speckled; his nose, long like Keira's, except Daddy's was bent from a break he'd suffered playing Rollerblade hockey; and his closed-lip smile, warm and kind. "Daddy? If I do the pageant . . . will you read a book?"

Daddy's eyebrows pulled together. "Hmmm. I'd have to think about that. I'm not sure I could hold up my end of the bargain."

"Me either. I *really* don't like talking in front of people."

Daddy put his hand on her crossed arms. "But . . . I'm willing to try."

Minni pushed herself up, feeling suddenly excited. "I know! I could help you—like Keira wants me to do with her." She grimaced, then quickly brightened again. "We could read it together!" She grinned.

Now Daddy showed his straight, white teeth. He and Keira had the same perfect smile, while Minni had gotten Mama's crooked teeth. She would probably be fitted with braces later this year, just as Mama had been as a girl. "Only if you pick the book."

Minni hugged Daddy's tree-trunk middle.

"But make it a good one. Maybe something with pirates, or airplanes. Not too many fairy princesses or silly, frilly, long dresses. Deal?"

She squeezed him harder. "Deal."

"Love you," Daddy said.

"Love you," Bessie Coleman twittered.

"Love you, too," Minni replied.

Chapter Four

The next day, Mama called Grandmother Johnson and told her Minni and Keira were coming. Grandmother Johnson would pay for the plane tickets as a birthday present and arrange the flights. They'd leave in a week and return approximately ten days later. Just like that, it was done.

"Okay," Mama said, after hanging up the phone. "Let's see what we have to do to get you girls ready for this pageant."

The three of them went to Minni and Keira's bedroom, where Keira had the Black Pearls of America Web site up in a matter of seconds.

The pageant had grown since Mama's day. They now had one contest for preteens aged eleven and twelve, another for girls thirteen to fifteen, and another for girls sixteen to eighteen, the age Mama had been when she had competed.

The program was only open to active Black Pearls or "legacy members," which was why Minni and Keira could be considered—because Mama had been a member. There were no state prelims, just the national contests. The applications served as the screening process, although Mama said anyone who met the membership criteria and put down the sponsorship money was basically guaranteed the opportunity to participate.

"Here's the application." Keira clicked on a link and a document opened.

Minni pointed to the screen. "This says the deadline has already passed." She tried not to sound too happy.

"What?" Keira cried. Apparently she hadn't taken the time to read any details.

"Mother assures me she's gotten an extension from the director. She said to bring the completed forms with you and she'll hand-deliver them to the Black Pearls office."

"Oh," Minni said.

"Yeah!" Keira printed a copy for each of them. "Maybe the old lady's not so bad after all."

Mama's lips turned down at the corners but she didn't say anything. Keira picked up the papers from the printer and handed one set to Minni and one to Mama. "What else does it say?"

"Let's go to the table and work on it together," Mama said. "Bring some extra paper to write out your answers and then you can copy them onto the application."

Minni got the extra paper while Keira picked through her pencil holder, obviously searching for the perfect writing implement. She pulled out her purple gel pen.

Minni grabbed a chewed-up, blue ballpoint and followed Keira and Mama to the dining room. Daddy was sitting in the living room watching his favorite TV program—a reality show about fishermen braving the dangers of life aboard a boat in the Arctic Ocean.

At the table, Minni stared at the application. She couldn't believe she was actually going through with this. She glanced at Daddy, sprawled in the comfy leather chair with his feet on the ottoman. A deal was a deal.

She read the words across the top of the page: "Miss Black Pearl Preteen National Achievement Program." She knew that firstborns were supposed to be the achievers, and she had won a few things—Student of the Month, the spelling bee, that state award for her poem.

But Keira . . . Keira was *driven* to succeed. Every time she got another gold medal at a gymnastics competition, or when she sold the most cookies of any Girl Scout in all five states of their region, or when she entered the national fashion design contest and won honorable mention, Minni was convinced all over again that Keira was supposed to have come out first.

She forced herself to look beyond the name of the contest to the information they wanted. Name, address, e-mail, birthday, grade level, school, parents' names. Basic stuff. She supposed she could fill out that much.

She wrote in her first name—Minni, not Minerva, of course. Then middle—she wrote the whole thing because she liked it okay, even if Eddie Moldanado had found out it was Lunette and told all the boys to call her Minni Lunatic. And finally, her last name, which she wrote in all capital letters because it was the best part of her name—being the same as Dr. King's—and because it just seemed to want to be written big and bold like that: KING.

She filled in her address, 1907 Bluff Drive, Port Townsend, Washington, then her e-mail address—Flyer Girl10@quikmail.com—and their birthday, June 23. Sixth grade. Crawford Elementary. Gordon and Lizette King.

Her eyes dropped to the next line. Grade average. Her heart thumped a little harder. The application only listed four options—and they weren't A, B, C, and D. They were A+, A, B+, B. The instructions said to circle one.

What was someone like Keira supposed to do?

It reminded Minni of the form she'd filled out when she tested for the Hi-Cap—or "high capability"—program this spring. The form listed six options for race and told her to choose one. Should she choose black or white? "Other" was an option, but she wasn't "other." She was black *and* white. She'd skipped it.

When she'd turned in the form, the woman said, "You missed one," and pointed to the race question.

"I didn't know what to put," Minni said.

The woman glanced at her, then marked "White."

"But I'm not just white," Minni said, suddenly hot and flustered.

"It doesn't really matter. It's just government stuff." The woman's voice turned bright and cheery. "Now, ready for the test?"

Minni focused again on the Miss Black Pearl application and the four grade options listed. She looked to where Keira and Mama sat side by side. Keira was still on their school name.

"Mama," she said.

Mama looked up.

Minni turned the application and pointed to the question.

Mama took the paper and read where Minni had pointed. Her lips pulled to the side. She glanced at Keira, then handed back the application. "Go ahead and circle your answer."

"But what's Keira going to do?" She had gotten a C average this year.

Keira's head snapped up. "About what? What's wrong?"

"It's not a big deal," Mama said.

"What's not a big deal?"

"They want our grade average," Minni said.

Keira searched the paper for what they were talking about. "Why do they only list four options?"

"I'm not sure," Mama said. "But don't worry. Academics is only one criterion they use for judging."

Keira looked crushed. "What if they have a rule about grades? What if they won't let me compete?" Her voice rose anxiously.

Minni felt herself getting anxious, too. There was no way she would do this without Keira.

Daddy walked into the room. "How're my beauty queens?" He kissed the top of Keira's lamb's-wool head.

"I'm no queen," Minni protested. "I'll always be a *King*."

Even if she ever got married—and that was a big if—she was keeping her last name. Now, *Minerva,* on the other hand . . .

"You have to have a B average or higher!" Keira wailed.

"What? Is that true?" Daddy looked at Mama.

"If things are still the same as when I participated, they don't exclude anyone based on grades, but they give extra points to girls with higher ones."

"But what if you have a learning disability?" Minni asked, feeling suddenly defensive about her sister.

"I don't know, but let's not worry about it. For now, we'll just leave it blank."

Minni knew what happened when you did that. It *didn't* make the question go away.

That evening, at Daddy's insistence, Mama pulled out a box from the bottom of a big stack in the closet. Mama wasn't one for taking strolls down memory lane. Minni had only seen a few pictures from when she was a girl.

Minni, Keira and Daddy sat on the couch craning to see as Mama leafed through her high school scrapbook. They saw a program from a play in which Mama had played the lead—the famous track athlete Wilma Rudolph, the first American woman to win three gold medals in a single Olympics, even though as a young girl she had walked with braces after having polio.

In the picture from Mama's junior prom, her date, a boy with chocolate-brown skin, wore a tuxedo with an electric-blue bow tie and cummerbund to match her satin dress.

"Do you have a *perm* in your hair?" Keira exclaimed. Minni had always been intrigued by the fact that a "perm" meant opposite things to blacks and whites. For black women, it meant having their hair chemically straightened, while white women got perms to put *in* curls.

"That was before I was liberated," Mama said. "Your grandmother has always been a devoted chemical user. I got my first perm when I was twelve. Mother saw it as an important 'rite of passage' and the key to my future social success."

Minni pointed to the boy's head. "Are those your initials shaved into his haircut?"

Mama looked closer. "Oh yeah. I had forgotten all about that." She flipped the page.

Minni and Keira looked at each other, then busted up.

"Where is the poor guy now?" Daddy asked with a wink. "Probably pining away somewhere, wondering why you dumped him." He put his arm around Mama and tickled her ribs.

Mama rolled her eyes. "I don't think so."

She found the pages with memorabilia from the Miss Black Pearl pageant. There was a program, and a small card that had come with flowers signed, "We are so proud. Mother and Gerald." Gerald Payne was Mama's stepfather, a light-skinned black man with wavy salt-and-pepper hair and a huge Adam's apple. They had only seen him in pictures—never met him. He was as skinny as a stork leg— so skinny that Minni and Keira thought he probably left their grandmother out of fear he'd be crushed if she rolled over on him during the night.

Mama said Grandmother Johnson only married him because he was an orthodontist. His profession plus her status as a teacher all but guaranteed her acceptance into some elite social organization, and, as a bonus, she could get Mama's crooked teeth straightened out for free. Mama was also convinced her mother had wanted to get herself a hyphenated last name. "More high-class and educated-sounding," Mama said, "to match her lofty view of herself."

Technically, their grandmother was still Minerva Johnson-Payne, even though she and Gerald had divorced at least fifteen years ago, but Minni and Keira just called her Grandmother Johnson. Or sometimes, Grandmother Johnson-Payne-in-the-Butt. Strictly between themselves, of course.

"Did you win anything?" Keira asked Mama.

"Miss Congeniality." Mama chuckled. She pointed to a photo of all the girls together. They stood in rows on risers. "Can you find me?"

Keira leaned over Mama's arm to get a closer look.

Minni scanned the photo from where she sat. Of course she had known Miss Black Pearl was a competition for African American girls. And because Grandmother Johnson had always talked about Minni's participation as a given, she had never questioned her right to be included—only her desire.

But now, seeing a photograph of the contestants—row after row of brown faces—it dawned on her.

Would she be included? How would the other girls see her? As one of them? Or as a white girl?

She tried to hear Mama's voice telling her she was black, too, but as Minni imagined herself up on a stage with a group of black girls whose blackness wasn't hidden—wasn't buried deep in the soil of their souls—well, she knew what would happen.

She would stand out. She would stand out too much.

Minni hated standing out.

What if the pageant people—or worse, the other girls—didn't think she belonged there?

Chapter Five

☀ ♡ ☾

Minni lay on her bed, reading the book about Martin Luther King, Jr., that Mama and Daddy had given her for her birthday. Keira had gotten a fashion design activity book that included paper, beads, ribbons and stencils to create a bazillion outfits and accessories. The kit even came with miniature hangers so you could display your finished products. They had both loved their gifts.

Minni gazed at a picture of Dr. King marching arm in arm with other civil rights leaders. All the faces in the photo were brown. What if she had been alive at that time? Would she have marched, too?

She believed she would have, if she had been old enough, but she couldn't help but wonder again—would she have stood out? How would others have seen her—as one of the black people fighting for their rights, or as a white person? White people had protested and participated in sit-ins, too. Would she have been counted among them?

Suddenly Minni wondered about Keira. Did Keira feel like she stood out at their mostly white school? In their mostly white hometown? How was it that they had never actually talked about it?

Minni knew from a school report she'd done on the 2000 census that Port Townsend was only point-six percent black, and it didn't seem to have changed much in the last ten years. There were no black families in their neighborhood—in the entire *town*, as far as Minni was aware. The handful of black children at Crawford Elementary came from interracial families, like her and Keira, or had been adopted by white couples, like Neil Moreland. Keira had been one of two dark-skinned children in their class this past year, and Sandeep was East Indian. Other years, Keira had been the only one.

Keira bounded into the room. She had sectioned the front of her hair into five or six parts, twisted the sections tightly and pinned them down. The rest of her hair flew free, surrounding her head in a curly halo. "Gigi's here! Let's go!" She grabbed the shiny red purse off her bed—the one that matched her sparkly red ballet flats—and rushed back out.

If standing out bothered Keira, she sure didn't show it. Besides, Minni would know if it did, being her twin and best friend and all. In fact, it was just one more way she and Keira were opposites. Minni avoided unwanted attention at all costs, but to Keira, "unwanted attention" was an oxymoron.

"Come *on*, Skinny!" Keira shouted. "You're holding us up!"

"Wish me luck," Minni said as she fed Bessie Coleman a sunflower seed through the cage bars.

Daddy's mama—who lived in a condo in nearby Discovery Bay, and whom they called Gigi, short for Grandma Gretchen because neither name suited her very well—was taking them twenty-five miles to Sequim, the closest big town and the only place in the area with a gown shop.

They were going shopping.

For silly, frilly, long dresses. *Yuck.*

The bird took the seed and cracked it with her beak.

Keira called down the hall. "*Min*-ni!"

When Gigi had heard about the pageant, she'd gotten so worked up about it you'd have thought it was the most exciting news she'd heard in twenty years. She'd insisted on providing the girls with their formal gowns and, of course, Marla Ray makeovers. Gigi was a Marla Ray consultant.

Minni fed her bird one more seed and slipped a plastic headband into her hair to keep it out of her eyes. "See ya later, Bessie."

"See ya!" Bessie replied.

Keira was saying goodbye to their parents in the kitchen.

"Nothing too racy," Daddy said, kissing Keira on the forehead. "You may be eleven, but that doesn't mean I've changed my mind about unchaperoned dates. Not until you're old enough to spring yourself from jail."

Keira threw back her head like always and said, "Don't be silly, Daddy."

And Mama added her usual "Don't be ridiculous, Gordon."

But Daddy just shook his head and said, "You think I'm joking. I'm not joking."

Then he saw Minni standing in the doorway, skinny as a piece of uncooked spaghetti, and said, "Same goes for you, Min. No solo flights until you're eighteen."

Minni knew he only said this because he didn't want her to feel left out or to think she wouldn't have boys calling her all the time like Keira would. But Minni was a realist. She wasn't nearly as pretty as Keira, and she knew it. She was lanky, like Daddy, with wavy red hair that frizzed in the rain, big feet and freckles—a description that sounded a bit too much like a clown. Keira was shorter, like Mama, and compact—the perfect gymnast's build—with smooth, clear skin the color of cinnamon sticks and, of course, that dazzling smile.

Fortunately, Minni didn't really care about the boy thing. The fewer boys she had calling her, the more time she'd have to read and study, which she would need to do a lot of if she wanted to get a PhD like Dr. Martin Luther King, Jr.

"Let's go!" Keira snatched Minni's arm and pulled her toward the front door.

"Have fun!" Mama called.

They went outside to Gigi's long, lavender Lincoln Continental with the white leather interior. She had won the car by selling Marla Ray cosmetics. Mama and Daddy joked that she had probably purchased most of the makeup herself—she wore so much of it.

Minni and Keira didn't care how Gigi had gotten the car. They loved to be seen driving around Port Townsend in it. They would sit in the back and pretend she was their chauffeur. "To the bead store," they would say, or, "To the ice cream shop," and she would play along and say, "Yes, my ladies. Your wish is my command."

Banjo was in front, as always. He did a few circles, then put his paws on top of the seat and panted at Minni in greeting. "Hi, boy," she said, letting him lick her mouth.

"That's so disgusting," Keira said.

Minni kissed Gigi's cheek.

"After the dog licked your lips? That's *totally* disgusting." Keira made a face.

"Gigi doesn't care." Minni slid back and fastened her seat belt.

"It's true. I don't." Gigi laughed and put the car in gear. "Put down your windows, girls. I'm taking Minni's advice about being environmentally friendly and not using the AC." She glanced at Minni in the rearview mirror, and they smiled at each other. "For *now*. The second I feel a hot flash coming, the AC's back on." She pulled the car away from the curb. "So . . . looking forward to your big trip?"

"Yes!" Keira bounced on the seat.

Minni sighed.

"Not so much, huh?" Gigi asked.

Banjo did a few more circles, jumped up on the door and stuck his head out the window.

"Minni doesn't want to go."

Minni kept her eyes on the houses they passed.

"You don't? But you get to see your other grandmother."
As if that should make her excited. "Hasn't it been a couple
years since she came out to visit?"

"She doesn't want to do the pageant."

"But why?" Gigi looked at her in the rearview mirror.
"You'll be fantastic, kiddo!"

Minni's eyes met Gigi's.

"Have you been out on your deck without sunscreen
again?" Gigi asked.

Minni looked away. "Maybe." She'd been trying to bring
out a little more color, was all. Too bad all it brought out
was more freckles. Why all her melanin had to clump together in tiny dots she would never understand. And no
matter what she tried—suntan lotion, olive oil—her skin
just turned pink in the sun, not brown.

"What have I told you about that, young lady?" Gigi's
dangling silver fan-shaped earrings with the turquoise beads
tinkled as she shook her head. "You're going to end up looking like a piece of venison jerky! Do you want to look like
you're seventy-five when you're thirty?"

She had just turned eleven and Gigi wanted her to think
about being thirty? The car kept motoring forward while
Gigi turned and looked over her shoulder. "Hmmm?"

"Look out!" Minni pointed with one hand and covered
her eyes with the other.

Gigi slammed on the brakes and Banjo shot to the floor-
board with a thud. They screeched to a stop just in time to
avoid the car in front of them. Good thing they all had their
seat belts on. Except Banjo, of course.

The dog jumped back up and licked Gigi's face.

"That's so gross," Keira said. "Why do you let him do that?"

"What can I say? He likes the taste of Marla Ray. And with our all-natural, one-hundred-percent purely botanical ingredients, it's good for him, too."

"But he's getting you all slobbery." Keira made a face.

"It keeps me cool. And when you're going through 'the change,' you need all the help you can get in that department."

Gigi was always talking about going through "the change" and how it made her hot. When they'd asked Mama what "the change" was she'd said it was an old-woman thing and they didn't need to worry about it for a long time. Gigi got offended when they told her what Mama had said. "You're only as old as you look. Do I look old to you?" Of course they knew to shake their heads no to that one. And with all the makeup she wore, and her short hair dyed as red as the sun setting on the Pacific Ocean, and her big silver and turquoise jewelry, she didn't look *that* old.

Minni often wondered what Gigi would look like without all that stuff. Would she still look like herself, or would she be someone else?

The light turned green and Gigi set Banjo on the seat.

"When I have my own fashion design company, I'll be able to help you stay cool, and it won't involve slobber," Keira said.

"How's that?" Gigi asked.

"Well, you know about global warming, right?"

"You don't even believe in global warming!" Minni said. She was the one who was always telling Keira about it, trying to get her to take shorter showers and turn off the lights in their room when she left so they'd burn less fuel and do less damage to Mount Rainier's precious glaciers.

"As I was saying . . ." Keira put her arms on the back of the front passenger seat, stretching the seat belt as far as it would go. Banjo jumped up and head-butted her. "Ow!" She fell back. "Dopey dog," she muttered.

"As you were saying . . . ," Gigi repeated.

"As I was saying," Keira said, eyeing the dog, "I'm working on a new line. I call it Global Chillin'. Get it? 'Cool fashions for a warming world.'"

Minni groaned. Leave it to Keira to take a global crisis and figure out how to make it into a new fashion fad.

Keira stared at Minni. "What? You wouldn't get so sunburned if you wore my ultrabreathable, sheer UV-protection jumpsuit and matching sun hat—in reflective silver or bronze."

"Sounds brilliant, Keira. Sheer genius!" Gigi looked back and smiled. She returned her eyes to the road just in time to avoid hitting a man crossing the street. *Screech!*

Thud. Banjo hit the floor again.

"Sorry!" Gigi yelled out the window. The man gave them a dirty look.

They weren't even out of town and they'd already almost gotten into two accidents. This trip was doomed.

Keira continued to describe her latest fashion line as they pulled onto Highway 101 and picked up speed.

Minni listened in awe. Keira was super-smart—something not all their teachers had understood, since she struggled so hard with reading. But Minni had always known her sister's intelligence, starting from when they were five and Keira had gotten the word "freedom" during a family game of Pictionary. She had drawn a picture-perfect version of the Statue of Liberty.

Banjo jumped onto the seat and stuck his head outside. His tongue flapped in the breeze. The air was warm, and fresh with the scent of evergreen. The highway skirted the Olympic National Forest. Pine trees came right up to the edge of the road, with only an occasional break for a cluster of tiny resort cabins.

At the wide spot in the road that was the "downtown" of booming Discovery Bay, they passed Fat Smitty's, a ramshackle joint with a giant plastic cheeseburger out front, and Discovery Bay Railroad—a line of parked train cars painted in pastels that served pizza and ice cream. Minni and Keira loved both places and had eaten at them with Gigi many times.

Minni was about to recommend that Keira could make her Global Chillin' line even hipper by using eco-friendly fabrics when a long string of slobber released from Banjo's mouth and flew in through Keira's rolled-down window—just as Keira opened wide to speak.

Keira practically hit the ceiling. "Ahhh! Banjo slaaah-buh im-mah mouw! Stah the cah! Stah the cah!"

"What?" Gigi said. The car careened toward the highway shoulder and Gigi jammed on the brakes.

Thud. Poor Banjo.

Keira shook her hands in front of her. They looked like rubber chickens. She scrunched her face. "Slaaah-buh!" Keira moaned. The way she was acting, you'd have thought she'd just swallowed a huge, hairy spider and not a little dog spittle. Minni stifled a giggle.

"What is she saying?" Gigi turned to look.

"Banjo slobbered . . ." Minni felt a laugh attack coming on. "In her mouth!" She stopped trying to contain her giggles and laughed so hard she snorted.

Gigi sounded like a parrot choking. "Wuh-ut!" Her shoulders jumped up and down with her guffaws.

"Thnot fuh-neh!" Keira cried.

Gigi kept laughing.

Minni put her hand over her mouth and tried hard to swallow her laughter, but she couldn't help it. It wasn't like Keira was going to die, even if she acted as if she were. Keira wiped her tongue on her shirt, then let it hang out of her mouth, as if it were a towel on a clothesline and she was trying to get it to dry.

Banjo put his paws on the seat in front of Keira. His shiny black eyes peered at her from under thick tufts of hair, and Minni swore his mouth formed a crooked little smile.

Gigi let out a big sigh. "Oh, I haven't laughed like that for ages. Whew, did that feel good!" She opened her glove box, grabbed a pile of paper napkins and handed some to Keira, who snatched them and wiped her tongue some more. Gigi took one and dabbed at her cheeks. "I knew there was a reason I reached for that waterproof mascara this morning."

Keira's eyelids lowered and her lips pooched out. "It wasn't funny," she grumbled.

"Don't be a Grumpy Gus. Banjo didn't mean to slobber in your mouth." Gigi held Banjo in the air between the front and back seats. "Did you, boy?" She waggled him so his head moved back and forth. "Say you're sorry."

Banjo barked.

"Apology accepted?" Gigi asked.

Keira glared at the dog.

"What if it had been me, Keira?" Minni said. "Wouldn't you have thought it was funny? Even just a little bit?"

Keira's mouth slid to the side of her face. She looked like Mama when she did that. "Maybe. But only a *little* bit." She ran the back of her hand over her mouth once more and shivered. "And I never, *ever* want that to happen again."

Minni put her arm around Keira's neck and squeezed. She was glad to be here, even if the last thing in the world she wanted was a silly, frilly, long dress. If she had to do this pageant, at least she'd be doing it with her twin sister.

Chapter Six

Fifteen minutes or so after what would forever be known between Gigi and Minni as The Slobber Incident, they pulled into a Sequim strip mall and parked. Keira immediately headed to the Burger Barn across the street to kill the dog germs with some fizzy cola.

Since Minni was boycotting Burger Barn (she'd read online recently about the treatment of animals sold for meat to its restaurants), she decided to start looking at dresses without them. *Might as well just get it over with*, she thought. The sooner she found something, the sooner she could rejoin Banjo in the car.

She entered the store and started walking along the rows of gowns, her hand occasionally reaching out to touch the fabrics. Satin . . . velvet . . . silk. She only knew their names because of Keira and her passion for fashion.

She reached out and touched a dress's hot pink taffeta bodice and its full tulle skirt.

Hideous.

With her pale skin and red hair . . . *No way.* Total Bozo the Ballerina.

The storekeeper, talking on the phone behind the counter, smiled and held up a finger to indicate she'd be with Minni in a moment. Her white teeth stood out against her fake-tan skin. Minni knew fake tan when she saw it. She had once taken Gigi's tube of the orange-brown stuff and rubbed it on her arms to see if she could get closer to Keira's shade.

Minni went back to her task, every once in a while pushing back a dress to take a look. The gowns pressed against one another like the books on her overcrowded bookshelf. It wasn't a bad comparison. Come to think of it, Keira read clothing like Minni read books. Everyone had a personal style statement, Keira said. What they wore spoke volumes.

Keira had dubbed Gigi's personal style Outlet Chic and Mama's Mother Africa Artiste. Minni's was Geek Chic, which Minni thought was funny. Keira had pronounced her own style Tween Haute Couture, which she always followed up with the explanation, "That means trendsetting fashions for preteens in *French.*"

The woman hung up the phone and started toward Minni. "Are you looking for something in particular, dear?"

Minni shook her head. She had no idea what she was looking for. She couldn't imagine herself in anything with sequins, puffy sleeves or a Cinderella skirt. And if she put on one of these strapless thingies there'd be nothing to keep it from falling around her ankles. If her chest were one of those maps with various colors for different elevations, it'd be all the same color.

She looked across the street to the Burger Barn. Where were Keira and Gigi? They were the experts at this stuff. Set them loose together in a mall and watch out. They approached stores as strategically as a search-and-rescue team, covering every square inch to make sure not one deal was missed. They would pile the clothes so high that they'd exceed the dressing room limit and have to leave most of them outside. Minni's task became watching the mountain of clothes and having the next ten outfits ready to go.

She pulled out a light turquoise gown that shimmered with a rainbow of colors, like the inside of an oyster. She held it up to herself and ran her hand down the full skirt.

"That would work wonderfully with your coloring." The woman stood back and looked her up and down. "Definitely. It brings out the blue in your eyes and highlights your lovely red hair." She reached for the dress. Minni handed it over. "I'll start a dressing room for you. Are you alone?"

"My grandma and sister are coming."

The woman nodded and took the dress to the back of the store.

Gigi and Keira came in the front. Keira went straight to the display window and the fire-engine red dress hanging on a mannequin.

Gigi walked toward Minni. "Find anything?"

Minni fingered the satin ribbon on a lime-green dress.

"Gigi, what if I trip and fall? Or forget what I'm supposed to say?" She had started having dreams of herself at the pageant. In one of them, when she tried to talk, all she could do was cluck like a chicken.

Gigi patted her shoulder. "Don't worry, honey. That won't happen."

The saleswoman came back. "I've started a room for your granddaughter in the back." She eyed Keira holding up a dress near the front of the store. "Excuse me!" the woman called out. She beelined toward Keira. "I'd rather you didn't handle the dresses yourself." She grabbed the gown from Keira's hands and stuffed it back onto the rack.

The woman might as well have pulled out a gun and shot it into the air. Minni's heart hammered in her chest. Her face and palms prickled with heat.

"Was she really hurting anything?" Gigi went and stood next to Keira.

"I just prefer that . . . people . . . not handle the dresses." The woman wrung her hands. "Skin oils can ruin the fabrics."

Minni held her breath. *Say something!* she shouted at herself, but she couldn't figure out what it should be. Her jaw felt locked in place.

Gigi put her arm around Keira. "Let's go, girls. I think we'll take our business elsewhere."

Keira's eyes blazed.

The woman's fake tan couldn't cover the pink flooding her cheeks.

They turned and headed for the door.

Gigi drove them toward the big indoor mall. "Never mind that rude woman," she said. "We'll find the perfect gowns— you'll see!"

"Yeah, what was up with that lady?" Keira asked. "It's not like I put the dress on the floor and stomped on it."

Minni replayed the store scene in her mind. What *had* happened back there?

One thing Minni was certain of—the woman hadn't re-alized Keira was her sister. Strangers always thought she and Keira were just friends, and they *never* believed they were twins. When they were alone with their brown-skinned mama, Minni was the "friend," and when they were with pink-skinned Daddy, it was Keira's turn.

Still, even if the woman didn't know they were related, there was no excuse for the way she had treated Keira.

A thought pushed its way into Minni's mind, even as she fought to keep it out.

She thought you were white.

So? Lots of people thought that.

She saw Keira as black.

Minni's insides tightened and coiled.

That's why she treated Keira differently.

Minni felt as though she might get sick.

They didn't return home until almost seven o'clock. They'd stopped at Fat Smitty's for cheeseburgers and fries, plus it had taken forever to find shoes. To Minni's horror, they'd had to go to the ladies' department for hers. Her feet were suddenly too big for the girls' sizes. She plopped on the couch next to Mama, limp with mall fatigue.

Keira hugged her sun-yellow sleeveless chiffon halter dress with a V neckline and buttons up the back, and spun in the center of the room. The double layer of ruffles at the hem floated upward with the breeze. "Don't you just love how the empire waist is decorated with this chiffon band gathered ever so delicately with pearl clusters?" Her face glowed with excitement. "Isn't it *breathtaking?*" She gave Gigi a big smooch.

"I told you we'd find just the right thing," Gigi said.

Keira's eyes narrowed. "No thanks to that crazy lady at the first store."

Minni stiffened. Hopefully Mama wouldn't ask.

"What crazy lady?"

Of course she would.

"All I did was take a dress off the rack to look at it. She practically ripped the thing in half grabbing it out of my hands."

"She said she didn't like people touching the dresses," Gigi said, "and she wasn't very friendly about it. So we left."

"She was rude." Keira's mouth turned down at the corners. She held the dress up again. "But, whatever, I got a way better dress than I would have found at her dumb store anyhow."

Mama listened quietly. She put her hand on Minni's knee. "What about you?"

Minni couldn't breathe. The shame she'd felt in the store

for not pointing out the lady's different treatment of her and her sister washed over her again.

"Yeah, where's your dress?" Daddy came up from behind and squeezed her shoulders.

Minni pointed to the garment bag hanging over the chair by the front door. She had chosen the least frilly dress she could find—an A-line sky-blue silk dress with a straight-across neckline and solid, sturdy straps. No pearl clusters, bows, rhinestones or fussy lace anywhere. A layer of sheer organza covered the skirt, but Minni actually liked how it made the dress shimmer like moonlight on the ocean.

"Well, let's see it!"

Holding up the dress wasn't enough. Daddy wanted a fashion show, so they went and put on the gowns. Keira zipped Minni, then found a matching pendant in her ballerina jewelry box and fastened it around Minni's neck.

Minni hoped Keira wouldn't ask how the woman had acted before she and Gigi came into the store. Then when she didn't, Minni almost told her. They never kept *anything* from each other. They were sisters, best friends—as wide open with each other as the ocean to the sky. But she just couldn't bring herself to do it. She zipped Keira's dress and they went into the hall.

Keira floated into the living room, stopped to pose at the side table topped by the framed black-and-white photo Daddy had taken of her and Minni on the beach, then whipped around and continued across the floor.

"Go on, girl. Show us what you got," Mama said.

Mama, Daddy and Gigi clapped. Banjo barked.

Keira swiveled at the opposite wall and raised her arms like a movie starlet. She stood in front of Mama's huge acrylic painting of purple, orange and red starfish, looking very dramatic. She batted her eyelashes. Even Banjo got a smile.

"Your turn, Little Moon," Mama said, looking to the doorway, where Minni peered out from behind the wall.

Minni took a few small steps. The sky-blue skirt swished back and forth.

Mama made a sound—sort of a gasp-sigh. *"Beautiful."*

Was she? Minni looked at her pink arms, crossed in front of the dress.

Daddy came and took her hand. He spun her under his arm. "Yes, you are. Both of you." He took Keira's hand as well. "Our twin beauties."

Chapter Seven

☀ ♡ ☾

"Am I black or white or what?" Minni sat in a beach chair next to Mama's stool on their large back deck, watching her work. She had put on sunscreen today. Keira was at gymnastics and Daddy was up in the air somewhere, giving a flying lesson.

Mama added more carmine to the brown-skinned lady's dress in her painting. "All of the above, and more."

"But I don't *look* black."

Mama rested her painting hand on her leg. "You don't?"

Minni rolled her eyes. *"Mama."*

"Where do you think you got those big round eyes?"

Minni knew her eyes were shaped just like Mama's. "But they're *blue*. Black people don't have blue eyes."

"Hmm . . . I see. . . ." Mama went back to her painting. "And those nice full lips that your sister's so jealous of?" She glanced at Minni from the corner of her eye. "Where'd you get those?"

Minni pulled in her lips and huffed. She looked longingly at Mama's beautiful kinked twists of hair held back from her face by a bright orange and fuchsia scarf tied at the nape of her neck. "What about this?" Minni held up the floppy end of one of her limp red pigtails. "I don't exactly have a black person's hair."

"Gigi had to get herself in there somewhere." Gigi loved to point out that she and Minni shared the same color hair, although Gigi only kept hers red with the help of dye. "That Irish pride runs deep and has some strong genes to go with it."

"Then where are Keira's Irish genes?"

Mama sucked in her breath, making a light whistling sound. "Don't ever let Gigi hear you say that. Where do you think Keira gets her feisty spirit? According to Gigi, that fire is pure Celt."

Minni had heard Gigi say that as many times as she'd pointed out Minni's hair. "Is that what you think?"

"Your sister's a lot more fiery than I've ever been, that's for sure."

Minni didn't think it very fair that she had gotten the fire hair but not the fire spirit to go with it. Keira was much more like Daddy and Gigi that way—they all laughed loudly, cried openly and expressed affection freely—whereas Minni had Mama's kind reserve and tendency to worry what others might think. It wasn't that she and Mama didn't feel things deeply or love intensely—these things just got expressed more quietly than they did with Keira and Daddy. She didn't know what, if anything, they'd gotten from Grandmother Johnson. Except, in Minni's case, The Name, of course.

Mama wiped her hands on a rag. She reached down and lifted Minni's face. Their eyes locked. "Where's all this coming from, anyway?"

Mama's fingers held steady. Minni shifted her eyes to avoid Mama's gaze.

A sharp memory pierced her thoughts, sending an aching pain all the way to the soles of her feet. She was sitting on the living room rug in the hollow of Mama's crossed legs, like a chicken in a soup pot. They were watching *Sesame Street*. Keira sat beside them with her elbow propped on Mama's knee. Minni felt safe with Mama's arms draped around her and her warm breath heating the top of her head.

That was when the song came on:

One of these things is not like the other.
One of these things just doesn't belong.

She saw Keira's brown arm on Mama's brown leg, and then her own pale skin against them both, and she shrank. She felt as though she was shriveling inside the protective shell of Mama's body until she was nothing.

"Hey." Mama shook her shoulder gently, bringing her back to their deck and the smell of the pulp mill on the warm summer air.

Minni blinked. What had they been talking about?

Mama cocked her head and squinted. "What's going on in that head of yours?"

"Nothing."

"Uh-huh."

Then Minni remembered the story they'd heard several times, from when she and Keira were babies, about the woman at the park who saw Mama holding Minni and asked if she was looking for more nanny work. Mama had been furious.

If only Minni had been born darker, people would know she wasn't someone else's daughter. And she wasn't just Keira's friend.

"Mama?"

Mama raised her eyebrows, as if to say, *I'm waiting.*

"People think I'm white when they look at me. Ever since the day I was born."

Mama put her brush down. "Maybe some people." She got off her stool and sat on the side of the lounge chair.

"What if the pageant people think I'm white? What if the other girls . . . ?"

Mama let out a low hum, as if all the mysteries of the universe had suddenly come clear. "You know, as much as I've soured on these pageants since the days when I partic-ipated, I'm actually glad you're going. Being in the South is going to be good for you."

"It is?" Minni was surprised to hear Mama say that, since it seemed she had gotten as far from the South as she could without falling into the Pacific Ocean.

"Growing up in North Carolina, I knew black people who were as dark as licorice and as light as cream. Some had doctoral degrees and some had farmed all their lives. Some had money and some didn't. Some even had *blue* eyes."

Minni's eyes opened a bit wider.

"Yes, they did. There were plenty of differences, but we shared a common ancestry, which you share as well. And no matter what a person's job or education or skin tone, in the end we all faced, and were united by, a common struggle."

Minni bit her bottom lip. She saw the image of Dr. King and the others, arm in arm.

"There are many ways to be black, Min. Down there, people will be able to see it's a part of you, too."

Minni turned Mama's words over and over in her mind as if they were gemstones. She wanted to see all the facets.

"Being in this pageant is going to be good for you, too." Mama put her arm around Minni's shoulders. It didn't matter that they were different colors. Mama was still her mama. "Like being in that high school play was for me." She gave Minni a squeeze. "I don't want you to be crippled by shyness like I was half my life. It's time for you to come out from the shadows, Little Moon, and shine."

Minni chewed on her lip. She hoped Mama was right about all this, but she didn't know. "I think I'll go read," she said. She scooted past Mama and headed for the sliding glass door.

"Daughter."

Minni stopped and turned.

"Oh, good. You haven't forgotten. You're my daughter. And your daddy's daughter. And Keira's sister. And your own strong *human* self. Not a color. Got it?"

Minni nodded, but her heart still wasn't sure.

"Good." Mama blew a kiss, and Minni went inside.

Chapter Eight

The morning they were to leave for North Carolina, Keira wanted to fix Minni's hair the way she might wear it for the pageant. Normally in the summer, Keira would sleep until nine or ten, but not this morning. She pulled Minni out of bed at five-thirty and made her put on her clothes so she wouldn't mess up her hair after it was done. Keira was already dressed.

Minni yawned and stumbled behind her sister to the bathroom, where she plopped down on the toilet seat. As Keira dragged the brush through Minni's hair, Minni slowly came to. They were really going.

Keira gathered Minni's red locks into a high ponytail, loosely twisting a few strands on the sides, and secured the hair with an elastic band. Then she took sections from the ponytail and twisted them until they coiled. She bobby-pinned the loose ends of the coils, making a heap of loops on the top of Minni's head. She used her fingers to mess the loops a little, then pulled a few strands free at the sides of Minni's face, and curled the strands with her curling iron. The final touch: two dainty flower-shaped clips, sparkling with rhinestones. She put one on either side of the crown of Minni's head. Then she sprayed enough hair spray to shellac a small boat.

Minni coughed.

Keira stood to the side, smiling widely. "I believe my work here is done." She stuffed barrettes, bands and bobby pins back into their compartments in her vanity case.

"What about yours?" Minni asked.

"I haven't decided for sure yet how I want to do it," Keira said, pulling her thick hair into a single pompon at the back of her head and clipping barrettes on either side to keep the hair in place. "But believe me, it will be knock-your-socks-off amazing."

They heard a dog's claws clicking on the wood floor as it skittered this way and that—then Gigi calling, "I came to say goodbye to my gir-r-r-ls!"

"If that little rat tries to slobber on me . . ." Keira slapped her palm with her wide-toothed comb.

Minni stepped around the corner. Banjo practically catapulted himself into her arms. She scooped him up and gave him a big kiss.

"My, oh my!" Gigi exclaimed. Mama closed the door and turned to look. Daddy smiled from across the room.

Gigi reached for Minni's hair and touched it lightly here and there. "Don't you look exquisite? I *love* it!"

"It was all Keira," Minni said.

Keira appeared in the doorway. "You like?" she asked. They all expressed their approval.

Minni smiled in spite of herself. It was just *hair*, after all. But she had to admit, the style made her feel almost glamorous—and very grown-up.

"With that Sunset Pink blusher and Touch-of-Pink lip gloss we tried on you the other night," Gigi said, "well, you and your sister are going to steal the show."

Mama stepped forward. "Both of you *are* beautiful, but remember this program is not primarily about how you look on the outside. It's about each girl getting to express who she is on the *inside*." She looked deeply into Minni's eyes. "Right?"

Minni nodded.

"But it won't hurt to look good, too!" Keira said. Banjo stretched his neck, trying to sniff her face. She shielded herself with her hand. "Isn't it time to go?" she asked.

"Yep!" Daddy said. "Let's get this show on the road."

Minni handed Banjo to Gigi, who plopped herself in the leather armchair. Mama followed them to their bedroom for one final check of their bags.

Bessie Coleman greeted them with a "Hello" and a whistle, as if she too had noticed Minni's hair. Minni let the bird climb onto her hand for one final pet. As well as finishing *Around the World in Eighty Days*, which they had started a few nights ago with Keira following along, Daddy had promised to spend a little time with Bessie each day—letting her out of her cage, talking to her and of course feeding and watering her.

Mama counted what they'd packed on her fingers. "You've got your dresses, your shoes, stockings, at least two skirt outfits each, nice pants, a couple of blouses, and plenty of shorts and T-shirts, right?"

"Right," Keira said.

"Underwear and socks?"

"Check."

"Hair care, deodorant . . ."

"Of course."

"Swimsuits and swim cap, just in case?" Mama looked at Keira, who wore a swim cap to keep her hair from having to be washed every time they went swimming. Minni didn't wear a swim cap. Her wavy, oilier hair could and *needed* to be washed more often.

"Check."

"Your tumbling costume for your talent routine?" Mama looked at Keira again. When Minni had discovered that the talent competition was optional, she had immediately opted out. Fortunately, Mama hadn't fought her on it.

"You're wearing your tennis shoes . . . what else? Oh, the applications. Where did they end up?"

Minni pointed to her backpack. "In my Dr. King book, so they won't get crumpled."

"Good. Your grandmother wouldn't approve of crumpled."

They had finished their applications the same day they'd started them, listing their hobbies, volunteer activities (Minni had gotten to help out at the animal shelter twice that week and would resume her duties when she returned) and awards and other achievements. They also had to write two essays—one on how they would use the title of Miss Black Pearl Preteen of America to bring attention to an issue they cared about, and the other on what they might like to do as a career.

Minni's issue of concern was the environment. She had already organized one class cleanup trip to the beach and planned to expand the project to include the whole school next year. When Keira had a hard time coming up with something, Minni suggested she could use the title to bring awareness to the struggles of kids with learning disabilities, like her, which Keira thought was a great idea.

Keira had no problem writing about her career plans— to be a fashion designer—but Minni wasn't so sure what to say. She decided on animal researcher—researching *about* them, not on them—or veterinarian. She would be happy with either of those jobs.

As for the grades question, Mama directed Keira to leave it blank. She had called the Black Pearls of America office and learned that the program still had the same rule about academic performance. Grades didn't exclude a girl from participation, but she would earn extra points and possibly the award for academic excellence if she included a copy of her report cards from the previous two years. Mama had slipped Minni's in with her application in spite of Minni's protests. She didn't like getting attention for her grades— she feared how it might make Keira feel—but then Keira sided with Mama about the report cards, so Minni gave in.

"There's just one last thing," Mama said. She disappeared

down the hall and returned a moment later with a gift bag in each hand. Minni put Bessie Coleman back in her cage. Daddy leaned against the door frame, a grin on his face. He sipped coffee from his KISS ME I'M IRISH mug.

Keira had the tissue paper out in two seconds. She squealed. Minni peeked into her bag. A cell phone? Wow! Just last month, Mama had insisted Keira and Minni were still too young.

Keira stripped the bubblegum-pink phone from its box and danced around the room with it over her head. Minni held hers in her hand, admiring its turquoise color and enjoying the grown-up feel of it.

"The deal is you only use them to call your dad and me, or each other. Your grandmother was less than excited to know you'd have them, but I don't care. I want us to stay in close contact while you're gone. We'll talk later about what happens to them once you're home. Got it?"

They nodded enthusiastically and thanked their parents—Keira with lots of cheek kisses—and then everyone grabbed a bag or two. Minni stayed behind while the others tramped down the hall.

"Well, Bessie Coleman, this is it. I have no idea what's going to happen—"

The bird squawked.

"But I'm going to try my best. Make sure Daddy's reading that book while I'm gone, okay?" Minni had picked *Around the World in Eighty Days* because the story involved flying—by hot-air balloon as well as airplane, not to mention traveling by train, steamship, sledge and even an elephant. She figured all the action should keep Daddy's attention. "He'll take care of you."

She looked around their room, trying to memorize it all—Keira's fuzzy lime-green throw pillows, the crystal sun catcher in the window, the sound of the ocean near the bottom of their bluff. She gazed at Keira's mural of a boutique-lined Paris street with the Eiffel Tower in the background, then hers of Mount Rainier. "Ten days isn't so long, right?"

"See ya!" Bessie Coleman stretched her marbled black-and-white wings, showing off her sky-blue body. She flapped them as if to say goodbye.

Minni touched the cage and looked into Bessie's tiny black eyes. "See you *soon.*"

Daddy flew them to Boeing Field in Seattle, and they took a shuttle to SeaTac International Airport. Minni was used to being in the sky, since Daddy took her up often, but she hadn't been in a jet since they were six—the last time they'd visited Grandmother Johnson. Seeing the big planes made her excited, but a little nervous, too.

They had to say goodbye to Mama and Daddy at the security checkpoint. An airline attendant would take them the rest of the way. Daddy squeezed them tightly. Mama hugged their necks and kissed their faces. She even had to wipe a tear from her cheek.

Then, just like that, they were off. On the other side of the checkpoint they waved to their parents. Daddy didn't stop blowing kisses until they were out of sight. Minni blinked to keep herself from crying.

Walking down the crowded corridor, Keira was glued to the attendant's side, asking her about the "glamorous life of a stewardess" and if she'd ever worked flights to Paris, which was where Keira had already announced she planned to study fashion.

On the plane, another attendant hung their pageant dresses in a compartment near the cockpit. They found their seats, and Minni pulled out her Dr. King book. Keira called Mama and Daddy on her cell phone, just because she could. "We're sitting on the plane!" she said, as if they didn't know. "There's a little TV at *every* seat!" Then she got out the disposable camera Mama had packed for each of them and took a picture of her and Minni, their shoulders and heads pressed together. Minni could only manage a small smile.

She opened her book. She had been surprised to learn that Martin wasn't even Dr. King's real name. It was Michael. Some of his friends called him Mike his entire life. His dad had changed his own name and his firstborn son's after visiting Germany and learning about some famous church guy named Martin Luther—a man whom he apparently had been very impressed with and wanted his son to be like.

Minni hadn't been named after anyone famous, just Grandmother Johnson—a woman who, as far as she could tell, she didn't want to be like at all. As the plane taxied toward the runway, she rested her head on the seat, closed her eyes and tried to think about anything other than where they were headed.

Chapter Nine

☀ ♡ ☾

A few hours after switching planes in Chicago, they bumped to the ground in Raleigh. In the Jetway, the warm, sticky air clung to Minni's skin, making her feel sluggish and slow.

She shuffled along behind the escort and Keira, who walked with clipped, sure steps and swiveled her bag around small children, a luggage cart and a guide dog with the smooth sophistication of a veteran flight attendant.

Minni found herself staring at people passing in the corridor and waiting for planes—the very thing she disliked having others do to her and her family. But she couldn't help it. This was *nothing* like Port Townsend, or even Seattle, for that matter. "There are so many more black people than at home," she whispered to Keira.

"I know. Nice, isn't it?"

Minni nodded, but she also suddenly felt about as pale as a flounder.

At the baggage claim area, a black man in a white button-down shirt with yellowish stains under his arms held a sign scrawled in black ink.

Drat.

Her name had been written in all-caps for the entire Raleigh airport to see:

MINERVA AND KEIRA

Keira nudged Minni's arm. "A hired driver. I always knew she was rich, in spite of her stingy cards." Grandmother Johnson sent two cards each year—one on their birthday and one on Christmas, with a twenty-dollar bill for them to split.

"You Mrs. Johnson-Payne's?" the driver asked.

"Unfortunately," Keira said under her breath.

Minni nodded. They got their bags and followed the driver to the garage.

They sat in the back of the black Town Car with tinted windows. They were being chauffeured for real! Minni eyed the card with their names lying on the seat between them. Keira had asked to save it as a souvenir.

As they left the airport, a sign welcomed them to North Carolina. Minni looked out across the lush green landscape, darkened by the dusky night air. It was as green as where they came from, but in a different sort of way. Bushier and overgrown, like the whole area needed a big buzz cut. There wasn't a single evergreen—Minni loved those trees for their elegance and streamlined appearance. The trees here were leafy and full, like the handful of deciduous trees around Port Townsend. They inflated in spring and summer, giving the illusion of being much larger than they actually were. Come winter, they would be stripped of their finery—nothing but spindly wooden skeletons left to shiver in the wind.

The driver exited the freeway near downtown. The Raleigh skyline consisted of eight or ten tall buildings, mostly concrete and brick and very drab. Three buildings outstripped the others in height. They contained more glass, looked more modern, and reflected the twinkling lights around them.

The man drove down a busy main street toward a lit-up, grayish-white stone building—blocky, with lots of columns and, in front, a lighted pillar topped by a statue of a man wearing a broad-brimmed hat and leaning on a rifle.

"Thought you might enjoy seeing the capitol," the driver said, stopping at an intersection and pointing.

That's the capitol? Minni thought. It wasn't nearly as impressive as theirs in Olympia. The roof was a dull bluish green and the dome on top was minuscule, although it did have an interesting decorative crown around its perimeter.

"It has a reputation for being the most"—he paused dramatically—"*haunted* state capitol in the country."

Well, that certainly made things a bit more intriguing. Minni took another look, this time with genuine interest.

They turned this way and that until the streets were no longer lined with high-rises and businesses but houses—old houses with pointy roofs and porches and lots of gingerbread-type decoration, painted in colors like light blue, yellow and mint green. "I see from Mrs. Johnson-Payne's address that she lives in the old Oakwood neighborhood, where all the well-to-do lived back in the eighteen hundreds."

Of course they knew this already. Grandmother Johnson liked to point it out. She was a member of the Oakwood Garden Club and sat on the board of the Historic Oakwood Neighborhood Preservation Society.

They turned onto Elm Street. Minni remembered the giant trees at once. They lined the street and reached far above the houses, shading each yard with their branches.

The car pulled up in front of a single-story white house. The porch light was on. A dormer with three square windows stuck up from the green-shingled roof. A green vinyl awning angled down from under the gutter and ran across the entire length of the porch, making it hard to see the front door or the windows on either side.

The house was set back and up from the street. A waist-high retaining wall covered with ivy separated the perfectly groomed front lawn from the sidewalk. Black iron railings on either side of four cement steps led to the front walk and a lighted lamp on a black iron post, also wound about with ivy. At the end of the front walk, another four or five steps led to the porch. The flower beds—front and side—displayed a huge variety of mostly pink, yellow and white blooms.

She didn't remember the awning. It looked shiny and new—perhaps one of the "improvements" Grandmother Johnson was supposedly always making to her home. Minni didn't remember the two-story lavender house next door, either, but then it had been five years since they'd visited, and they'd just been little kids.

The driver opened Minni's door. "Thank you . . . sir," she said, remembering the instructions Mama had given them to use "sir" and "ma'am" when addressing adults. It was the polite, Southern way. She got out and hitched her backpack over her shoulders.

He handed them their dresses and pulled their suitcases from the trunk. He even walked their bags up to the porch and set them by the door. When he came back to where they still stood near the car, he checked the address on a slip of paper. "This is the right place, isn't it?"

"Yes, sir."

"And she's expecting you?"

Minni nodded, but neither she nor Keira moved.

The man raised an eyebrow. "Okay, then . . ." He waited for another moment, as if he wasn't sure whether to go. "Enjoy your stay in Raleigh." He walked to his door, glanced once more over the car's roof at them and then drove away.

They stood on the sidewalk, looking up at their grandmother's house. It was as if they were being born all over again. Neither one of them wanted to be first.

Something in the front window of the lavender house caught Minni's eye—had the curtain moved?

"I guess we should go to the door, huh?" Keira said.

"I guess we should," Minni replied. They took the cement steps to the front walk together.

Seeing the porch swing hanging from its chains, Minni felt Mama's hand stroking her hair as she lay, rolled in a ball, with her head in Mama's lap. The swing was completely silent in the still night air, but Minni could hear it—like the creaking of a dock swaying in the ocean—as she, Mama and Keira rocked back and forth on the warm summer nights of their first and only visit.

Minni looked up at the baby-blue porch ceiling. Yes, she remembered that, too. It had been painted to resemble the sky, and something else . . . some old wives' tale their grandmother had told them.

The dead bolt unlocking made a thunk. The front door swung open. Grandmother Johnson appeared behind the screen, filling its frame. "Finally. I was beginning to wonder." She pushed the screen door toward them.

She wore a navy blue suit jacket and skirt that came to her knees, sheer blue stockings and practical navy blue pumps, which added at least a couple of inches to her already imposing height.

She looked them up and down, stopping at their heads. "I'm pleased to see you are putting more effort into your hair these days, Minerva."

Minni had noticed her hair in the Town Car's tinted windows. Thanks to Keira's ultra-strong hair spray, the elegant updo looked almost exactly the same as when they'd left their house that morning.

Grandmother Johnson's eyes shifted to Keira. The lines around her lips deepened. "You, on the other hand . . ."

Keira's eyes narrowed.

"How can your mother allow you to go out with your hair looking like that?"

Minni started to say that Keira had been the one who put her hair in its fancy style, but Grandmother Johnson waved at them to come in. "Get inside, then. In spite of what my grandmother thought, a blue porch ceiling does *not* keep away flies."

Keira entered with a huff, jerking her wheelie behind her.

Minni stepped inside and tugged on her suitcase, which seemed to have gotten stuck on the doorjamb. She looked down just in time to see her wheelie bump over one of Grandmother Johnson's extra-long navy blue pumps. "Sorry," she said, nearly tripping over her own long feet in her hurry to get inside. So she had Grandmother Johnson to thank for her humongous feet as well as her clunky name.

"I think I'll survive." The door shut with a thick *clump*, enclosing them in the stuffy, dimly lit living room. "I keep the curtains closed during the day to help it stay cooler in here." Grandmother Johnson's strategy didn't seem to be working.

Not only was it hot, it smelled like rotting bananas and disinfectant spray. Behind two wingback chairs, a long strip of Oriental rug created a path across the hardwood floor to the dining room through a large opening in the living room wall. The chairs faced a baby grand piano in the front corner of the living room and a fireplace surrounded by a floor-to-ceiling wall of built-in bookcases—stuffed full of books!

Minni suddenly remembered being six and staring up at

the wall of books, filled with awe and a little fear that if she pulled one out they'd all come crashing down. When she'd been alone in the room, she had tried anyway, tugging one free from its tight space. She'd only started to read a couple of years before, and the book she'd pulled down was full of small print and big words, but she sat and read as much as she could anyway. Grandmother Johnson had discovered her there on the floor, and after that, everywhere they went, she bragged to anyone who would listen about her six-year-old granddaughter who read at a college level.

"Your trip was uneventful enough, I expect."

They both mumbled, "Yes, ma'am."

"Good. Give me your gowns and I'll hang them in my closet."

They handed over the dresses and Grandmother Johnson inspected them through their clear plastic covers. "I see your mother followed my instructions to keep them appropriate."

Minni and Keira eyed each other. Mama had told them not to let their grandmother know Gigi had taken them shopping. She would say she didn't like the dresses even if they were fine.

"First things first. Go to the lavatory and wash your hands." Grandmother Johnson pointed to an opening that led to a hallway on the right. "Airplanes are a bacterium's paradise. And wash your faces as well. You will see the washcloths on the shelf."

Lavatory? She still talked like a teacher, even though she'd been retired for a while now.

"In my teaching career of forty-five years, I encountered every communicable disease known to mankind, and not a single one ever brought me to my knees." Grandmother Johnson picked up a spray can from a small table by the door and released its contents into the air. "It's a constant battle, but I know how to keep germs in their place."

Minni choked back a cough as a cloud formed around her head.

They had entered a war zone, and for the next week and a half, this stern, disinfectant-spraying woman would be their commander in chief.

Chapter Ten

The pink sink, bathtub and toilet—with a fuzzy pink seat cover—huddled together in the tiny mint-green room. A shelf unit on the wall across from the sink held baskets of dusty perfume samples, lipsticks and gold jewelry, and various bottles and cans of things like rubbing alcohol, mouthwash and room deodorizer. Stacks of pink and green towels stood on the middle two shelves.

Minni turned on the water to cover their voices. "She's so *snotty*. I'm sorry about what she said—about your hair."

Keira stood next to her in front of the sink. "Whatever. It doesn't matter."

Minni looked at her sister in the mirror. Would people in North Carolina be able to tell they were sisters?

Probably no more than at home. All because of eight genes. Eight invisible genes.

"How are we going to deal with her for ten days?" Minni asked.

Keira held out her fist. "Together."

Minni pressed her knuckles against her sister's. Yes, together. They had gone through everything together. *Together* was the only way Minni knew how to be.

She washed her hands and face, but Keira just wet a washcloth and hung it on the shower door rail. "I won't mind if she gets some of my germs."

Minni opened the door and jumped with surprise. Grandmother Johnson was standing right outside. Had she been listening? She looked over their heads to the wet washcloths, then turned and opened the door to a stairwell. "You will be staying in the attic."

Minni stepped into the dark hallway, which led to the kitchen at one end (she could see the linoleum floor) and, she was pretty sure, led to their grandmother's bedroom at the other. She peered up the steep wooden stairs. The attic? That sounded creepy.

Grandmother Johnson started up the steps, which creaked and groaned under her weight. Once in the single upstairs room, she pulled on a string that turned on a light-bulb hanging from the ceiling. The ceiling sloped to meet the walls, but not too sharply or quickly.

"Put your clothes in the dresser—hanging garments can go in the armoire—and then join me in the dining room *with* your applications. We will take them to the Black Pearls office tomorrow."

She went back down the creaky stairs, which cut through

the center of the room, forming a rectangular hole in the floor that they would need to walk around carefully. There were no guardrails to keep a person from plunging headfirst to certain death below.

Curtainless windows stood over the twin beds on either side of the room. The air was thick and hot. Minni yanked on the window by her bed. "I don't remember coming up here before," she said.

"Mom was probably afraid we'd fall down the stairs."

Yes, Minni remembered now. Mama had banned them from exploring any part of the house where she wasn't. And they were not to touch anything, even when in a room with her.

The window finally up, Minni sat on the bed to test its firmness and looked around. At the other end of the room, the three square windows she'd seen from outside twinkled with light. They were made of that leaded glass that Mama liked. A bench seat filled the dormer space, making a perfect place to read.

Minni lifted her suitcase onto the gingerbread-colored bedspread. She sniffed the warm breeze. Her senses must have been playing tricks on her. The more she looked at the gingerbread color, the more she smelled the sweet scent of actual gingerbread. She pressed her nose into the quilted cover.

"What are you doing?" Keira had already hung up her blouses and skirts and was lining up her five pairs of shoes in the bottom of the armoire near her bed.

"Something smells like gingerbread. I thought maybe it was the quilt."

Keira put her nose to her bed and inhaled. Her nose wrinkled. "Yuck. All I smell is bleach."

They put all their clothes away and headed downstairs. At the bottom, Minni sniffed again. No gingerbread. Just rotting bananas and disinfectant spray.

How silly. She'd actually let a small seed of hope take root that they would find Grandmother Johnson in an apron, a plate of warm gingerbread in one hand, the other extended to welcome them into a grandmotherly embrace.

When they turned the corner to the dining room, the little sprout completely shriveled up and blew away.

Three tall glasses of thickish white liquid.

Buttermilk.

Minni's tongue curled, remembering its sour taste.

Grandmother Johnson strode through the kitchen door with a tray of round, plain cookies that looked as if they were made from wood pulp. "You may be seated. I thought you might like a bit of refreshment after your travels."

Keira sat with her elbows on either side of the glass. She sniffed the milk. "I can't drink this."

Grandmother Johnson sat at the head of the table. "Please remove your elbows from the table and refrain from any further canine behavior."

Keira slumped in her chair.

"And sit *straight*. Young ladies—especially those contending for the title of Miss Black Pearl Preteen of America—must always think of their posture."

Minni's eyes darted between Grandmother Johnson

and her sister. Keira's back got straighter, but her mouth still drooped with disgust.

Grandmother Johnson raised her glass. "Low-fat buttermilk. Excellent for the digestion." She took a sip. "It's a miracle drink, really. Kind on the arteries, good for the skin, and so many other health benefits."

Minni stared at the thick milk.

There was no way out of this except through an empty glass.

She held her breath and took a drink. Then another. And another. She might as well just get it over with. She squeezed her eyes shut and drained her glass.

She let out her breath in a loud gasp as her glass clunked on the table. She tried to keep her face from contorting, but she couldn't stop her muscles from twitching any more than she could keep her eyes open when she sneezed. A long shiver, like a mini-earthquake, shook her body from the back of her tongue to the base of her spine.

Grandmother Johnson's eyes narrowed and her nostrils flared, but she didn't say anything. She turned her attention to Keira, who sat staring at her full glass.

"Keira." Grandmother Johnson's eyebrows pulled together. "Your sister has finished hers—with less gentility than she will employ the *next* time . . ." She took a sip, eyeing Minni over the rim of her glass, then setting it quietly on the table. "But finished nonetheless."

Keira lifted her glass. Her nose wrinkled, and she set it back down. The clock on the corner hutch ticked.

"We will not move from here until you have finished." Grandmother Johnson's voice was forceful.

Minni gripped the sides of her chair. *Come on, Keira. You can do it.*

Every time the milk got close to her face she gagged and pulled it away. "I can't. It's too disgusting."

Grandmother Johnson's lips pressed tighter. She was losing patience.

Minni fidgeted. Pressure had built beneath her ribs. It traveled upward—against her breastbone, the back of her throat. All the air she'd gulped along with the buttermilk was struggling to find its way out.

At home if they needed to let out some gas, they just did it. Minni was sure Grandmother Johnson's house rules did not permit burping at the table, even after gulping a full glass of buttermilk, but maybe this was her chance to get Keira out of the hot seat.

Should she do it?

What would their grandmother do if she did?

Grandmother Johnson would be seriously shocked and appalled, no doubt, but Minni and Keira had already decided: They would only get through this together.

She opened her mouth and belched like a toad.

Keira laughed.

Minni's relief was instantaneous—until she saw the look on Grandmother Johnson's face. Her stare pinned Minni to the back of her chair. Perhaps she had underestimated their grandmother's disdain of the public airing of bodily gases.

"*What* was that?"

Surely she knew what a burp was.

"I might expect this kind of behavior from your sister, but never from you . . . *Minerva*."

Keira's smile flipped into a frown. She glowered at their grandmother.

"If you need to *do that*, you will cover your mouth with your hand and, most of all, keep your mouth closed." Grandmother Johnson's mouth snapped shut, but she wasn't done talking. "This is exactly why I wanted you here this summer. I knew your mother wasn't giving you proper home training. You are eleven now. It's time you learned how to behave properly—like ladies. Don't ever let me hear you do that again, at the table or anywhere else for that matter."

Minni was grateful the trapped air hadn't decided to use the lower escape route. If Grandmother Johnson felt this way about burping, what would she say about letting loose from the other end?

Maybe that was the source of Grandmother Johnson's foul disposition—all the farts she'd held up inside herself. The gas had to go somewhere, so it had leaked into her blood and turned her sour as her nasty buttermilk.

Minni bit the side of her mouth to keep from smiling. She would tell Keira her theory later, and she'd make sure Keira knew she didn't agree with Grandmother Johnson one bit—that thing she'd said about her expectations of Keira versus her. How dare she say that? Grandmother Johnson didn't know Keira. She didn't know either one of them.

One thing she clearly didn't know about Keira was how stubborn she was. Keira would stay at this table for their entire visit if she had to. She would sit in front of that buttermilk until it went bad, as if buttermilk could get any worse.

To Minni's surprise, Keira raised the glass with her first

two fingers and thumb, lifted her pinky in the air and drained the milk without a single gulp, gasp or shudder.

When she was done, she set the glass gently on the table, picked up her cloth napkin and dabbed the corners of her mouth. She looked at Grandmother Johnson with just a hint of defiance.

"Very good," Grandmother Johnson said, nodding. "Now, let's talk about the pageant."

"Yes, let's. Since that's the only reason we're here," Keira said with more than a little attitude, which Minni hoped somehow their grandmother hadn't noticed.

Grandmother Johnson's lips clamped together, revealing the tiny wrinkles around her mouth. She pulled a pair of thin rectangular glasses from her jacket pocket and perched them on the end of her nose. She extended her arm. Her fingernails were well manicured but polish-free. "Your applications?" She took the papers and put Minni's on top. She murmured her approval as she worked down the page and onto the next.

With their grandmother absorbed in her reading, Minni could observe the woman undetected. Her hair was immaculately pulled back from her chocolate-brown face and gathered into a tight bun at the back. She kept it so straight and slick that if not for its dark color, she might have appeared bald from a distance. She had a perfectly oval face—her hairstyle emphasized the shape—and her skin was amazingly wrinkle-free for a sixty-nine-year-old, although this, too, could have been at least partly the result of her tightly pulled-back hair. Maybe that was why she wore it like that.

Still, she definitely looked older than she had two summers ago. Her cheeks sagged more, pulling the corners of her mouth down even when her lips curled into an occasional smile. The last time they'd seen her, she had come to Port Townsend. It had ended very badly; Minni and Keira never really understood why. Grandmother Johnson had said something to set Mama off, but Minni couldn't remember what now.

Minni continued her inventory of Grandmother Johnson's face. It was at least one-third forehead. Her eyes were set evenly on either side of her triangular nose under straight eyebrows that were filled in with a makeup pencil. Her earlobes sagged from years of wearing heavy earrings. All her jewelry was gold—a gold watch, a gold class ring on her right ring finger, a gold necklace with a rectangular gold locket. She wore her glasses for reading only—never in pictures. Mama said she was too vain for that. Instead she posed with them in her hand because it made her look smart. She called herself "full-figured." *Like Queen Latifah*, Minni thought, *except without any of the glamour or beauty.*

Grandmother Johnson finished reading. She nodded at Minni. "You have done an excellent job. I am especially pleased with your A-plus average."

Minni glanced at Keira, whose eyes roamed over the ceiling.

"There's just one thing. You will write in your *full* first name." Grandmother Johnson went to the desk behind Keira and pulled out a bottle of Wite-Out. She set it, along with the application and a pen, on the table in front of Minni.

She returned to her seat and picked up Keira's application. "*Purple* ink?" She *tsk*ed, then ran her finger down the page. She stopped about halfway. "You forgot to circle your grade average."

Uh-oh. Hadn't Mama told her?

"No, I didn't."

Grandmother Johnson cocked her head. "Then why has it been left blank?"

"Because none of the options apply." Keira looked directly at Grandmother Johnson.

"And what exactly *is* your grade average?"

"C-plus." Keira's chin was level, her neck long. She didn't blink once. "Mom was happy."

Grandmother Johnson looked as if she'd swallowed a spider. "Your mother doesn't understand that children rise to the expectations placed upon them." She sat back in her chair and crossed her arms. "How is it, exactly, that you have earned no better than a C average?"

Mama hadn't told her.

"*C-plus*. I have a learning disability." Keira said it just like that—no shame at all. "Severe dyslexia."

Minni hadn't thought she could admire her sister any more than she already did, but as she watched Keira be herself without apology, Minni's pride swelled like an ocean wave.

Grandmother Johnson didn't look proud. Her face had grown so tight Minni waited to hear it crack. "Severe dyslexia?"

Keira shrugged. "It's not that big of a deal."

Grandmother Johnson nearly rocketed through the roof. "Not that big of a deal?" She paced. "Not that big of a deal? I'm an educator! I have two master's degrees in education!" She planted her palm on the table near Keira. "And your mother didn't think to tell me my granddaughter has a learning disorder?"

"Disability," Keira corrected.

Grandmother Johnson tossed the application onto the table.

"She's been doing a lot better since they figured out what was wrong," Minni said.

Grandmother Johnson scowled. Minni scrambled for the Wite-Out and got busy changing her name.

"How will you get anywhere with grades like that?"

"I can't help it that my teachers just saw me as dumb and didn't try to help."

"Did you ask?"

"Mom did, every year. But no one seemed to take her seriously. She kept hearing that I just needed to apply myself more. I think they were being racist, because this year when *Dad* went in—"

Grandmother Johnson snatched up the application. "Never blame others for what is *your* problem."

Keira crossed her arms. "I can't help the way my brain is wired."

Grandmother Johnson straightened her glasses and put her hand to her heart as if trying to slow it from the outside. She sat, took a deep breath and thrust out her ample chest. "Perhaps not. But there is always plenty that *is* within your control." She started again to read Keira's application, then stopped and put it down. "Academic excellence has always been critical to the success of our race. It is how we have lifted ourselves from poverty to positions of power and influence. We will have to do something about your performance, but for now, let us focus on the matter at hand."

While Grandmother Johnson finished reading, Minni snuck her cell phone from her pocket and quietly texted her sister:

i luv u dont listen 2 her

She pushed Send.

Keira fidgeted with her pocket, keeping her eyes down and her phone out of sight. Minni could tell she was checking her messages. Keira looked up. They smiled at each other.

*L*ater that night, Minni and Keira sat on Keira's bed in their nightshirts with their backs against the wall and their straight legs touching. Keira put her phone on speaker, and in hushed voices they told their parents the whole buttermilk story, including Minni's burp. "You did *what?*" Mama said. Then they all laughed.

"Grandmother Johnson freaked about my grades," Keira said.

The other end of the line was quiet. "Oh, Keira. I'm so

sorry," Mama said finally. "Of course she would scrutinize your applications."

"Why haven't you told her?"

Silence again. "I know I should have, baby. Don't worry—I'll be sure she knows we're on top of things—and to leave you alone about it. Have you done your reading for the night?"

Minni and Keira looked at each other. "It's kind of late," Minni said. "We'll start tomorrow, when we're fresher." Keira nodded.

They said good night to their parents and got into bed. Lying in the dark, Minni told Keira what she'd been thinking after Grandmother Johnson had come down on her so hard, including her trapped fart theory. Keira laughed, of course. "You're not going to let her get to you, right?" Minni asked.

"I *so* don't care what she thinks."

"Good." Minni was about to say good night when something rumbled below. It sounded as if someone had dragged a piece of furniture across the wooden floor.

The rumble came again.

Minni sat up and pushed her ear toward the sound. It kept coming, like waves crashing on the beach—except more jarring, not relaxing like the ocean.

Keira's covers rustled as she sat up as well. "She's snoring!" Keira said with glee. "Grandmother Johnson snores!"

She was right. The jagged sound was snoring. *Grandmother Johnson's* snoring.

Minni clapped her hand over her mouth, trying to keep

herself from laughing, but Keira didn't bother She just laughed.

Minni was sure they'd wake Grandmother Johnson with their carrying-on, but the snoring kept going and going. The longer it went, the harder they laughed, until Minni forgot all about the pageant and the applications and Grandmother Johnson's apparent approval of her over her sister.

Chapter Eleven

☀ ♡ ☾

Way too early the next morning, Grandmother Johnson yanked open the door leading to the attic. "Time to get up!"

Minni rubbed her eyes and looked at her watch. Four-thirty. She planned to keep her watch on Pacific time.

Keira groaned. "What time is it?"

"Seven-thirty."

"That's only four-thirty our time!" Keira rolled over and put her head under her pillow.

Grandmother Johnson hadn't left the bottom of the stairs. "There is no time other than the one you're in. Now, get up and get dressed. We need to turn in your applications at the Black Pearls of America headquarters."

That worked. Keira got up.

"Put on skirts and sandals." Grandmother Johnson shut the door.

Keira slipped on a tangerine-orange camisole and covered it with a crisp white button-down shirt. She advised Minni to wear her light blue cardigan over an aquamarine spaghetti-strap tank. They both put on flowery skirts, and Keira donned her red ballet flats.

Then they went to the bathroom to do their hair. Minni sat on the edge of the tub and watched Keira wield her fork comb the way Mama worked her paintbrushes. First she picked out her hair. Then, at her hairline, she sectioned off a two-inch strip, made a center part and slicked down the front on either side of the part with gel. She used bobby pins to hold the hair even tighter to her scalp, then hid the pins beneath a bright pink satin-covered headband.

Minni wound a strand of her own hair around her finger, admiring Keira's puffed-out curls. Her sister looked even more like a model when she wore her hair like this, big and wild and free.

Minni quickly pulled her own hair into her usual two low ponytails and left her bangs to do whatever they wanted.

"Wait," Keira said. She took the ends of the ponytails and put them back through the elastic bands without pulling the hair all the way through. Then she gently pulled the loops until they were the same size. "There. That has *twice* the funkiness factor."

They went to the dining room table, where Grandmother Johnson fed them oatmeal and dry toast. Minni was thankful that this time they got orange juice instead of buttermilk. She dipped her spoon in the slimy cereal, trying hard not to think of slugs or mucus.

"Can we have some butter?" Keira asked.

"'*May* we,' and no, you may not. Terrible for the arteries."

Keira crunched on the toast. She made her eyes big and exaggerated her chewing, as if trying to moisten the bread enough to get it down. Fortunately, Grandmother Johnson didn't notice.

They ate mostly in silence, although the bread was so crunchy and dry and the cereal so slimy it was hard not to hear every swallow. Minni felt as if she was on the verge of another laugh attack their entire time at the table.

Just when she thought she couldn't hold in her giggles a second longer, Grandmother Johnson finished. She picked up her empty bowl and looked at Keira. "Before we leave, you will make that head of yours presentable."

"What's wrong with my head?"

"You need to get that unruly hair of yours under control, preferably locked up in some braids. Two will do."

Why did Keira have to "lock up" her hair to be presentable? Grandmother Johnson made even a simple hairdo sound like prison.

"I haven't worn braided pigtails since I was in second grade!"

Grandmother Johnson's left eyebrow arched high. Her glare would have sent a bear running for cover, but Keira held her ground.

Minni was about to jump up and pull her sister away

when Keira stalked off, but not before muttering, "At least I don't snore."

Grandmother Johnson's prune lips got even more wrinkled. "How dare . . . I don't snore—" she snapped, but Keira was gone. Grandmother Johnson smoothed her jacket like a hen trying to get its feathers unruffled. "I just breathe heavily."

She turned to Minni. "Are you finished?"

Minni still had plenty of oatmeal in her bowl, but if Grandmother Johnson wasn't going to make her eat it . . . "Yes, ma'am."

"Then go wash up. And let your hair down. I want the program director to be able to see how nice it is."

"But you just told Keira—"

"Never mind what I told your sister. Now, go finish getting ready."

Minni went to the bathroom and took out the loops Keira had given her. She hated that she would have to go through the day brushing her scraggly, flat hair out of her eyes and mouth. She put the elastic bands in her skirt pocket for later and stepped into the hallway.

Keira appeared from the attic carrying her brush, spray conditioner and barrettes. Her eyes took in Minni's loose hair. She opened her mouth to say something, but Grandmother Johnson called Minni to the kitchen.

Minni shrugged at Keira and scooted down the hall.

"Much better," Grandmother Johnson said, eyeing Minni's head. "Now we just need to do something about your sister's tight curl." She made it sound as if Keira's hair were a problem of global significance, like greenhouse gases or something. "Bring this chair and come with me."

Grandmother Johnson held a ball of twine and a huge pair of clippers with thick metal blades.

Minni looked at the chair she'd been told to carry. Did their grandmother plan to tie Keira down and cut off her hair?

Grandmother Johnson stepped out the back door.

Minni thought about running to warn her sister.

"Hurry up, now!"

Grandmother Johnson was no small woman, but if she tried to nab Keira, Minni would jump her. It was still two against one, and Grandmother Johnson was old.

Minni lugged the chair down the back steps, noticing the neighbor's lush garden with cornstalks already sprouting, a gnarled old apple tree, and a compost pile next to a toolshed. Whoever lived in the lavender house must be all right. Composters were earth-friendly by definition. Two bird feeders hung from branches in the apple tree and one hung outside the back window. A small bird with a yellow head landed on the feeder near the window. She thought of Bessie Coleman, and a wave of homesickness swept over her.

"Minerva!"

Minni jolted.

"The *chair*." Grandmother Johnson leaned over a rosebush in the side flower bed near the front of the house.

Minni dragged the chair behind her. A warm breeze stirred up the pink roses' sweet scent.

"With all that hair, your sister's going to be a while."

Grandmother Johnson pulled on a pair of gardening gloves and sat in the chair. "And idle time is wasted time."

Minni was relieved the woman just wanted to prune her bushes and not Keira's head. She pretended to watch, but her attention was fixed on the house next door. The second-story balcony would be a great place to escape to with a book and some iced tea.

The breeze picked up and the neighbor's many and varied wind chimes tinkled and clanged. A *clink-clunk*ing wooden sound made Minni think of one of Mama's recordings of African music. "Those chimes sound pretty," she said.

"Unneighborly inconsideration is all I hear." Grandmother Johnson closed the shears on a thick stem with a grunt. *Snap!* "That woman is single-handedly bringing down the property values of all the homes on this street, with those cornstalks—they attract raccoons, you know—and that disgusting compost pile; her hideous yellowing yard; and the dishes of pet food all over her porch, attracting every kind of mangy mutt and tattered cat to tramp through *my* perfectly groomed grass. I work hard to keep my yard looking respectable, and I *will* protect my investment."

From the looks of the lush green grass, the only hard work Grandmother Johnson had done was to lift a pen and write a check for someone to come spray a bunch of yucky chemicals. Very environmentally *unfriendly* chemicals.

"Next thing you know, she's going to have vagabonds showing up for handouts. Not to mention she practices voodoo. I've seen the shrunken heads in her kitchen window. And she's always burning candles—probably doing some kind of ancestor worship or séances. She's going to burn our houses down one of these days."

Snip, snip.

She peered at a flower. "She doesn't even garden with *gloves!*"

Snap!

"Has she lived here a long time?" Minni asked. She had become more intrigued with each new bit of information.

A scruffy dog with floppy ears and wiry, matted fur slunk up the woman's front steps and disappeared.

"*Here* as in next door? Only a year or so. But she's a Raleigh-Durham native, same as me."

"Did you know each other growing up?"

"Our families were friendly, I suppose, but I never liked her. Too brash for my tastes. Spent her whole career at Shaw University—the historically black college here in town— teaching African studies and anthropology. Very strange people, those anthropologists. Why she had to move next door to me of all places, God only knows."

The dog appeared on the steps again. He trotted into Grandmother Johnson's yard. Minni smiled, hoping to make a friend. She held out her hand and tiptoed toward him. He sniffed around the grass, and . . . he wasn't about to . . . *was he?*

Grandmother Johnson looked up just as the dog hunched into a position that could only mean one thing. "Don't you dare do your dirty deed on *my* grass!" Grand-mother Johnson jumped up and ran toward the animal, pumping her fists and bellowing.

The dog turned to look, but he was smack-dab in the middle of his business, which was to use Grandmother Johnson's pristine green grass as his own private lavatory.

"Get!" Grandmother Johnson waved her shears in the air. "Get, I said!"

Minni watched through her fingers as the dog left three neat little packages—signed, sealed and delivered—on Grandmother Johnson's TruGreen chemically treated, blemish-free lawn.

Grandmother Johnson shook her shears. "Shoo!"

The dog let out a low growl. If the animal attacked, Minni wasn't at all sure which way she would run. She should probably do something—try to scare him off—but there was a little bit of her heart—a mean part, she knew—that wanted the mutt to frighten the old woman. Payback for how she'd treated Keira last night and again this morning.

Somehow Grandmother Johnson made herself even taller. She jabbed the shears as if she were a sword fighter.

The dog bared his teeth and growled again.

Minni's heart flopped around her chest like a fish out of water. The ends of her fingers tingled with fear.

Grandmother Johnson lunged.

The dog tore across the yard, leaped from the cement wall to the sidewalk and scampered away.

"What's going on?" Keira had pulled her hair into two knots—like cinnamon buns—one behind either ear. She'd decorated them with rhinestone bobby pins. The front was still held down with the pink headband.

Minni grabbed Keira's arm with shaking fingers. What had happened was so scary and hilarious at the same time that all she could do was laugh. Nervous laughter that bubbled up inside her chest as if she were a glass of Gigi's sparkling mineral water.

"What's so funny? What'd I miss?"

Grandmother Johnson called out, "Keira, get me a paper sack, second drawer down to the right of the sink!" She stood over the dog's "dirty deed." "And bring the hammer and a nail."

"Why does she need a hammer and a nail?" Keira asked.

Minni was afraid to guess.

"Hurry up, child!"

Keira looked miffed, then walked back to the house.

"Minerva, fetch me that trowel from the flower bed." Grandmother Johnson pointed to an area near the roses.

Minni had no idea what she was being asked to do.

"The spade. There. In the dirt." Grandmother Johnson waved her hand, scowling.

Minni looked again. All she saw was a small shovel, its sharp point sticking into the ground. She pulled it up by its handle as if she were yanking a weed. "You mean this?" Now that she could see the whole thing, she realized it looked very much like the spades she knew about—the kind on Daddy's playing cards.

"You don't know what a spade is, child? I don't suppose your mother's teaching you about tending flowers out there, either."

"Mama doesn't like gardening." Minni handed

Grandmother Johnson the tool. "She just lets whatever shows up grow wherever it wants."

Mama always said if something took hold in a particular place, its roots must have found what they needed in that plot of ground, and who was she to remove it? There was a pine tree almost two feet tall in their front yard that had gotten blown there by the wind. Minni had hung tiny ornaments that she made out of Mama's shiny Mardi Gras necklace on the tree last December.

Keira returned. She started to hand everything over, but Grandmother Johnson traded her the spade for the hammer and nail. "Now, be a good granddaughter and put it in the bag," she said, pointing to the ground.

Keira's face contorted. Her lips parted and her tongue flew to the back of her teeth. She was about to give Grandmother Johnson a big, fat NO.

Minni grabbed the shovel. "I'll do it. I don't mind."

Keira set the open bag on the ground and backed away. "Be my guest."

Minni crouched. Grandmother Johnson stood over her muttering. "That woman . . . putting out food for every stray animal in Wake County . . ."

Minni held her breath as she scooped the dog's excrement, but she really didn't mind doing it. If she became one of those scientists who observed animals in their natural habitat, tracking their movements and recording everything about their daily activities, including their elimination habits and the contents of what came out, she'd be doing this for a living.

". . . creating a health hazard . . . should have had a fence built the day she moved in . . . this time I'm calling Animal Control."

Minni closed the bag and stood. "What do you want me to do with it?"

"Follow me." Grandmother Johnson crossed the boundary between her TruGreen yard and the neighbor's dry, yellowing one. "Next time I get the lawn treated, she's getting the bill."

Minni held the package by its folded-over top. It could have been a bologna sandwich and some carrot sticks. Looks sure could be deceiving.

She glanced at Keira, who stayed a couple of steps behind, pinching her nose and looking thoroughly disgusted.

Grandmother Johnson stomped up the front steps and kicked aside one of the dishes. Pet food scattered everywhere, sounding like hail on a roof. "Hold it up here." She pointed to the large, heavy-looking door. Wind chimes tinkled and clanked around them.

Minni and Keira exchanged glances. They didn't have to be twins to know what the other was thinking. *Grandmother Johnson has flipped.*

"What are you going to do?" Minni asked, even though it was more than obvious what Grandmother Johnson intended, standing there holding a hammer and nail.

Grandmother Johnson raised the tool, a crazed look in her eyes. "It's time for Laverna Oliphant to get potty trained."

"You'll ruin her door," Minni said, aware that she could

no more stop Grandmother Johnson from doing what she pleased than she could hold back a freight train falling over a cliff. But she had to try. The old door was beautiful—painted a dark, shiny purple the color of an eggplant, and topped by three leaded squares of glass.

"'An eye for an eye,' I say. Actually, a small hole is nothing compared to how this crazy woman is ruining our neighborhood."

Who was crazy exactly? Making her granddaughters scoop poop and hang it on her neighbor's door—in skirts and sandals, no less.

"Hold it up, now!"

Minni clutched the bag in her sweaty fist.

"Child, my patience can't get much thinner."

Minni pressed the bag against the door, one hand on either side.

Grandmother Johnson placed the nail at the top center of the bag. Minni squeezed her eyes shut.

Bang!

Minni jumped and her heart took off racing.

Bang! Bang! Bang!

"What if she's home?" Keira asked. She cupped her hand around her face and peered into the large front-room window to the left of the door.

"Then she'll get it that much quicker." Grandmother Johnson lowered the hammer.

Minni let go of the bag. It hung there like a poor man's door decoration. Her hands felt dirty, not from picking up the poop, but from what she had just helped her grandmother do.

She listened for the sound of footsteps, expecting any moment to be standing face to face with a very angry, voodoo-practicing neighbor.

The door remained closed.

"My first dung-a-gram." Grandmother Johnson sounded almost gleeful. "Let's see what the neighborhood wrecker has to say about this 'welcome home' surprise." She slapped the hammer against her palm, looking very satisfied with herself.

As she spun to leave, she slipped on a round piece of dog food. Her feet fluttered and her arms flailed as she fought to keep herself from falling.

For sure Grandmother Johnson was being paid back for her meanness this time. Minni knew she probably shouldn't mess with fate, but she grabbed her grandmother's flapping arm and held on until the woman had her footing. Even that little bit of her heart that wanted Grandmother Johnson to get it couldn't let an old lady fall and hurt herself.

Their grandmother growled, kicking another dish with her pointy-toed shoe. The food went flying. She stomped down the stairs and across the grass.

"Geez, what got into *her?*" Keira asked. They stared at Grandmother Johnson as she marched away.

Minni shrugged, then turned her attention to the mess on Miss Oliphant's porch. She bit into her bottom lip. "Maybe . . ." She had started to say they should take the bag down and clean up the kibble, when a long silver-gray car with a peeling black roof and rusty patches on the hood and driver-side door turned into the driveway alongside Miss Oliphant's house.

Before the car could get close enough for them to see who was driving, Keira yanked Minni's arm and they raced down the steps to Grandmother Johnson's yard.

Minni's body buzzed with the fear that they had been seen. Had it been Miss Oliphant behind the wheel? What would she do when she discovered Grandmother Johnson's surprise package?

Grandmother Johnson, seeing the car, pushed them in front of her to the garage. "Faster!" she said, clip-clopping up the cement walk. "I'll retrieve your applications from the house. *You* get in the car."

Minni and Keira climbed into the backseat of a perfectly buffed and shined Cadillac, breathing the smell of disinfectant and waiting to see what their crazy grandmother would make them do next.

Chapter Twelve

They drove downtown. Keira made a crack about being chauffeured, but Grandmother Johnson gave her The Eyebrow and that was the end of that.

They circled the blocky capitol with its spiked crown and passed the fancy, historic Hotel Lamont, where Miss Black Pearl Preteen of America would be held in only eight days. Just looking at the multiple-story white building with the uniformed man standing in front made Minni's pits sweat.

"When we arrive at the Black Pearl headquarters, I expect you to be on your best behavior." Grandmother Johnson eyed Keira in the mirror.

That sounded pretty strange coming from a woman who had just nailed a bag of dog poop to her neighbor's door.

"I want to hear 'ma'am' after everything that comes out of your mouth."

"Even if we're talking to a man?" Keira asked. Minni giggled.

"You know that's not what I mean." Grandmother Johnson's mouth snapped shut like a stingy person's coin purse.

Minni pushed out her lips and shushed Keira without sound. Her sister was pressing her luck again.

Keira made a zipping motion across her mouth and grinned at the back of Grandmother Johnson's head.

"The president of the organization is Dr. Billie Hogg-Graff. I've met her at several functions here in Raleigh."

"Hog as in pig?" Keira's nose wrinkled.

Minni hit her sister's leg.

Grandmother Johnson glanced in the mirror. "It's unfortunate, I know. Luckily for her, her maiden name wasn't Goat."

Keira's eyebrows popped up. "Billie Goat-Graff?"

The girls looked at each other wide-eyed. Had their grandmother just made a joke?

Grandmother Johnson looked over her shoulder as she backed the car into a space along the curb. The turned-up corners of her mouth and eyes seemed to be saying she thought what she'd said had been pretty clever.

Minni peered out the window. They had pulled up in front of a mansion. And Minni didn't think that just because of the tall second-story windows, or the two chimneys coming out of the flat roof, or even the parapeted tower that rose above the front entrance. A sign in the front yard actually said, BROOKMORE MANSION—1838. Beneath that, it said, HOME OF BLACK PEARLS OF AMERICA, INC. EST. 1946.

"It used to be a plantation"—Grandmother Johnson nodded toward the big house—"but look who runs the place now!" She let out a sharp laugh.

Grandmother Johnson slipped on a pair of white gloves, picked up her purse and the folder with their applications and checked her face in the mirror. She turned and looked back and forth between them. "Remember, first impressions are everything. From the moment we step through that front door, the competition has begun." Just like that, she was all business again.

The girls lagged behind as long as they could, walking hand in hand. Minni leaned into Keira, whispering. She described Grandmother Johnson's face when she'd seen that mutt squat in her yard—"I thought her eyeballs were going to shoot from their sockets and explode in a burst of fireworks." Keira tilted back her head and laughed toward the Easter-egg-blue sky.

Holding Keira's hand, being able to make her sister laugh—these were the things that made Minni feel that everything would be okay, no matter what happened with this silly pageant or how crazy Grandmother Johnson got.

Bells on the door tinkled when they walked in, but no one was behind the front desk.

Keira zoomed toward the coffee table and snatched up a magazine. She plopped into one of the cream-cushioned wicker chairs and started flipping pages. *Essence*. She was always begging Mama for a subscription so she could look at the fashions, but Mama said the content was "too mature" for girls their age. Keira tried to use her learning disability to convince Mama she wouldn't bother trying to read the articles, but Mama hadn't been swayed.

Grandmother Johnson picked up a pen and started writing in a visitors' log.

The wicker chairs, leafy palm plants and gauze-curtained windows reminded Minni of Gigi's Caribbean-inspired living room. A ceiling fan created a light breeze, and she thought she smelled coconut. She sniffed the large white candle in the center of the coffee table. Definitely coconut.

"*Tch.*" Grandmother Johnson shook a finger at her. "No canine behavior." She hung her purse from the crook in her arm and clasped her white gloves in front of her as if she were the Queen of England.

Minni sat in the chair next to her sister. A container of seashells sat on the glass-topped table between them. She picked out the shells one at a time, noticing each one's unique beauty. How she would love to be walking barefoot along the beach, letting the water lick her toes and the sea breeze tickle her face.

Grandmother Johnson pulled out their applications and flipped through them once more. She cleared her throat. She yanked a tissue from the box on the counter and dabbed it against her upper lip. "Where in the world . . . ?" she muttered. "Hel-*lo!*" No wonder their grandmother had said earlier that her patience couldn't get much thinner. She hardly had any to stretch.

Minni looked into the container again. When she saw it, it took her breath away. The shell spiraled into a perfect circle—starting at the outer edge as pearly white and turning browner and browner, curling into a near-black center. It was just like her family—white, brown and black all swirled into one round whole. She pushed it into her skirt pocket, feeling a little guilty about taking it, but on the other hand, hadn't someone taken the shell from the beach? There were so many in the dish, no one would notice if one went missing.

"The nerve of these people." Grandmother Johnson plunked her purse on the counter. She reached over and rattled the doorknob on the divider door.

"Can I help you?" a woman said.

So much for making a good first impression.

Grandmother Johnson pulled back her hand as if she'd been bitten by a snapping turtle. "I should hope so. We've been waiting for quite some time."

Their grandmother was as sour as the buttermilk she drank. Didn't matter who she was talking to.

Whom, Minni heard Grandmother Johnson say in her head. *It doesn't matter to* whom *I'm talking.*

"I apologize. We were in a meeting."

"Well, I guess that's understandable, but perhaps next time you could leave a sign." She shoved the used tissue into her purse. "I've brought my granddaughters' applications for the Miss Black Pearl Preteen pageant."

"The deadline for the Miss Black Pearl National Achievement *Program* has already—"

Keira looked up with alarm.

Another woman entered the area behind the counter.

"Dr. Hogg-Graff," Grandmother Johnson said, reaching

to shake the president's hand. "It's a pleasure to see you again."

Dr. Hogg-Graff didn't look anything like a pig—or a goat, for that matter. She was tall and beautiful, with mahogany-brown skin and shiny black hair that flipped and curled down to her shoulders and lay across her forehead in solid bangs. She wore a red pantsuit with a black pearl stickpin in the lapel. "Have we met?"

"Why, yes, at the Black and Silver Tea last month. I made a contribution—a *significant* contribution." Grandmother Johnson gripped her gloves.

"Well, we certainly appreciate your support."

"And I spoke to you on the phone last week about my granddaughters coming from Washington State to participate in the pageant."

"*Program*," the first woman said. "A pageant is focused on externals. We, on the other hand, seek to inspire our girls to become young women of *character*." She sounded as if she were reading from a Black Pearls of America brochure.

Grandmother Johnson muttered, "Of course, of course," then focused again on the president. "You said they could have an extension on the applications, as long as I brought them in no later than today." She held out the folder.

Dr. Hogg-Graff took it and looked through their paperwork.

Grandmother Johnson gestured around the room. "What a lovely old home you've acquired for your offices. On the state historic registry, I assume. I'm working to get mine on as well. But what a lot of red tape. They don't make it easy."

"Grandmother Johnson's house a historic monument?" Keira whispered. "Maybe if they want to preserve old *smells*."

Minni giggled.

"I suppose they don't want just *anyone* getting the designation," Grandmother Johnson said.

"No. I suppose not."

An awkward pause filled the space between them.

Dr. Hogg-Graff smiled at Keira. "So, is this Keira or . . ." She looked at the papers again. "Minerva?"

Minni winced.

"I'm Keira, ma'am." Keira rose and walked to the counter. She shook the woman's hand.

"And where is your other granddaughter?"

Minni wanted to shrink to the size of a snail and crawl into one of these shells. The woman could see her sitting right there.

Keira turned and gestured. "This is Minni, ma'am."

Dr. Hogg-Graff stared blankly. "This is . . . ?"

"*Minerva*," Grandmother Johnson corrected. "My namesake." Her lips curled into a proud smile.

Minni sat on her hands, afraid to move or speak.

Grandmother Johnson's lips flattened and her eyes bugged a little. "What do you say to Dr. Hogg-Graff?"

"How do you do?"

Grandmother Johnson's eyes bugged more. She held her hand below the level of the counter and waved her over.

"Ma'am," Minni added. She walked lightly across the room and stood beside Keira.

Dr. Hogg-Graff's eyes darted back and forth between them. "Are they . . . sisters?"

Minni found the shell in her pocket and traced its circular form with her finger.

Grandmother Johnson cocked her head at the woman. "Most certainly."

"Biological?"

"As opposed to zoological?" Grandmother Johnson said curtly.

Dr. Hogg-Graff glanced up, then looked back at the applications, as if searching for some clue to explain what she saw standing before her.

"We're twins," Keira said proudly.

"Twins?" the other woman exclaimed. "I've seen everything now."

Keira locked arms with Minni. They stood like links in a chain.

Grandmother Johnson puffed out her large chest and crossed her arms. "In fact, they are fourth cousins to the venerable Reverend Dr. Martin Luther King, Jr., himself."

Keira made a sound like a whale coming up for air. *"Phuh!"*

Minni stared at their grandmother. Was it possible? Why hadn't she ever told them this before?

Wait a second. The King name came from Daddy's side of the family. Grandmother Johnson was at it again, doing anything she could to impress.

"Is that so?" Dr. Hogg-Graff didn't sound too convinced. "Amazing! That means we've got descendants of Frederick

Douglass, Thurgood Marshall, Madam C. J. Walker, and now Dr. *King* in this year's competition." She looked at the other woman and rolled her eyes.

"As well as sharing my name, this one"—Grandmother Johnson pulled Minni to her side—"was given Dr. King's initials to honor his memory. She's a very bright girl."

"I can see that," Dr. Hogg-Graff said, studying Minni's face. "*Very* bright."

"If you look on her application, you'll see she has an A-plus average. You're looking at a future Dr. King right here."

Dr. Hogg-Graff's lips scrunched as if she was trying to decide what to say next. "So, I take it their mother is white?"

"Their mother is just as black as you," Grandmother Johnson said sharply. "Furthermore, she is an alumna of the Black Pearls. I mentioned that at the Black and Silver Tea."

"Oh, yes. I must have forgotten."

"Our father is white," Keira said, lifting her chin.

"Is that a fact? I didn't know Martin Luther King had white cousins." Dr. Hogg-Graff's eyes slid over to Grandmother Johnson.

Minni pulled in her lips to keep from smiling. So much for what their grandmother would likely say was only a "little white lie" about their relation to Minni's hero. Clearly Dr. Hogg-Graff hadn't believed her anyway.

"Of course he does. Most of us do," Grandmother Johnson snapped. She pulled her checkbook out of her purse. "Now, as for the sponsorship fee, shall I make the check to Black Pearls of America, Inc.?"

"Yes." Dr. Hogg-Graff continued to scan the applications. "Based on what I'm reading here, I see no reason why your granddaughters wouldn't be allowed to participate. Deirdre will get the girls their opening-number outfits before you leave. The sponsorship fee covers those as well."

Dr. Hogg-Graff looked up again. She gave them a tight smile. "I apologize if I've offended with my inquiries into the girls' relatedness and background, but with all the blended families these days, I had to ask. This is a program for *black* girls, after all, and we feel very strongly about our mission in that regard."

Keira put her fist on her hip. "My sister *is* black."

Grandmother Johnson cut Keira a look, then turned to Dr. Hogg-Graff. "Of course. I understand fully." She smiled ingratiatingly. "But surely you know our people run the gamut when it comes to skin color and other features."

Minni's blood rushed to her head, leaving the rest of her body shaky and weak. From the heat in her cheeks, she could tell she had turned as pink as one of Grandmother Johnson's roses. Mama had promised that people would be able to see her blackness down here in North Carolina.

The woman's gaze roamed over Minni's face, but she never looked directly into Minni's eyes—eyes that had never felt so blue.

Chapter Thirteen

☼ ♡ ☾

Grandmother Johnson took them for lunch at a fifties-type diner. "In celebration of being officially entered into the Miss Black Pearl Preteen of America pageant. Excuse me, *program*." Their grandmother obviously hadn't appreciated the woman at the office correcting her.

Minni ordered a cheeseburger, onion rings and a chocolate malt with whipped cream. They hadn't even been there twenty-four hours and already Grandmother Johnson's culinary abilities had her starving. Had the woman's mother taught her *nothing* about cooking?

Grandmother Johnson butted in. "You may have the burger with*out* cheese, and the malt—but hold the whipped cream. Scratch the onion rings. Too much artery-clogging fat."

Minni clenched her teeth.

"I'll have the Healthy Heart Special," Grandmother Johnson said, pointing to the menu. "But substitute tuna for the cottage cheese, and no tomatoes. They give me indigestion."

The waitress pinched her lips together. She kept her eyes on her pencil as she wrote on her pad.

Keira was allowed to order her French dip sandwich, but the fries became a side salad. The waitress picked up their menus and walked away without a word.

Minni excused herself to go to the bathroom. She wanted to call Mama in privacy, plus as soon as they had scooted into their seats, Grandmother Johnson had commented on a man talking loudly on his cell phone two booths away. "And people call all this gadgetry *progress*. Those things should be outlawed in public places."

Grandmother Johnson wasn't big on technology or electronics. That was clear. They hadn't yet found a single television in her house, and they knew she didn't have a computer. She took pride in the fact that "her children" (as she called her students) never used calculators. Minni had once heard her tell Mama, "Children need to know how to use their *brains*, not just punch buttons. We must always remain smarter than our technology."

Minni stepped into a stall and pushed the button she'd programmed to speed-dial home. Someone came into the bathroom. "Skinny?"

The phone on the other end of the line started to ring. "I'm in here," Minni replied.

"Are you okay?"

Minni thought for a moment. "Yeah."

The answering machine kicked in.

Keira turned on the water in the sink. "Why did you leave me alone with Payne-in-the-Butt? She started harping on the grades thing again."

"Mama? It's me." Minni glanced at her watch. Nine a.m. Mama was definitely up. She was a morning person, like Minni. They often shared the sunrise over a hot cup of cinnamon spice tea. "I'm just calling to let you know we're entered. We took in the applications." She fingered the shell in her pocket.

Pick up, Mama. Please. I need to hear your voice.

"Okay. Guess you're not there. Talk to you later." Her voice faltered, as if tripping on a crack in the sidewalk. "Say hi to Bessie Coleman for me."

She came out of the stall. Keira took Minni's hand and peered at her. "Are you sure you're okay?"

Minni nodded. She washed her hands quickly, trying not to see her red hair or pale skin in the mirror.

At the table, the waitress was setting down their food. Keira slid into the booth behind her French dip sandwich. When the waitress left, Grandmother Johnson turned to Minni. "Never mind that ignorant Hogg-Graff woman. She's obviously blind if she couldn't see the black in you."

Minni studied the pickles on her plate. "Yes, ma'am."

"My grandmother was as fair-skinned as any white person, and she was black all her life."

Minni looked up at the mention of her great-great-grandmother, who had also been a Minerva—another reason Grandmother Johnson had insisted that her eldest granddaughter receive The Name. Minni didn't remember ever hearing about the woman's skin color. "Your grandma looked white?"

Grandmother Johnson pursed her lips and nodded. "But as the saying goes, 'One drop of black blood . . .'"

"Could we see a picture of her?" Minni asked.

Grandmother Johnson glanced at her food, then rubbed at a spot on her blouse just below the hollow in her neck. She pulled out her rectangular gold locket and released the tiny latch. It popped open.

Minni and Keira leaned across the table to get a better look.

Maybe the black-and-white photo accentuated it, but this lady definitely looked more white than black—possibly part American Indian, with her squared-off jaw and high cheekbones. Thick black bangs swept across her prominent forehead, and a perfectly round mole nuzzled the front edge of one of her dark eyebrows. There wasn't a hint of a smile anywhere on her face.

Minni sat again, wondering about this great-great grandmother she had never met but who apparently had been of enough importance to Grandmother Johnson that she wore her around her neck.

Their grandmother returned the locket to its place beneath her blouse. "She was a strict woman, and *proud*. Oh, was she proud. Made most of her clothes, and she was always dressed to the nines." She rested her hands on either side of her plate. "She raised me in church, taught me about saving money, wouldn't even buy a *thimble* on credit. I wouldn't be the woman I am today had it not been for this lady." She touched the spot on her chest again.

Minni and Keira glanced at each other. Minni knew what her sister was thinking. She was thinking the same thing. *Am I glad I never had to meet her!*

"She was a domestic worker all her life—spent thirty years cleaning the very home I live in now."

"She used to clean your house?" Keira asked.

"It wasn't mine then, of course. Or hers. It belonged to a white man—Old Man Buchanan. Buck, she came to call him. She took the bus twenty miles from Durham to Raleigh and was his live-in housekeeper five days a week. They had a rather unconventional arrangement. He was a widower without any children. When he died, he willed her the house. When she died, it became mine." She sipped her iced tea. "I went to live with her in Durham when I was seven."

Minni felt her forehead bunch. "Where were your parents?"

Grandmother Johnson's lips pursed, and for a moment Minni didn't think she would answer. "My father disappeared mysteriously when I was only two. My mother was sure there was foul play—whites angered by my father's unwillingness to submit to the laws of the day. I've been told he was quite the rebel. Then my mother died suddenly, and my grandmother took me in. My grandfather had already passed on."

"Oh," Minni said, because she didn't know what else to say. She hadn't known any of this family history.

Grandmother Johnson laughed suddenly, loud and harsh, almost like a bark. "Seemed like no matter how tall I got, my grandmother was always taller. I finally realized she was buying higher heels to stay ahead of me. I don't think she gave up until she was seventy-one. I was eighteen and starting college at North Carolina State." She gazed out the window next to their booth. "I loved her as if she were my mother. That is what she was, after all."

Thank goodness nothing had ever happened to Mama and Daddy. The thought of having to live with Grandmother Johnson for good made Minni feel fidgety inside, as if a colony of red ants were swimming in her bloodstream.

"When she got sick, I wanted to quit school and care for her full-time, but she wouldn't hear of it. She was always pushing me to excel academically because *that*, she said, would be my ticket to independence. I can hear her voice as if she were sitting right here. 'Minerva, you're not a natural beauty, but you're *smart*, and you're going to use that brain of yours to get ahead. You'll be a domestic worker over my dead body.'"

"How did your mom die?" Keira asked.

"Oh, now, we don't want to get into all of that." Grandmother Johnson opened an orange plastic vial from her purse, shook out a small pill and swallowed it with a sip of iced tea. She lifted a forkful of tuna salad. "Now eat up. We have some serious work to do before this *pageant* begins."

Minni took a bite of hamburger. They had learned more about Grandmother Johnson in the last five minutes than in the last five *years*. She thought of the whirling sprockets in Gigi's clock. Was it possible that being in North Carolina might actually help her understand better the complicated inner workings of Grandmother Johnson?

Chapter Fourteen

☼ ♡ ☾

Back at the house, the chair was still toppled in the yard after the run-in with the dog and their hasty departure. Minni offered to get it.

She stopped next to the chair and glanced over her shoulder. Grandmother Johnson shooed Keira inside. Minni tiptoed across Miss Oliphant's dry grass to her front walk.

The bag was gone. The porch had been swept. The food dishes sat full and ready to welcome more strays.

The nail still poked from the door—a sharp reminder of the awful thing they had done.

Something nudged her leg and she jumped. A gray cat rubbed its head against her calf. "Oh! Hello there." Minni bent over and stroked the cat's side. Its left eye appeared to be sewn shut, but the other shone a brilliant green, the color of algae.

The big purple door creaked open.

Minni froze, barely breathing. Someone stepped onto the porch. "I see you've met Billie Holiday."

Minni looked up into the powdery, pale face of an old woman. Laverna Oliphant? Two gray braids sat pinned atop her head like a bird's nest. She wore a knee-length purple and white tunic made of swirly African-looking fabric. Intricate woven white appliqué bordered the neckline.

"She's had some hard knocks, but she's a fighter. And a sweetie. That one there's as sweet as sweet tea."

Billie Holiday . . . She was a singer Mama listened to when she painted.

"I've taken a special liking to her, I suppose partly because of her bad eye." The woman pointed to her own right eye. It was cloudy and near-white, as if covered with a thin layer of opal. "Together, though, we've got a perfectly good set."

The cat climbed the steps and snaked around the woman's skinny ankles and sandaled feet. She lifted the cat in her arms. Did she know who had put that nail in her door? Had she seen them?

"I . . . I have to go," Minni stammered, backing away.

"You're Minerva's, aren't you?" The woman beckoned with her hand. "Come on in and have some homemade gingerbread. We're neighbors now and neighbors should get to know each other." Her thin lips stretched into a smile.

Minni recalled the gingerbread scent she'd smelled the previous evening. Hadn't the old woman in "Hansel and Gretel" made gingerbread? *Out of little boys and girls?*

"Thank you, but I really have to go. My grandmother

will wonder what happened to me." She turned and ran, then realized she'd forgotten the chair, went back and picked it up, and ran again as fast as she could manage.

In the kitchen, Grandmother Johnson popped up from behind the open refrigerator door, holding a carton of buttermilk. *Drat.* "What in the world took you so long?"

Minni tried to hide her huffing. "Sorry."

"All right, then. Go sit at the table." Grandmother Johnson moved toward the three glasses on the counter.

Keira sat at the table looking disgusted. Apparently she already knew what was coming.

"I met the neighbor—Miss Oliphant," Minni whispered, setting the chair down.

Keira's eyes got big, but there was no time to talk about it now.

Grandmother Johnson set a glass in front of each of them, then sat at the end of the table. "Drink up. You need something to settle your stomachs after that lunch."

"But I'm so full," Keira complained. "If I drink that, I'll explode!"

"Has anyone ever told you you can be quite dramatic?" Grandmother Johnson took two small capsules with a sip of buttermilk, then shook out two antacid tablets from a plastic bottle and popped them into her mouth as well.

Minni smiled, remembering Mama's comment that Grandmother Johnson should have gone into theater. Their grandmother was apparently unaware of her own drama queen tendencies.

"Now we must discuss your talent performances."

Keira sat up, excited. "I'm doing a tumbling routine. It's one I've done before, so it's all worked out. I designed my costume myself. Mom sewed it for me."

The wrinkles around Grandmother Johnson's mouth deepened again. "I'll need to see the outfit to make sure it is appropriate."

Keira's eyes narrowed slightly—probably not enough for Grandmother Johnson to notice, but Minni could tell that her sister was annoyed.

"And you, Minerva?"

"I'm not doing the talent competition. It's optional."

Grandmother Johnson shook her head. "Oh, no, no. That will never do. You must maximize your chances of winning. You will enter a talent. I expect you can sing?"

Minni shook her head quickly—she could never stand in front of a crowd and sing. The only person who ever heard her sing was Keira. And not very often. Mostly Minni sang to the ocean.

"What are you good at, then?"

Thanks to Daddy, she was good at playing poker, but she wasn't about to say that. This past year, she had discovered she was pretty good at badminton, but she had no idea how to turn that into a stage performance, particularly by herself. And she'd already ruled out animal impersonations. She shrugged.

"There must be something you're good at. What about the clarinet—weren't you taking lessons?"

"I stopped."

"And your mother let you, of course."

"I wasn't very good, and I wasn't enjoying it."

"Enjoyment comes from mastery. It's difficult to improve if you quit. So what do you enjoy?"

"I like to read."

"Well, that's good, but you can't just stand on the stage and read to yourself."

"Minni doesn't like to perform in front of people. It makes her skin get blotchy." Keira set her elbows on the table.

Grandmother Johnson frowned and shook her finger at Keira's elbows. "Everyone gets nervous in front of a crowd, but it's a fear that must be conquered if you want to succeed in life."

Keira crossed her arms over her stomach. "When she gets that kind of nervous, it makes her pits stink."

Grandmother Johnson took a deep breath. "That's why people wear antiperspirant."

"It also makes her butt sweat. Do they make antiperspirant for that?"

Minni giggled.

"That's enough," Grandmother Johnson said sharply.

Minni bit her bottom lip.

"Well, I, for one, refuse to let your abilities go to waste." Grandmother Johnson's stomach grumbled as loud as an elephant warning its herd. She stood quickly. "I will be back momentarily. Your buttermilk should be gone by the time I return."

No problem there, Minni thought.

"And if you think you can get away with emptying your glasses in the kitchen sink, you underestimate me. If you hadn't noticed, the floor creaks." Grandmother Johnson rushed to the bathroom. The floor groaned under her heavy steps.

"Hand me your glass," Minni whispered as soon as the bathroom door had shut. She turned in her chair and poured both glasses into the ferns in the window seat.

When Grandmother Johnson appeared, Minni and Keira sat quietly behind their drained glasses. Minni's hands were folded properly in her lap.

Grandmother Johnson glanced at the table, then walked to the piano in the living room. "I've decided. You will sing. Just as your mother did when she competed for Miss Black Pearl." She flipped up the lid, pulled out the bench and perched on its edge.

When neither Minni nor Keira moved from her seat, Grandmother Johnson eyed them over her shoulder and cleared her throat. Keira rolled her eyes at Minni and they trudged to the piano.

Grandmother Johnson picked out a piece of sheet music from a stack on the piano, opened the folded paper and leaned it against the stand. She put her fingers on the keys and started to play. The notes came out jerky and with a lot of pauses, as if she were an out-of-shape person trying to talk while walking up a long, steep hill.

Minni shifted her weight back and forth, trying to figure out what, if anything, she was supposed to be doing. After several torturous minutes, Grandmother Johnson plunked the same note a few times. Minni stared at her grandmother's jawline, set and firm. "I can't sing."

"Of course you can. It's in your genes."

"Really, music is my worst subject in school. I don't even know this song."

"Your mother hasn't taught you 'His Eye Is on the Sparrow'?" Grandmother Johnson removed her glasses and stared at them.

The girls shook their heads.

Grandmother Johnson looked aghast. "But she loves this song! She used to perform it all the time in church. Women would faint in the aisles as if we were Pentecostals. Even grown men were known to shed a tear or two."

"Our mama?" Minni couldn't imagine it. Mama had taken them to a church exactly one time, and the only thing anyone would have fainted from there was boredom.

"I always felt some of the women were being unnecessarily emotional and histrionic, but nonetheless, my girl could sing. So I'm sure you can, too. You just don't know it yet." Grandmother Johnson turned back to the keys and played the opening again.

Minni couldn't sing—she was as sure of that as Grandmother Johnson was of the opposite—but she knew Mama could. She often sang them to sleep at night. Still, Minni had a hard time imagining her in front of a big, swooning crowd. Mama didn't like being up in front of people any more than Minni did. If she had gotten any genes from Mama, the not-liking-crowds gene was definitely one of them.

In the end, Grandmother Johnson plucked out the melody and made Minni follow along. Minni slid from note to note like a fish trying to swim on ice.

"Now, that wasn't so bad, was it?"

It was horrible, Minni thought.

"You sing as sweetly as a bird, just like your mama."

Was the woman deaf?

"But I don't want to sing in front of a bunch of people."

"You don't have a choice." Their grandmother placed her glasses in their case and closed the piano. "Now, go upstairs and get out what you plan to wear for your talent. We may need to do some shopping if what you've brought is less than satisfactory." Her stare followed them to the attic door.

Minni felt sorry for all the children who had ever had Mrs. Johnson-Payne-in-the-Butt as their teacher. And how in the world would she get out of having to sing before hundreds of strangers?

Chapter Fifteen

☀ ♡ ☾

That night in the attic, Minni had a flash of inspiration. She sat up in bed. "I've got it!"

"What?" Keira sat on her own bed, tying the satin scarf she slept in to keep her hair from frizzing.

"You can break my leg!"

"*What?*" Keira finished the knot and dropped her hands.

"I *have* to get out of this contest."

Keira's eyelids lowered. "You made a deal with Dad. Remember?"

Minni forced breath through her nose. "I know. But I *can't*. I can't walk around in a long dress and talk and sing in front of a bunch of people. Don't you think a broken leg is a lot better than having a heart attack?" She knelt next to Keira, grabbed her sister's knee and begged with her eyes. "You've got to help me."

"You're not going to die of a heart attack, and you can't quit. Besides, Grandmother Johnson already put down the money."

Minni plopped beside Keira on the bed. The springs squeaked. She looked at her bare shins crossed in front of her. "It wouldn't be very hard." She stretched out her legs, holding her feet in the air.

"I'm not going to break a single one of your skinny bones—not even your pinky."

"I know." Minni pulled her knees to her chest and wrapped herself around them. She had a sudden urge to jump under her covers and hide. Why had she ever agreed to this? "Speaking of making deals, we should probably do some reading."

Now it was Keira's turn to huff.

Minni got her backpack from under her bed. She pulled out the book she'd picked for them to read together and handed it to Keira, then climbed onto Keira's bed again and scooted back against the wall.

"*Black Be-a*—" Keira tried to sound out the word. "I can't even read the title," she moaned.

"Beauty," Minni said. "Don't worry. I don't mind going slow."

"You told me about this one, didn't you? Doesn't the horse tell the story?"

Minni nodded. "The author wrote it to make people more aware of the need to be kind to animals."

"Thanks for picking out a book about horses, at least." Keira loved horses. She'd even taken riding lessons at a stable outside Port Townsend.

Minni liked horses, too, and had tried one lesson, but when the dopey horse kept dropping to the ground to roll in the dust she'd decided to stick with smaller animals. "I think you'll really like it. Ready?"

"I guess."

"I'll read the first chapter, just to get us into it."

Keira listened to Minni read. When the master caught the plowboy, Dick, throwing sticks and stones at the horses, and clocked him on the ear as punishment, Keira cheered. "Serves him right, the little brat!"

Minni smiled. Her plan had worked. Keira was now wrapped up in the story, rooting for the horses and booing the bad guys. She handed a bookmark and the book to Keira for chapter two. "Use the bookmark to follow the lines, instead of your finger."

Keira exhaled loudly. She placed the guide under the first line of text. "'Be-fore I was two ye-ars—years—old a'... I have no idea what that word is."

"Try to sound it out. I'll help you."

"Kur—"

"Sur—" Minni corrected.

"See, that's the problem." Keira tossed the bookmark in the air. "Why is the English language so complicated? Why does the letter 'c' sometimes sound like 'k' and sometimes sound like 's' and how in the world are you supposed to know when it does what?"

"Eventually you'll know, just by looking at the word. In this case, the 'c' is soft before the 'i' and hard before the 'u'— as in 'circus.'" Minni picked up the marker and handed it back to her sister.

"I can barely keep the letters from flipping and flopping around on the page, let alone remember a bunch of rules for when I finally get them to stand still."

"Try again. Think 'circus.'"

Keira placed the bookmark and squinted at the word. "Sur-kum-stan-seh. Circumstance?"

"Exactly!" Minni held up her palm and they slapped high five.

Keira smiled. "One line down. How many to go?"

"Don't think about that. How do you run a marathon?"

"I *wouldn't*. Those people are crazy."

"One step at a time." Minni pointed to the next word in the story.

Keira plugged along, slowly, and after about fifteen minutes or so, they had gotten through four or five good-sized paragraphs. Minni leaned into her sister. "You're doing great," she said.

Keira leaned back, pushing Minni in the other direction. "Thanks, Skinny."

After a little while longer, Minni took the book and finished the chapter, a harrowing account of a rabbit hunt with yelping hounds and galloping horses. In the end, a horse, being driven too hard, tripped and tumbled, throwing its rider to the ground, breaking his neck and killing him instantly. The horse ended up no better off. It broke its leg. A man came with a gun and put him out of his misery.

"That was so *sad*," Keira said. "I don't think I can take any more tonight."

Minni closed the book and put it on the nightstand at

the head of Keira's bed. She pulled the cord on the light-bulb and got under her covers. They were quiet for a while.

Minni turned her face toward Keira. "It doesn't matter how fast you can read. You'll always be the only sister I'd ever want."

"Me too."

"Good night, Sun."

"Good night, Moon."

Minni sighed and looked out the window at the few stars she could see from where she lay. The sheets might be stiff and smell sort of like bleach, but she was still falling asleep in the same room with her favorite person in the world, and that was all that mattered.

Chapter Sixteen

☀ ♡ ☾

"We're going to the beauty parlor this morning," Grandmother Johnson said at the table the next day. "Normally, we wouldn't have been able to get in on a Saturday, but they had a cancellation."

Minni stopped and thought about this announcement. Grandmother Johnson was old. And "beauty parlor" sounded suspiciously like a place where old ladies went to get their hair done. Would she and Keira leave there with old-lady hairdos?

"Will they know what to do with our hair?" she asked.

"They're not doing anything with yours. The appointment is for Keira."

Keira's eyebrows pulled together. "I don't need help with my hair. I can do it myself just fine."

"Can you give yourself a relaxer?"

Keira dropped her spoon in her cereal. "Really?" Her smile took up half her face.

"Mama doesn't let Keira get relaxers," Minni said.

Keira's lips were suddenly doing a backbend. She gave Minni a stink-eye so fierce Mama and Daddy could probably smell it all the way out in Port Townsend.

"I mean, she told her she couldn't get her hair texturized until she was eleven," Minni said, trying to get her sister's mouth to flip. "And we're eleven now, so I guess . . ."

Keira grinned, nodding.

"She said no such thing."

Keira's smile went south again. Her lips were getting a serious workout today.

"I am fully aware that your mother is committed to this natural nonsense, but as I told her, God wouldn't have given Madam C. J. Walker the wisdom and knowledge to create products to smooth out our hair if he didn't want us to use them."

"You talked to her about it?" Keira asked.

"I spoke with her last night. She's agreed to let you try it."

Keira jumped up from the table and bounced around the living room, pulling at her pompon ponytails and letting the tight curls snap back toward her head. Her voice rose up and down with her springing body and hair. "I'm getting a relaxer! I'm getting a relaxer!"

"You'll get yourself a bad case of trouble if you don't stop that nonsense. Get back in here and clean up your dishes."

Keira came back, still smiling in spite of being bossed around by the Wicked Witch of the South.

Grandmother Johnson had done it again—worked her strange magic on Mama. They must have talked after Mama returned Minni's call yesterday. Mama had asked Minni several times if things were going okay, and although Minni had wanted to tell her what had happened at the Black Pearls of America office with Dr. Hogg-Graff seeing her but not seeing her, in the end she didn't want Mama to worry or be mad, so she kept it to herself.

"You can thank your father this time. In spite of his severe *lack* of education, he helped me convince your mother that you should be allowed to make your own decision about this. Perhaps he's smarter than I perceived."

Minni ignored the dig on Daddy. "What about me?" she asked.

"Your hair is too delicate for those harsh chemicals. No, child, you don't need all that. Just thank the Lord for sparing you the trouble."

Instead, she thanked the Lord that Grandmother Johnson had drunk all the buttermilk last night and hadn't gone to the store for more before this morning.

They washed their dishes, then headed downtown. Minni brought her MLK book, since according to Grandmother Johnson the procedure would take at least three hours. She had actually called it a "procedure," as if Keira were having her appendix removed or some other problem fixed.

Salon D'Vine was one of several businesses inside an old brick building that had been fixed up. They walked through an indoor courtyard with lush green plants growing everywhere.

Right before they stepped into the salon, Minni pulled her sister back. "Are you sure you want to do this?"

"Are you kidding? I've been begging Mom for years to get a relaxer."

"What if the chemicals ruin your hair?"

"They won't. Mom just says that."

"But your hair is beautiful!" Minni suddenly felt like crying.

Keira grabbed one of her Afro puffs. "You don't know what it's like to have to take care of all this, Skinny."

It was true.

"It'll be okay," Keira said. "Trust me." She gazed into Minni's eyes in that way that reminded Minni she would always have at least one other person in the world who knew what she looked like deep down inside. "Okay?"

"Okay." She followed Keira into the salon.

The front room was painted a deep lilac, and everything, from the jewel-encrusted lamps to the black iron curtain rods to the red velvet chairs, screamed hipness. Tendrils from potted plants in the corners trailed along the walls. All the chairs in the waiting area were taken. A few women sipped wine from real glasses. Others drank coffee. The air smelled of heat and hair products and the dried lavender Mama hung in all the windows of their house.

Most of the women waiting looked on the younger side— not even as old as Mama, who insisted she wasn't old even though she was already pushing forty-three. Then there were some women who looked around Mama's age. Grandmother Johnson was definitely the oldest person there.

"This is where you get your hair done?" Minni asked.

"No. But I thought Keira might appreciate having hers done by someone a little—what do you young people say?—'cooler' than my stylist. This is also supposedly the best salon in all of North Carolina for African American hair."

Keira smiled. A genuine smile. For a second, Minni thought her sister might even give their grandmother a hug. Keira squeezed Minni instead. "Isn't this so exciting?" She jiggled up and down.

But as hard as Minni tried, she couldn't be excited for her sister. She loved Keira's hair. How many times had she wished hers could be as curly and dark? As many times as she'd wished her skin were browner so that people would see they were sisters and not just friends.

Minni looked around. All the stylists, whom Minni could see in the other half of the salon, were black. All the women sitting in the chairs around them were black. Standing in the center of the room, she suddenly felt like a marble statue on display, even though none of the women had looked up from their magazines to notice them.

The receptionist walked up. "Would you like a soda?" she asked the girls.

Minni started to say, "Yes, please!" but Grandmother Johnson butted in. "At ten o'clock in the morning? I don't think so. Besides, children drink way too many empty calories these days. Not to mention all that carbonation and acid—very hard on the digestion. Water will be fine."

She couldn't just say no. She had to go and give the woman a lecture about the evils of carbonation. The receptionist looked at Minni and Keira as if she felt very sorry for them, then walked over to a small refrigerator.

A chair opened up and Grandmother Johnson went to sit.

The receptionist returned with two bottles, leaned over with a definite twinkle in her eye and whispered, "It's sparkling." She winked. "Do you want to sit over here?" She pointed to two hair-drying chairs on the opposite end of the room from where Grandmother Johnson had sat.

"Sure! Thanks," they said together. They sat and twisted off their bottle caps. The carbonation let out a small *tshhh*. They looked over at Grandmother Johnson just in case she'd heard it. Like all the other ladies, she was flipping through a magazine. Unlike the other ladies, she *tsk*ed at each page and shook her head.

Minni sipped the fizzy water. It tickled the insides of her mouth and made her feel like laughing. In the room where the stylists worked, a stand held hot combs and pressing irons for straightening curly hair. Why did women want to get their hair pulled straight? She would have given any-thing to have thick, kinky black curls.

Port Townsend didn't have any salons for black women. Whenever Mama needed to get her hair washed and retwisted or she wanted to change up her look, Daddy would fly them to Seattle and they'd all make a day of it.

Mama went to a woman who did natural styles in her living room by appointment only, so they were always the only ones there, not at all like being here at the crowded Salon D'Vine.

The first time Minni could remember going with Mama

to her stylist's house, she and Keira had been six. That visit, she had learned two things that would stick with her forever.

One, it was possible to get rid of your name if you didn't like it and become a whole new person. The stylist told them she had changed her name in college from Diane to Kenya. She'd gone to a government office and signed papers and everything, and no one was supposed to call her Diane any longer. Minni had decided then and there that as soon as she got to college she would do the exact same thing—she would head straight to that government office and unload the burden of "Minerva" once and for all.

The second thing she'd learned was about her hair.

Mama had asked Miss Kenya on the phone if she would do her daughters' hair while they were there—"Clips-n-Snips is no longer 'cutting it,'" she had said with a laugh, "especially for my one daughter's hair." Minni had known she meant Keira, since the last time they'd been to the budget salon, Keira had cried all the way home that her head looked like a pyramid.

Miss Kenya scheduled them all for appointments, but as soon as they walked in the door, the woman said she wouldn't be comfortable doing Minni's hair. She specialized in black hair. She could do Keira's, but Minni would be better off with Clips-n-Snips. She apologized to Minni and told her not to feel bad—there was nothing wrong with her hair. The texture was just finer than she was used to working on.

But Minni *did* feel bad, because she understood what Miss Kenya was saying: She had white-people hair.

Once again, she felt too different from her mother and sister. *One of these things is not like the others. . . .*

Afterward, they had gone down to the pier with Daddy. Minni insisted on walking between Mama and Keira. She gripped their hands tightly, not wanting either of them to let go. They had been to the city many times, but she had never been so afraid of getting lost in the crowd.

Minni's attention was brought sharply back to Salon D'Vine. Keira had poked her in the arm and was pointing at Grandmother Johnson with a look of glee. Their grandmother had nodded off. Her chin rested on her chest.

Minni was about to wonder aloud if they should wake her before she got to log sawing and embarrassed herself (and them) too badly, when Grandmother Johnson snorted.

Keira had just taken a sip of her drink. *"Pffft!"* Water sprayed from her lips. Women looked up from their magazines.

Grandmother Johnson's head jerked. She glanced around to see if anyone had been watching. Minni and Keira looked away quickly but ended up looking at each other. They jumped in surprise and then busted up.

Grandmother Johnson rose.

Minni pinched her sister's arm.

Keira choked down the water she'd been holding in her mouth.

Grandmother Johnson beelined toward them. Minni could see it in their grandmother's eyes: Her embarrassment over her*self* was about to be taken out on *them*.

Fortunately, a stylist in an apron arrived at the same

moment as Grandmother Johnson, sparing them from another lecture. "Are you Keira?" the stylist asked. Her hair was sleek and shiny, pinned into an elaborate twist at the back of her head.

"Yes, ma'am." Keira was suddenly full of Southern manners.

"I'm her grandmother, Minerva Johnson-Payne." Grandmother Johnson bent her extended hand at the wrist, almost as if she expected the woman to kiss it.

"Pleasure," the younger woman said, shaking the ends of Grandmother Johnson's fingers. "I'm Angelique. Now, let's see what we've got to work with here. Can you take these out?" She pointed to Keira's Afro puffs.

Keira pulled out the ponytail holders and shook her head.

Angelique picked out a curly strand, pinched the hair near Keira's scalp, then yanked the other end. "No breakage. Good. You've got a healthy head of hair, young lady."

"I deep-condition twice a month."

Angelique nodded.

"What are you going to do to her hair?" Minni asked.

"I think we have you down for a relaxer, am I right?"

"That's right," Grandmother Johnson said.

"How do you do it, though? Make really curly hair so straight?"

"First of all, relaxers don't make hair all the way straight."

"They don't?" Keira looked disappointed.

"That's why they're called relaxers. They relax the curls—get them to chill out a bit."

"I need them to chill out a *lot*," Keira said.

"Don't worry. The difference will be dramatic."

"Dramatic goes well with this one," Grandmother Johnson said.

Keira narrowed her eyes.

"But how does it work?" Minni asked once more. She felt her sister glaring at her, as if to say, *Would you stop talking already?*

But Minni needed to know. What if this ruined Keira's hair forever, the way Mama seemed to think chemical straighteners did? She had told them the process was so harsh, a person might as well put a match to her head.

"Basically, the chemicals break the bonds inside the hair shaft, then reset them in a new, looser arrangement. Is that a good enough explanation?" Angelique put her hands in Keira's hair and felt around some more. "With the texturizer, you'll be able to wear it curly or straight."

"Straight hair, here I come!" Keira exclaimed.

"Can I get a perm?" Minni blurted. She'd always wanted to have Keira's tight, springy curls. Maybe now was her chance.

Angelique looked at her. She felt the end of one of Minni's pigtails. "Your hair's pretty fine. And it's already nearly straight. If you perm out what little curl you have—"

"Not a straight perm. A curly one. *Really* curly. Like my sister's is now."

Grandmother Johnson interrupted. "And ruin your perfectly good hair? No."

Keira's face wrinkled up almost as much as one of the prunes Grandmother Johnson had been making them eat every day. "Ruin?" She crossed her arms. "Do you think there's something wrong with my hair the way it is?"

Angelique's eyes slid back and forth between Grandmother Johnson and Keira.

"You seemed more than happy to have it relaxed," Grandmother Johnson said.

Women in the waiting area were starting to stare. "Mama says we both have good hair," Minni said.

Grandmother Johnson looked down her nose. "Well, some of us need a little more help to have that good hair than others."

Keira huffed. Then she turned and walked straight out the door.

Grandmother Johnson's mouth flew open, but nothing came out. She looked about as shocked as if she'd just heard a donkey talk. So, the woman could be silenced after all.

Minni ran after her sister. It appeared that Keira would be keeping her curls, and for that, Minni was very, very glad.

Chapter Seventeen

☀ ♡ ☾

On Sunday, Grandmother Johnson woke them early to shower. She had informed them the night before that as long as they were staying under her roof, they would be attending church.

No more had been said about the salon or how the excursion had ended. Grandmother Johnson must have known it was no use trying to get Keira to go for the relaxer once she had soured on the idea. Their grandmother couldn't exactly drag Keira back to Salon D'Vine and chain her to Angelique's chair.

Keira bathed first, since her thick and still kinky-curly hair took extra long to wash. When she came back to the attic, she looked as if she'd discovered buried treasure. She pulled a plastic bottle from under her shirt and sat next to Minni on Minni's bed. "Look what I found in the medicine cabinet."

Minni had almost peeked behind the mirror herself but had been too scared that the sound of it clicking open and shut would alert Grandmother Johnson to her trespassing.

Keira handed the container to Minni. "I didn't feel like figuring out everything the label said, but I could read a few of the words, no problem: 'gets rid of' and '*gas*.'" She made a fart sound with her mouth.

Minni snickered at the name of the medicine. "Flatulex?"

As she read out loud about gastrointestinal distress and embarrassing odors, the need to laugh built—just like the air trapped in Grandmother Johnson's colon. "It works by making you burp and fart your gas out!" She dropped the bottle of pills on the bed, grabbed her pillow and smashed it against her face. She laughed until her stomach ached and she felt as though she would suffocate.

Keira took no such precaution. She just fell out on the bed, hooting and hollering. Her feet pounded the footboard.

Minni was too busy trying to suppress her own laughter to shush Keira. She flopped alongside her sister. Whenever she felt a giggle attack coming on, she shoved her face into the pillow again. She shook uncontrollably . . . like that dog pooping on Grandmother Johnson's TruGreen lawn.

Thinking about the dog and Grandmother Johnson running toward it like a crazy Amazon woman made Minni laugh even harder. The pillowcase was getting wet from tears and drool. She felt as though her laughter had been piling up like snow on a mountain; the antigas medicine had set off an avalanche.

Keira snorted, sending them into another fit. The bottle

bounced on the bed between them. Minni laughed so hard she gave herself the hiccups.

"What's going on up there?"

Minni bolted upright. Grandmother Johnson's voice worked like her pills. They both knocked the air right out of you.

The door below cracked open. "Minerva, have you showered?"

Minni opened her mouth to speak, but all that came out was a hiccup.

"She'll be down in a minute," Keira said.

The door closed and Grandmother Johnson clip-clopped away.

"She really knows how to *make a stink*," Keira said. They clapped their palms over their mouths and laughed some more.

"That's because she's so full of *hot air*," Minni replied. More giggles.

How would they get through the rest of the day—the rest of the trip, for that matter—without breaking into inexplicable laughter at the slightest mention of anything gas- or odor-related? Grandmother Johnson would never stand for the rudeness of such outbursts. And if Keira snorted in church, Minni didn't know what their grandmother might do.

Keira's arms flopped from her stomach to the bed. She let out one last giggle and sighed. Hearing the air rush from her sister's lungs helped Minni to exhale, too. Her stomach muscles finally relaxed.

"I've got an idea." Keira's eyebrows danced the way they did when she was thinking something devious. "Grandmother Johnson may need some gas relief while we're at church. We'll just slip a couple of these into her oatmeal—"

"Yes!" Minni sat up. "After yesterday, she deserves it." They grinned at each other.

Justice for Grandmother Gasbag Johnson.

Sweet, sweet justice.

All the way to church, Minni worked hard not to look at Keira or think about the plot they had executed flawlessly. Keira had dropped in the pills and Minni had given the cereal a quick stir while their grandmother retrieved something from the kitchen. She had eaten the whole bowl without comment or a single raise of The Eyebrow. Keira had returned the medicine to the bathroom before they left the house.

As they drove along, Grandmother Johnson's stomach gurgled like a swamp monster. Each time, she let out a small gasp of surprise. Minni pressed her lips together, stared out the window and pretended she hadn't heard a thing.

Finally, they arrived at the church—Good Shepherd African Methodist Episcopal. The front rose steeply toward the sky, solid as a rock-climbing wall, with big, castlelike wooden doors. Families with boys in suits and girls in frilly dresses, couples and older people came from all directions.

Grandmother Johnson parked in a gravel lot a block away. Before getting out, she reached across the seat to the mystery box she'd brought to the car. She removed the lid and pulled out a hat covered in spiky white feathers. Somewhere a crested ibis was flying around with a naked behind.

She put on the hat and with four quick jabs pinned it to her head. "Let's go. No dillydallying." Her stomach rumbled again. "Ooo," she said, holding her belly. "The oatmeal's not settling so well today."

Keira smirked at Minni, who clambered out of the car. She didn't know how long she could maintain her poker face.

"She looks like she's wearing a feather duster on her head," Keira whispered as they followed behind.

"And a nurse's uniform," Minni whispered back. Grandmother Johnson was dressed completely in white.

She strode ahead of them down the sidewalk, commanding them to keep up. Her dress, gloves and hat feathers glowed in the humid gray air. Minni watched the sky, expecting any second to be dive-bombed by a flock of angry seagulls avenging one of their own.

"Deacon Barnes," Grandmother Johnson said with a curt nod to a man on the front steps.

"Deaconess Johnson," he said, tipping his hat.

They passed through the large front doors into a reception area. People milled about, chatting and laughing. All the women wore fancy dresses. Two boys in suits chased each other. No one wore a hat that looked like a blow-dried bird.

A picture of a husband and wife hung on the wall. Minni

could tell they were married by the way the woman leaned into the man and had her hand on his shoulder. An engraved gold plaque read, THE REVEREND DR. JAMES JULIUS AND HIS FIRST LADY.

Grandmother Johnson stopped to talk to another woman. Minni peered through the propped-open door that led to the inner part of the church—the part that had rows of pews all facing the front and a kind of stage with a podium. The part that made you feel like you had to be quiet. The *altar*, Minni seemed to recall it was called.

A large stained-glass picture high on the wall over the altar showed a brown-skinned shepherd with a staff in his hand and sheep around his feet. A light glowed around his curly black hair as if the sun were coming up behind his head. Was the shepherd Jesus?

She didn't really know much about Jesus, except that he was supposed to be God's son. She'd never seen him pictured with brown skin but she liked the idea that he could change colors depending on where he was, like a chameleon. She'd like to be able to do that.

"This way," Grandmother Johnson said, walking toward the open door. A smiling man handed them each a folded program; then a lady in white gloves led them down the aisle, keeping one hand locked behind her back. Grandmother Johnson held her chin high and walked the red carpet as though she were on a runway in Paris.

The cavernous space smelled of varnish, old carpet and the dust, sweat and tears of at least five generations. The woman led them farther and farther down the aisle until

Minni was afraid she was taking them to the pews on the altar, next to the man who had just come out to play the organ.

Just before they reached the front, the lady stopped and held out her hand—her other hand still firmly behind her back—directing them to sit in the second row. Grandmother Johnson went in first, pulling Keira in beside her. Minni scooted in last.

The lone woman in the front row sat in her seat as if it had been hers since the day God had made the earth. Her hat was the only one in the place that rivaled Grandmother Johnson's in its plumage. With all the yellow feathers and netting, it looked as though she had a whole flock of chicks nesting on her head.

A girl, old enough to be in high school, came and sat next to the lady. Minni got a glimpse of the woman's profile. This wasn't just any lady. It was the lady from the picture in the reception area—the *first* lady! Minni didn't know what that meant exactly, but if she had the same name as the president's wife she must be pretty important.

Several women and men in long blue robes filed out from a side door up front. The choir, Minni figured.

Then a large man in a black robe came out and stepped to the podium. She recognized him from the picture as well. The Reverend Dr. James Julius. He asked them to stand and then he said some fancy words and everyone read some words together off the program—except for Keira, who didn't like to read out loud, and Minni, who stayed quiet so her sister wouldn't feel alone. Then Grandmother Johnson handed them a big book opened to a song and the organ cranked up, and everyone sang, except for Minni and Keira again.

Minni couldn't see around the first lady very well. She wondered how many people didn't have a clear view of the reverend doctor because of Grandmother Johnson's hat. The song ended and everyone sat.

"Now is the time in our service when we welcome all those who are joining us for the first time." The reverend doctor smiled and held out his hand in their direction. "Deaconess Johnson, would you like to introduce your guests?"

Minni's heart banged against the walls of her chest as if it were trying to run from the church, which was what *she* felt like doing. Her palms turned moist, and if she didn't calm down quickly, her pits would soon have everyone around her wondering who had brought an overripe cantaloupe into church.

Grandmother Johnson rose to her feet like snow-covered Mount Rainier. "Stand up," she said under her breath. "Giving all honor to God, the reverend doctor and his first lady, and all my fellow saints here today . . ."

Minni swallowed, trying to unstick her dry mouth. She hoped Grandmother Johnson didn't expect her and Keira to say a bunch of fancy words like that.

"I have the pleasure of having my granddaughters with me this week. This is Minerva"—she reached across Keira and touched Minni's shoulder, looking around the crowded room—"and Keira. They will be competing in the Miss

Black Pearl Preteen of America pageant in exactly one week from today. I invite everyone to come out and give your support."

Please don't! Minni wanted to shout.

The reverend doctor welcomed them, then turned to a lady nearby who had stood while Grandmother Johnson was speaking. Minni sat, giving all honor to God that she hadn't had to speak in front of all these people.

"Yes, Sister Russell?"

The woman stood alone. She was tall and stylish and wore a huge diamond ring.

"I want to add that my granddaughter, Alisha, will *also* be competing for the title of Miss Black Pearl Preteen." The woman smiled at Grandmother Johnson from across the aisle.

The corners of Grandmother Johnson's mouth turned up as well, but it was hard to tell if she was smiling or snarling. Her eyes narrowed as if she were inviting Sister Russell to duel.

After a few more introductions, the choir stood. The man at the organ played a few chords that sounded familiar. Minni couldn't place them—until a girl in the choir started singing.

"Why should I feel discouraged?" she began.

The sparrow song. It sounded so much better than when she and Grandmother Johnson had practiced it.

The longer the girl sang, the more entranced Minni became. The music wrapped around her again and again until she could hardly move. It squeezed her heart so hard that a tear popped out of the corner of her eye and trickled down her cheek before she even knew what had happened.

The choir joined in on the chorus. *"I sing because I'm happy. I sing because I'm free . . ."*

Their voices dipped, dove and soared together, like a roomful of swallows, separate and yet one. Minni wasn't sure if heaven actually existed, but if it did it would sound like this. Like the ocean, Keira's laughter, Mama's singing, and Daddy's "I'm home!" all at once.

The belting voices sliced through her and made her insides melt like one of those chocolates with the liquidy centers, until she wanted to leap up with the people around her, who swayed and shouted to the music, and at the same time fall to the ground in a puddle of tears.

This was what the song was supposed to sound like? This was what it could make another person feel? She was at once overwhelmed with the knowledge that she could never make the song sound anything like this and inspired to give it everything she had the next time she tried.

She didn't want the music to stop, and for a long time it didn't. The organist kept returning to the chorus, and the soloist kept letting her voice slide up and down and all around, and people all over the church were shouting and some were even slumping to their seats and needing the ladies in white gloves to come and fan their faces.

When finally they reached the last chord, they held on to it so long that Minni expected some of the choir members themselves to faint. The choir director shook her hands in the air, encouraging the singers to keep the wall of sound coming, and they did, like a roaring waterfall, and then, just like that, the director brought her hands down and the waterfall stopped.

The entire church—even Grandmother Johnson—was on its feet, applauding. Minni and Keira stood and clapped, too. Choir members shouted out, "Hallelujah!"

The organ kept playing as the reverend doctor came to the podium. "His eye is on the sparrow!" he shouted.

"Amen!" people shouted back.

"And I know . . . say, 'I know!'"

"I know!" everyone said together.

"I *know* he watches me!"

"Yes, sir!" a man exclaimed.

"If I go up to the heavens, he is there."

"Yes!"

"If I make my bed in the depths, he is there."

"Thank you, Jesus!"

"If I settle on the far side of the sea, even *there* his hand shall guide me, his right hand shall hold me fast!"

"Amen!" people thundered. More applause and lots of organ playing.

Minni and Keira looked at each other and smiled. Maybe this church thing wouldn't be so bad after all. This was a whole lot more exciting than the church they'd visited in Port Townsend where everyone sat with their hands in their laps and seemed to like things very quiet, as if God were sleeping and they didn't want to wake him.

The organ stopped and everyone finally sat, but the music had worked like a charger, connecting the place to a giant electrical outlet, and though the room had quieted down, it was still full of energy.

The Reverend Dr. James Julius looked out at them all. "As we read in the Scriptures, God is like the hen that gathers her chicks under her wing."

Grandmother Johnson put her fingers to her lips and belched. Not loudly enough for anyone to notice—except Minni and Keira. They looked at each other out of the corners of their eyes. Minni stifled a giggle.

The reverend doctor kept talking. The longer he went on, the more Grandmother Johnson shifted and squirmed in her seat. She crossed her legs one way and then quickly crossed them the other. At one point, the air around them turned funky. Minni grabbed the fan from the back of the pew in front of her and waved it in front of her face the way other women were doing around the church.

Meanwhile, Keira had started to shake with held-in laughter. Minni pinched her sister's arm. She couldn't control herself much longer. She held her breath and fanned harder. Grandmother Johnson glared at them until, thankfully, Keira got ahold of herself.

The pastor got louder and louder, and faster and faster, and Grandmother Johnson looked more and more uncomfortable, as if she were sitting on a pinecone. Then, quite unexpectedly, in the midst of the singsong rhythm he had established, the reverend doctor decided to add a dramatic pause. He stopped—just as a high-pitched squeak came from underneath Grandmother Johnson's wide bottom.

Minni squeezed her sister's arm. She tried to swallow her

laughter, but some of it escaped through her nose, making a sound like a snorting horse.

Suddenly Keira was on her feet. Grandmother Johnson scooted them into the aisle. "Move. Now!" she whispered fiercely.

If the reverend doctor had noticed, he didn't show it. He picked right back up where he had left off, calling people to come forward who needed God to touch them and make them well. People filled the aisle, moving toward the front of the church. Minni, Keira and Grandmother Johnson were suddenly walking upstream.

Did God know how to deal with gastrointestinal distress? Perhaps Grandmother Johnson should join the people going forward.

Minni stumbled alongside their grandmother, who dragged them to the end of the red carpet and through the first door, past the picture of the honorable Reverend Dr. James Julius and his first lady and down the front steps.

The glowing Jesus must have worked some kind of miracle, because Minni and Keira kept all their laughter inside until they were safely in their room, their faces buried deep in their pillows.

Chapter Eighteen

☀ ♡ ☾

"She's old and wrinkled and her skin looks like puff pastry. And one of her eyes is all cloudy and pale, almost glowing. It's spooky." Minni sat cross-legged on her bed. She was finally getting a chance to tell Keira about Laverna Oliphant. The past two days, they'd barely had a moment to themselves, and at bedtime they'd spoken to their parents, and one night to Gigi as well. They'd fallen asleep before Minni remembered to describe her encounter with the mysterious neighbor.

Now, after an afternoon of reading *Black Beauty*, with Grandmother Johnson watching over their shoulders and doing far too much intruding, then dinner and a game of hearts, they were at last alone in the attic. Recounting Grandmother Johnson's untimely emission in church had made them roll with laughter and left them wide-awake.

"Do you really think she practices voodoo?" Keira asked, slipping into her nightshirt.

"Grandmother Johnson said she saw shrunken heads hanging in her kitchen window."

"Shrunken *heads?*"

"I guess they have something to do with voodoo."

"Sounds gross."

Minni bolted upright. "I know. Let's sneak out tonight and peek in her window!"

"You mean spy on her?" Keira sounded dubious.

"Not really. Just look and see if we can find anything to back up Grandmother Johnson's claims. Like I said—she's old. Really old. She probably won't even be up." Minni's curiosity about this stray-loving, possibly voodoo-practicing neighbor had been piqued, but truth be told, she was too spooked—*and* concerned that Miss Oliphant might know of their involvement in the poop-on-the-door incident— to have any kind of real conversation with her.

"Okay. You got me. Let's do it."

They changed back into their clothes. As soon as the snoring started, they snuck downstairs. As they passed the bathroom, the floorboards creaked so loudly, Minni was sure they would be caught. They grabbed each other, their eyes glued to the door at the end of the hall. The snoring kept on like a small aircraft engine, and they tiptoed toward the kitchen, practically tripping over each other to get outside.

A soft glow came from the first-floor windows alongside Miss Oliphant's house. "They're too high," Keira said, peering up. "There's no way to see in."

Maybe it was how well their scheme had worked this morning. Maybe it was the bright, shining moon. Whatever it was, Minni was feeling brave. "Stand on my shoulders," she said.

It was a stunt they did all the time at home—something Keira had learned in gymnastics. She had taught Minni how to be the "under-stander," the person on the bottom who needed to be strong, balanced and trustworthy. Minni had shown promise from their very first attempts, although it had still taken them several times to execute the mount flawlessly.

"Good idea."

Minni spread her feet and bent her knees. She focused on being as rooted to the ground as the elm trees lining the street. Keira put a foot on Minni's thigh and grabbed Minni's hands, and up she went. Then step, step and she had a foot on each of Minni's shoulders. Minni grasped her sister's calves and worked hard not to sway. "What do you see?" she whispered.

"Candles—everywhere. Do you think she's having a séance?"

"How would I know? I can't see anything! What's she doing?"

"She's at her dining room table, surrounded by candles. She's got some cards in a circle in front of her."

"Playing cards?"

"No, they're big. She's flipping one at a time, with lots of pausing in between."

Minni's pulse quickened. "Tarot cards! She's reading someone's future!"

"Or trying to find out who put that bag of poop on her door."

Minni's arms and legs suddenly felt weak.

"Let me down! You're shaking!" Keira lowered one leg and then the other so that she sat on Minni's shoulders. Minni started to kneel, but her legs buckled. Keira tumbled to the ground.

"Sorry." Minni grabbed Keira's hand and pulled her up. They hurried into their house, up to the attic, and fell onto Minni's bed, chests heaving from exertion and the thrill of their escape. They had collected some very intriguing intelligence about the enigmatic Miss Oliphant.

Perhaps Grandmother Johnson hadn't exaggerated. Could her neighbor actually read futures and cast spells?

The next morning, Grandmother Johnson was limping. She hobbled into the dining room, where Keira and Minni sat pushing soggy bran cereal around their bowls, waiting for an opportunity to dump the buttermilk in the ferns.

"Are you all right?" Keira asked.

Grandmother Johnson set her teacup on the table and lowered herself into her chair, wincing. "Arthritis. It flares up when storms are moving in."

Minni glanced out the window behind their grandmother. The sky was as clear and blue as a perfect piece of beach glass.

"Are you sure it's not your neighbor?" Keira looked at Minni with a sly smile.

"What kind of nonsense are you talking now, child?"

"Maybe she's got a voodoo doll over there and she's poking it in the knee."

Minni choked back a laugh.

Grandmother Johnson looked at Minni sternly, then turned to Keira. "Hogwash. I wouldn't put it past her to try—vengeance for my act of justice the other day—but that witch doctor foolishness is just that—*foolishness*." She waved her hand toward Keira's bowl. "Now finish up. I want you to sit with Minni and do some more reading."

Again, already? Minni thought. Although their lessons were going okay so far, she still felt awkward about tutoring her sister.

"Could we see more pictures of your grandmother, or other relatives of yours?" she asked quickly. Surely Keira wouldn't mind if she got them out of having to read. Plus, now that Minni knew what their great-great-grandmother had looked like, she was curious to see other pictures of Grandmother Johnson's extended family.

"They're your relatives too, you know."

"Oh, right. Other relatives of *ours*."

Grandmother Johnson looked at Minni intently, sipping her tea. "I suppose . . . if you're really interested." Minni and Keira both nodded. Their grandmother's lips curled into a small but pleased smile. She pushed back her chair and rose stiffly. "All right then, finish your breakfast and meet me in the living room." She limped to her bedroom.

Minni poured their buttermilk into the ferns while Keira tiptoed into the kitchen and disposed of the bran cereal.

They arrived in the living room at the same time as Grandmother Johnson and sat on either side of her on the straight-backed couch.

"Has your mother shown you this one?" Grandmother Johnson held up a framed photo of a man sitting in a stuffed armchair. A girl about Minni's and Keira's age sat in his lap, leaning back against his chest. Minni recognized the girl's round brown eyes and full lips, parted in a big grin full of crooked teeth. Her hair looked different braided into two plaits, but it was clear who it was. *Mama.*

Minni took the picture and pondered the man. Twinkling eyes set in a honey-brown face and framed by rectangular black glasses looked straight back at her. The man's arms circled Mama's shoulders and his long legs jutted out underneath her sprawling ones, which were covered to the knees by fitted striped pants. They looked as if they were laughing at a joke that only they shared.

"Isn't that Grandpa Johnson?" Keira reached for the picture and Minni gave it to her. Their grandfather, a government employee, had died before they were born. Mama still received money from interest earned off a big asbestos settlement he had won. A bitter reminder, she said, but a helpful supplement to her modest artist's income nonetheless. He had always encouraged her artistic abilities, she said, and would be happy to know he was helping make her career possible.

"Your mother worshipped the ground that man walked on. Always told her she could be anything she wanted." Grandmother Johnson took the frame and laid it on the coffee table. "I blame *him* for her fanciful pursuit of painting. She has the brains to be a doctor or lawyer. Even a successful business executive."

Mama in a suit? Carrying a briefcase to a board meeting? Never in a million years.

Grandmother Johnson opened the old album resting in her lap. "Here's a portrait of the lady I showed you the other day—your great-great-grandmother Minerva Louise Harris. This is the only portrait for which she ever sat. She half believed cameras had the power to snatch your soul from inside you."

The woman wasn't actually sitting. She stood straight and tall in a long, dark skirt and tailored jacket over a white blouse with a wide ruffled collar. Her shoulders were as broad as a man's. A lacy black hat perched at an angle on her head, and she wore black leather gloves. Wire-rimmed glasses framed her eyes. Her face looked paler and even more serious than in the locket picture.

Grandmother Johnson turned the page. In a square black-and-white photo, the same woman stood on the porch of a small, shacklike house in a housedress and apron, holding the hand of a much darker-skinned little girl in braids and a checkered dress. Minni pointed to the girl. "Is that you?"

Grandmother Johnson nodded. "Can you believe I was ever that small?"

It *was* hard to imagine their grandmother—formal and serious and bossy—as a young child. When had she become so obsessed with ladylike behavior and achievement? Had she ever enjoyed splashing in puddles, or eating an ice cream and letting it melt down her arm, or pretending her bicycle was a horse and she was a rider on the Pony Express? Had she ever put her toes in the ocean? If she hadn't, Minni felt very bad for her.

"We were extremely poor. In fact, at times, when my uncle brought me to Raleigh to visit Grandma Harris during the week, I'd look at these grand homes as we drove past and wonder if God cared for black people at all. I decided he must certainly love us less, or why would we be so much poorer than the whites?"

"Do you still think that?" Minni asked.

"Of course not. But seeing the disparity between black and white made a deep impression on me. Still, we had each other—we had family."

As she moved through the album, their grandmother pointed out the people who made up this family. Her mother and father when they were first married. Aunt Flossie, who eventually left with her husband and children to go north. Cousin Meaner, who ran the best soul-food restaurant Durham had ever known—so good, even white folks would venture into the black part of town to get themselves some of Miz Meaner's spicy ribs and buttermilk corn bread. Uncle Booker, who helped raise Grandmother Johnson, and whose farm's well produced such clean, fresh water, people traveled all the way from the big city of Raleigh to fill their jugs with the "Adam's ale."

"He was bottling water before there was such a thing," Grandmother Johnson said. "A true entrepreneur."

"So *that's* where Keira gets it," Minni said, smiling across Grandmother Johnson's large chest at her sister. Keira stared at the photos. She was being very quiet. Much quieter than normal. What was going on in her head? Minni wondered.

"I learned two things from my uncle. One, quality is colorless."

Minni noted with interest that Uncle Booker was significantly darker than his mother, Minerva Harris. All their relatives, other than their great-great-grandmother, had looked black.

"And two, white people will probably never accept you as an equal, but if you show them how industrious, intelligent and civilized you are, you may at least earn their respect."

Never accept you as an equal? Was that true?

Keira's forehead bunched, but she stayed quiet.

Some of the later pictures showed Grandmother Johnson as a young woman, just out of college. Then there were some of her with Grandpa Johnson and Mama as a baby. The final several pages contained class photos, just like the ones Minni and Keira got every year—the ones in which Minni was always in the back row, as tall as the boys on either side of her.

Grandmother Johnson stood to the side in each photo, with a faint but proud smile on her lips. These were all the classes she'd ever taught—"her children."

Right away, Minni noticed that Grandmother Johnson's earliest classes were all white. Or at least, all the children *appeared* to be white. As the years progressed, more black children were sprinkled throughout. By the last dozen or more pictures, all the children were black. She wanted to ask about this but wasn't sure how.

"Did you teach at an all-white school?" Keira's nose wrinkled. She looked puzzled—maybe even a little put off. It was hard to tell.

"At that time, yes, there were only white children at Lowell Elementary. I was one of five African American teachers handpicked by the superintendent to integrate the staff. It had been over ten years since *Brown versus the Board of Education*, and the government was pressing the city to integrate or forfeit federal funding."

Keira was thinking something serious. Minni could see it in her eyes.

"I was honored to be selected and I accepted, remembering what my uncle had taught me: Quality is colorless."

Grandmother Johnson closed the album. "I'll admit there were difficult times—always being watched, knowing I needed to perform flawlessly to prove that I was just as good as any white teacher."

Keira cocked her head as she listened. She nodded a little.

"Undoubtedly, part of the reason the superintendent chose me was because he knew I wouldn't make waves. I had sat on some district committees. I worked well with white people. I would come in and instruct the children, because that was my highest concern—educating children."

"But what about the black children? What about educating them?" Keira's eyebrows drew together sharply.

"I was looking at the bigger picture. And the bigger picture was that the white schools had more resources and better materials. Those kids were getting a higher-quality education—not because the teachers were any better, mind you." Grandmother Johnson sniffed. "Black children deserved to be let in, but someone had to pave the way."

She stood abruptly and tugged on her jacket hem, clutching the album to her chest. "Anyway, what are we doing sitting inside this stuffy house on such a nice day? Shall we dine out for lunch?"

"How about Thai?" Keira suggested, seeming to return to her lighthearted self again. "Panang curry is the best!"

Minni nodded in agreement. Now *she* felt like being quiet. Questions flooded her mind. Grandmother Johnson a way-paver? What had it been like to teach in a school that wouldn't allow black children to sit in desks next to white children? And if she, Minni, had been alive at that time, which school would *she* have attended?

Grandmother Johnson patted the photo album. "All this talk about family has put me in the mood for some good down-home cooking. I'll take you to Dinah's. Their ribs can't hold a candle to Cousin Meaner's, but the buttermilk fried chicken is delectable. Before we partake of lunch, however, I want to take you to a very *special* and important place."

They got their shoes and met up in the kitchen. Grandmother Johnson inspected their faces, hair and clothes in her usual brisk manner, but when she opened a compact mirror and applied a fresh coat of lipstick her hands trembled. And when she went to pick up her car keys from the counter, she picked up the metal measuring spoons instead. Had their trip down memory lane shaken her somehow?

Minni followed her sister outside, wondering what kind of place Grandmother Johnson considered "special and important." Probably just some big garden with fancy flowers growing everywhere, or that old cemetery in Oakwood where all Raleigh's rich people were buried.

At least they had some good food to look forward to.

Chapter Nineteen

☀ ♡ ☾

Grandmother Johnson didn't take them to a garden or a cemetery. She took them to Raleigh's African American Museum of History and Civil Rights. "A museum?" Keira whispered. Her nose wrinkled with disappointment.

Minni was not disappointed at all. This would be much more interesting than looking at a bunch of hydrangeas and azaleas, or worse, a bunch of dead people's grave markers.

Grandmother Johnson parked the car and they walked toward the building, which was surrounded by a sprawling lawn and trees. To the right of the entrance was a large brick courtyard, at the center of which was some kind of sculpture. It looked like a big upside-down pyramid sunk onto a base of two smaller right-side-up half pyramids.

Minni read the plaque at the entrance to the courtyard. "The Martin Luther King Water Monument!" she said excitedly. Grandmother Johnson called out something about needing to get inside, but Minni ignored her and ran to the monument.

She stood at the short brick wall that separated the sculpture from the rest of the courtyard. A steady flow of water rising from a hole in the center covered the black surface with a thin glossy layer. The water rippled from its source, then ran over the edge of the large inverted pyramid, clinging to the sides all the way down. She read the inscription on a smaller pyramid sitting at the far corner of the large, water-covered table: "'Until justice rolls down like waters and righteousness like a mighty stream.' Dr. Martin Luther King, Jr."

Keira had caught up with her. Grandmother Johnson slowly made her way toward them, still limping a little.

Minni read the writing on the surface of the glistening table. Listed were the names and roles of twenty-five local citizens who had made "significant contributions in the fields of civil rights, race relations, community improvement and education equality." She scanned the list.

One name hooked her attention just as Grandmother Johnson walked up. Minni pointed. "Laverna Oliphant!" She read the words under Miss Oliphant's name out loud. "Champion Civil Rights Leader, Longtime Professor, Shaw University."

"Wow," Keira said.

"Wow is right," Minni agreed.

Grandmother Johnson's lips pinched together and she exhaled loudly through her nose. She didn't look very impressed. She pulled a handkerchief from her purse and dabbed her forehead. "Time to get inside. This sun is too hot."

Keira looked at Minni out of the corner of her eye. A small smile turned up one corner of her mouth. "Sure you're not just going through 'the change'?" she asked.

"The change? What in heaven's name are you talking about, child?"

"Mom says it's an old lady thing," Keira replied seriously, but her eyes were full of mischief.

Grandmother Johnson's jaw tightened. "If I'm old, then that's all the more reason to show some respect." She grasped Keira's elbow and pulled her toward the museum. "Let's go."

Minni followed, glancing over her shoulder. She wished she could have read all the names and inscriptions.

Inside, large panes of glass made the lobby bright and almost as warm as outside, but it cooled down considerably when they entered the first exhibit hall. Minni's skin rippled with goose bumps.

"This way," Grandmother Johnson instructed. She seemed to have a particular destination in mind. Minni tripped along behind Keira, feeling the tug of all the photographs and captions she wasn't being allowed to stop and ponder.

They passed through a large entryway. Lettering over the entrance said, THE SIXTIES. Grandmother Johnson made a beeline to a blown-up black-and-white photo mounted on the wall. Even from a distance, Minni could tell who it was.

She would know that oval face, prominent forehead, intense gaze and well-kept mustache anywhere.

Dr. King.

He stood at a podium in what looked like a church.

"This was taken during one of his few visits to Raleigh, not too long before that fateful day . . ." Grandmother Johnson looked at the picture and then at the girls. Back to the picture and at the girls again—as if she was waiting for them to notice something.

And then Minni did. She noticed stained-glass feet above Dr. King's head. The glowing Good Shepherd's feet. "Is that your church?"

As soon as the words were out of her mouth, she saw something even more astonishing. Her jaw dropped.

There in the far right corner of the photograph, sitting in one of the choir's pews, was Grandmother Johnson! Her hair was pulled back in the same tight bun. Her eyebrows arched high. Her face was thinner and less saggy, and she was smiling an actual smile. But it was undoubtedly her. "That's *you*," Minni breathed excitedly. "Sitting behind Dr. King!"

Keira stepped closer and looked. "Wow," she said again.

"Did you meet him . . . talk to him?" Minni asked, bursting with questions. "What was it like to hear him speak?"

Grandmother Johnson gazed at the photograph. "Like rocketing into outer space . . . being lit on fire but not being consumed . . . receiving water on a parched and withered tongue . . . all at the same time." For a moment, it seemed as if she had left her body and entered the picture. "He gave us so much hope."

Suddenly her eyes turned moist. She spoke quietly. "When we heard the news that he had been shot, some of the children at Lowell cheered." Her breath seemed to catch in her throat. "It about tore me to shreds."

Cheered? Minni's face and chest burned with anger. *Cheered?*

"The following day, I just couldn't go in—couldn't face those . . ." Grandmother Johnson's voice trailed off. "My one absence in forty-five years . . ." She closed her eyes. Then she blinked, and just like that, she was ready to move on.

Minni lingered in front of the photo awhile longer. Her grandmother had sat in the same room as Dr. King!

They spent another hour or so wandering from room to room, but Minni didn't take in much after that. One group of photographs that *did* catch Minni's attention featured black people she never would have known were black had the captions not said so. *Just like me*, she thought.

The display talked about something called "passing," where blacks would take on white identities by day so they could find work, then return to their black families at night. Some people even cut themselves off from their families entirely, choosing to live as white and never seeing their loved ones again.

These pictures both drew her in and pushed her away. To live as white and never see Keira or Mama again? The very thought of it made her reel, like a satellite spinning into outer space, disconnected and alone. Reading about what these people had done—or felt they needed to do—to have a good life made her feel sad and afraid and even a little ashamed, although she didn't know why. She had never done—never would do—anything like that.

What about in the dress shop?

The question caught her off guard.

You didn't exactly let the woman know you weren't the white girl she thought you were.

She pushed the accusation from her mind and hurried out to the hall, searching for Keira and wishing she hadn't seen the exhibit on passing.

When they returned from their scrumptious lunch at Dinah's Soul Food restaurant, Minni clambered to the attic and called home.

Mama picked up on the second ring. "She met Dr. King! She shook his hand!" Minni blurted.

"Sounds like you went to the museum."

Minni ran all her words together as if they were one sentence. "Mama, it's amazing! I just can't believe it, but of course I do, because I saw the picture with my own eyes. It's incredible! Why didn't you ever tell me?"

Mama let her catch her breath. "Believe me, I've wanted to many times. But she asked me not to. She's been looking forward to showing you that picture for a long time."

Keira climbed the stairs and flopped onto her bed.

"Your grandmother may not have gone for staging sit-ins and letting herself get arrested, but she revered Dr. King from the beginning. And she tried to make a difference in her own way."

Minni supposed that was true, given that Grandmother Johnson had been willing to be one of the first black teachers to work at a white school at a time when white people didn't want black people there.

"You and Keira doing all right?"

Minni glanced at Keira, who lay on the bed twisting one of her curls around her finger. "Yeah. We're good. Oh—and after the museum, she took us out for soul food!" Minni put the phone on speaker so Keira could hear.

"Mother took you for soul food? Wow. Did you go to Dinah's?"

"Yeah, how'd you know?"

"That place is legendary. We went there all the time when I was a girl. Did you enjoy it?"

"The mac and cheese was incredible," Keira said.

"And could you make us greens like that at home?" Minni asked. The last and only time she'd had greens was the first time Mama and Daddy took them for soul food in Seattle. She'd only tried them this time because Grandmother Johnson had made her. And then she devoured the whole mound.

"Mmmm . . . I'll never forget the taste of Dinah's greens." Mama paused as if she was remembering their tangy flavor. "I'm sure mine wouldn't turn out anything like Dinah's, but I suppose I could try. I didn't exactly learn how to cook growing up."

"We had mushy tuna casserole last night." Keira stuck her finger in her mouth.

"With stringy pieces of celery." Minni shuddered.

"Hang in there. Only three days to the orientation. How you feeling about it?"

"Can't wait!" Keira shouted.

"Minni? You feeling all right about it?"

"Mm-hmm." She wasn't really, but she wanted Mama to be proud of her for not being too scared, and seeing the photograph of Dr. King and Grandmother Johnson had momentarily inspired her to at least try to overcome her fear of speaking in front of groups.

"Is Daddy reading his book?" she asked.

"He's working at it. How about you, Keira? Are you reading every day?"

Minni chimed in. "She's doing great." They hadn't read yet today, but they still had time. Tonight they would read the Dr. King book instead of *Black Beauty*.

They said their goodbyes. Minni rolled onto her back. She was still in shock. Yes, Grandmother Johnson was a pain at times, but she had been in the actual presence of Dr. Martin Luther King, Jr.

Amazing. Absolutely amazing.

Chapter Twenty

When Minni opened her eyes the next morning, bright light streamed into the attic. She looked at her watch. Seven a.m. Pacific time. It was *ten o'clock* and Grandmother Johnson hadn't woken them?

"Keira! It's ten already."

Keira pulled the blankets over her head. "So? Leave me alone."

They had stayed up late the night before, reading. Keira had gotten really caught up in the stories of teenagers who had been jailed for marching like Dr. King.

Minni listened for their grandmother's clip-clopping shoes or some indicator of her presence below. Nothing.

Minni's chest constricted. What if their grandmother's health complaints weren't minor after all? What if they were something serious and she'd . . . No, it wasn't possible.

She crept downstairs and tiptoed toward their grand-mother's closed bedroom door. She imagined the woman lying lifeless on her back, one arm dangling over the side of the bed. She put her ear to the door and listened. Silence. Her heart thumped steadily in her chest. She turned the knob slowly, holding her breath. *Creak.*

The covers lay flat and smooth, tucked crisply around fluffed pillows. Not a wrinkle in sight. Minni exhaled.

She went to the dining room, where bowls of bran had already been poured, with sliced prunes on top. A note leaned against the fruit bowl in the middle of the table. *Gone to a meeting of the Oakwood Preservation Society. See you at noon. P.S. Eat the bananas. They're going bad.*

Going bad. They were long gone. Minni was pretty sure these were the same bananas that had been here when they arrived. She called Mama and got her banana bread recipe.

A while later, Keira shuffled into the kitchen, rubbing her eyes. "What smells so good?"

Minni handed her a slice of banana bread on a plate. She'd known the aroma would get her sister out of bed.

Keira took a bite. "Mmmm. This is delicious."

Minni started to wash the mixing bowls and measuring cups. "Wasn't that totally amazing, what we learned about Grandmother Johnson yesterday? I still can't believe she actually *met* Dr. King." She looked at Keira out of the corner of her eye. "And all that stuff about integrating a white school." She paused. Would Keira tell her what she'd been thinking as they'd listened to their grandmother talk about her past?

Keira concentrated on her bread, still chewing. "I know how it feels."

"What?"

"Being the only one. I mean . . . I could relate."

Minni knew Keira meant the only *brown* one. She wanted to be able to say, "Me too," because she didn't like the idea of her sister feeling alone, but that would sound ridiculous. Not to mention, it wasn't true. "Do you feel like you're being watched all the time, like Grandmother Johnson did?"

"No, not really—I don't know." Keira shrugged. "It's more like . . . sometimes . . . well . . . it's just that sometimes I look around and everyone has this shiny, silky straight hair and light skin, and I feel *wrong*. Like there must be something wrong with me because I look so different."

Minni kept her eyes on the suds—the white suds that almost blended in with her white skin. She wished so badly she could tell her sister she understood, but how could she when apparently she was a part of the problem?

"You're a good listener, Min. Thanks." Keira put her plate in the dishwater. She peered at Minni. "You know I never feel that way around *you*." She threaded her arm through Minni's and pulled her down so she could kiss her cheek. "Right?"

Minni was quiet.

"Right, Skinny?"

"Okay." She glanced at Keira, then back at the water.

Keira grabbed a handful of bubbles and smashed them onto Minni's face.

"Hey!" Minni yelled, scooping up more suds and blowing them at her sister.

Then they were running and shrieking, first around the kitchen and then around the house, every once in a while returning to the sink for more ammunition, until they collapsed on the couch, panting and laughing in a wet, sudsy embrace.

By the time Grandmother Johnson returned, they'd thrown the bran cereal and prunes into the trash can and covered them with coffee grounds, dried off from their water fight, and dressed for the day. They'd also eaten about half the banana bread.

After eating a piece herself and murmuring her approval of Minni's baking, Grandmother Johnson opened her desk drawer and pulled out a portable tape recorder. "Have you been practicing your personal introductions?"

Minni had written hers out at home and hadn't looked at it since.

"Of course!" exclaimed Keira, who'd committed hers to memory. Keira had a memory like digital tape. It *had* to be strong, since her reading wasn't. Sort of like how a blind person develops a superpowered sense of smell and can identify people by their individual scents.

Grandmother Johnson turned The Eyebrow to Minni, who looked at the crumbs on her plate. "Uh-huh," she murmured.

"Good." Grandmother Johnson clip-clopped into the

living room. "But as there's no such thing as too much rehearsal"—she set the tape recorder on the coffee table—"let's do some more."

Keira traipsed behind. "Actually, you can peak early if you practice something too much. Coach told us that."

"Coach?"

"My gymnastics coach, Ron."

"*Ron?* Your mother allows you to call your instructor by his Christian name?"

"That's what he wants us to call him. Ron or Coach."

Grandmother Johnson shook her head, muttering to herself. "Well, perhaps your coach's rule about practicing too much applies to the execution of physical maneuvers, but never to elocution. Please come here."

"Electrocution?" Keira's nose wrinkled.

"*Elocution.* The art of effective public speaking. Minerva, pray tell me, why are you still in your chair?"

Minni shuffled into the other room.

"We will record you performing your introductions for the purpose of evaluation. Critical analysis of one's faults and weaknesses is the most effective way to improve oneself. And improving oneself is of *utmost* importance in improving one's station." Grandmother Johnson pointed to the area in front of the wall of books. "Minerva, you may start."

"Me?"

"Yes, you."

"Now?"

"No, tomorrow. Of course now!"

"Uh, I'm not really ready. I mean, I have an introduction but it's not memorized."

"Did you write it down?"

"It's in my backpack." She started toward the stairs.

Grandmother Johnson held out her hand to stop her. "If you wrote it down, the words are here." She tapped Minni's head. "You just need to access them." She nudged Minni toward the bookshelf.

Minni glanced at Keira, who looked back at her with an expression that said, *You can do it. Show* her.

Minni's armpits tingled. She ransacked her brain for the introduction she had written, but all she could come up with was "My name is Minni King," and something about flying.

Grandmother Johnson pressed a button on the recorder and its wheels started turning. The machine made a little clicking sound.

Words flew through Minni's mind, but not the ones she was supposed to be saying. A line from a poem she wrote . . . Keira's voice saying, *You can do it, Skinny!* . . . Her own voice pleading, *Please let me get my paper!*

Grandmother Johnson turned off the recorder. "It is much better to fail inside the four walls of one's own home than on a stage in front of hundreds of people. Would you not agree?"

Minni nodded.

"Then you must at least try. You're with family here, remember?"

Minni nodded again. *Family.* She had written a line about Mama and Daddy, and about Keira being her best friend.

The recorder's wheels clicked.

"My name is Minni—"

"Minerva," Grandmother Johnson corrected.

Minni clenched her teeth. "Minerva . . . ," she mumbled.

"Speak more clearly," Grandmother Johnson ordered.

Minni took a breath, lifted her chin and raised her voice. ". . . Lunette King. I am eleven years old and going into the sixth grade at Crawford Elementary School, home of the Fighting Crabs."

"You don't need to tell them your school mascot."

"I thought it was an interesting detail."

"Proceed."

"I have lived in Port Townsend, Washington, since the day my sister, Keira, who is my best friend, and I were born in the back of our daddy's plane—"

Grandmother Johnson shut off the recorder. "You certainly will *not* say anything about that!"

"But it's memorable."

Grandmother Johnson peered at her over the rims of her eyeglasses. "It's *common*, is what it is."

"It's not common! I bet no one else in the pageant was born in an airplane. Except Keira, of course."

Keira smiled.

Grandmother Johnson huffed. "That's not what I meant. I meant . . . Oh, never mind. Get your speech. I will read it and make changes and then we will recommence with this exercise."

Minni headed toward the stairs.

"Telling the judges you were born in an *airplane*! Where's your sense, child?"

Minni's choice of details might not have pleased their grandmother, but at least for now she had gotten out of having to practice her speech, and that was good enough for her.

Keira's elocution was perfect, but of course Grandmother Johnson-Payne-in-the-Butt had to find some little thing to correct. She told Keira she sounded like a toy wound too tightly. She needed to slow down and "*e-nun-ci-ate.*" Keira did what Grandmother Johnson asked, but it made her sound stiff and unnatural. Not like herself at all. More like Grandmother Johnson.

After Keira had done it Grandmother Johnson's way, Grandmother Johnson just nodded curtly and said, "Fine."

The lack of praise didn't seem to bother Keira, but it made Minni mad.

Over lunch, Grandmother Johnson fixed her introduction, and a couple of hours later Minni had learned it well enough to say it into the tape recorder—with far too many *ums* and *uhs*, according to their grandmother, but at least she had done it.

That night, Keira sketched while Minni lay on her bed, reading her MLK book out loud. Keira had convinced her that after four days in a row of working hard at sounding out words, she needed a break.

Minni lingered on the final page—sad that it was over, sad that he was gone, but inspired, too—by his courage and by the assurance that she could read the book again, as many times as she wished. She closed the book and looked up.

"Thanks, Skinny. That was great." Keira's eyes gleamed. "Now, are you ready for a drawing lesson?"

Minni shrugged. She drew even worse than she sang.

"We'll draw *her*." Keira pointed to the floor and then flipped the page in her sketchbook. Minni got up and sat next to her, smiling in anticipation.

Keira drew Grandmother Johnson bent over a steaming pile of dog poo with her mouth turned down in a scowl and her fingers pinching her nose.

"Let me see the pencil," Minni said. She reached for the spiral-bound book and put it in her lap. She wrote "Grandmother Johnson-Payne-in-the" and drew an arrow pointing to her behind. They laughed.

Keira drew another picture of Grandmother Johnson asleep, her huge feet sticking out at one end of the bed and a string of "z's" coming out of her nose at the other. A dribble of saliva dripped from her open mouth.

"Girls!"

Keira shoved her sketchbook under her pillow.

"Lights out!"

Minni pulled the string on the lightbulb and crawled into her bed. A while later, as she listened to Grandmother Johnson's log sawing, an idea sprang into Minni's head. A deliciously wonderful and sneaky idea.

She rolled over to tell Keira, but she knew from her sister's deep breathing that she was already asleep. She'd save it for tomorrow night. Keira was going to *love* this one.

Chapter Twenty-one

☼ ♡ ☾

The next day, Grandmother Johnson kept Minni and Keira busy practicing for the pageant. In the morning, she drove them to a community center where she had reserved the stage for Keira to rehearse her tumbling routine. Fortunately, Keira's gymnastic costume had passed inspection. Grandmother Johnson had also agreed to the skirt and blouse Minni had picked out for when she would sing. Or at least attempt to sing.

They sat in metal folding chairs on the gym floor, watching Keira leap, flip and dance to her music, a house version of Beethoven's Ninth. She was brilliant. Even Grandmother Johnson applauded at the end.

Back home, Minni stood by the piano, wincing as Grandmother Johnson stumbled through the accompaniment to the sparrow song. "Who's going to play piano for me at the pageant?" she asked when they were done.

Grandmother Johnson closed the sheet music and took off her glasses. "It's against the rules for anyone to be on-stage with the girls—"

"You mean I'll be singing without music?" This would be even worse than having Grandmother Johnson's awful playing.

"I plan to record myself, once I get it down a little better. You will sing to the tape."

"Oh. Okay." Minni felt a terrible case of laryngitis coming on. She was almost positive it would strike early Sunday morning.

After lunch, Grandmother Johnson told them to put on their gowns, and they walked around the living room with books on their heads. Minni felt ridiculous. Not only did her book keep sliding off, her toe snagged the hem of her dress, causing her to lurch every once in a while. Why was she *balancing* a book when she could be *reading* it? "Chin up, Minerva," Grandmother Johnson instructed.

Then they ran through their personal introductions again—without the tape recorder, thankfully—and finally they were done.

Or so Minni thought.

"Our final preparations for the Miss Black Pearl pageant address the issue of *character building*." Grandmother Johnson led them to the long cabinet near the back door. She pulled out her gardening gloves and some small digging tools. She placed them on the counter, then pulled down a bottle of sunscreen.

"We get to write a story?" Minni asked with a burst of excitement.

"No. Character as in integrity and a commitment to hard work."

They looked at her blankly.

"Your mother hasn't taught you the definition of character? What *is* she teaching you out there?"

Important things, Minni thought. Like how to see the beauty in a sunset and pull out a sliver without it hurting. How to take leftover rice, an egg and frozen vegetables and fry it all up into a whole new meal. How to turn empty containers into bird feeders, pen holders and soap dispensers. How to enjoy people and art and life.

"Character is the strength to make the right choice," Grandmother Johnson said. "As that meddlesome woman at the Black Pearls of America headquarters pointed out, it is the most important attribute for a Miss Black Pearl to possess."

Minni wanted to ask how much character it took to nail a bag of dog poop to your neighbor's door, but she decided Grandmother Johnson might not appreciate the question. Minni sure would love to hear her answer, though.

Grandmother Johnson handed Keira the bottle of sunscreen. "Now, put this on. *Thick.* You don't need to be getting any darker."

Keira scowled.

Minni gasped. How could their grandmother say something like that? Especially when she was just as dark as Keira—darker, even?

And yet she had done it before, hadn't she? On her last visit to Port Townsend, two years ago.

Suddenly it all came back—the comment before

spending time on the beach, the eruption between Mama and Grandmother Johnson, Keira and Minni wondering what was going on. Grandmother Johnson had left early the next morning, cutting her stay by two days.

"You too, Minerva. I don't want you showing up to the pageant pink as a Christmas ham."

Keira rubbed on some lotion, then shoved the bottle into Minni's hands and stomped outside.

Grandmother Johnson stood over Minni, pointing to spots she'd missed. Eventually Grandmother Johnson took the bottle, squeezed a mound into her palms and slathered the smelly stuff all over Minni's face, neck, ears—even *behind* her ears. Minni felt as *oiled* as a Christmas ham.

Grandmother Johnson applied lotion to her own face and arms, pulled down a straw hat with a broad brim from the hook near the back door, then told Minni to follow her. She took them to the flower bed alongside the house and showed them which plants were weeds and which to leave alone.

She handed Keira a forked digging tool and Minni her gardening gloves. "You'll have to work out who gets these. I've only got one complete pair left. We seem to have a glove snatcher in the neighborhood. And whoever it is, is very good. The last time, I hadn't looked away for two seconds and the glove was gone." She put the hat on Minni's head and marched back to the house.

A few minutes later they heard her plunking on the piano, practicing her accompaniment.

Keira started to yank on a stem.

"That's not a weed. That's a flower," Minni said, pulling off the ridiculous hat and tossing it to the ground.

"So?" Keira answered.

"She told us to leave those alone. Remember?"

"She meant *that* one." Keira pointed to a spreading plant with tiny lacelike leaves—clearly a weed. "Not this one." She ripped the long-stemmed yellow flower from the ground.

"Don't! She's going to be mad."

"Not with you, she won't. She never gets mad at you." Keira yanked another of the yellow flowers.

Minni felt herself crumbling like a sand castle under the waves of her sister's anger. "If you hadn't noticed, she's making me do the exact same work as you."

"Yeah, but who got the gardening gloves?"

Minni shoved the gloves at her sister. She didn't care about sticking her hands in dirt. "I was going to give them to you all along."

Keira growled and threw down the gloves. "You're Little Miss Perfect with the perfect grades and the perfectly good hair. Apparently now you have the perfect *skin*, too!"

Minni's body tingled all over, as if someone had taken one of those wire brushes used for scraping peeling paint to her arms, legs and face. She dropped to her knees and pulled out weeds as fast as she could. She couldn't help the color of the skin she'd gotten. It hadn't been her choice.

She dug her hands into the ground, letting the deep brown get under her fingernails. Mama always told them there were no ugly colors, but Minni knew differently.

Her skin was the ugliest color she had ever seen. *Buttermilk ugly*.

When she had a pile of weeds the size of a molehill, she dumped them in the waste bin, then turned to her sister. "Don't follow me," she said, feeling cross. She walked down the front steps, turned at the elm tree and marched down the sidewalk—all the way to the corner store, where she bought herself a soda, guzzled it right on the sidewalk for anyone to see and belched as loudly as she pleased. After that, she went back in, bought a soda for Keira and returned to Grandmother Johnson's.

When she got there, Keira was sitting at the bottom of the cement steps, far enough down that Grandmother Johnson wouldn't be able to see her if she looked out the front window. "Where did you go?" she asked.

Minni held out the soda.

Keira kept her hands tucked under her arms. "No, thanks."

Minni sat on the step below her sister. "Please, Keira . . . I can't help the things she says."

"You didn't exactly speak up and tell her she was wrong." Keira's eyes flashed. "And after I shared how I feel at school sometimes. I never should have told you!"

The words sliced Minni's heart, sending shooting pains down the insides of her arms. Her eyes prickled with tears. She set the bottle next to her sister, trying to get Keira to look at her. When Keira refused, Minni trudged up the steps, just in time to see the gray, one-eyed Billie Holiday slink away with one of Grandmother Johnson's gloves.

"Hey!" Minni shouted, and ran after the animal, but it raced around the corner of Miss Oliphant's house and disappeared under the back porch. She looked for a way to follow the cat but didn't see a hole large enough to crawl through.

A knock from inside the kitchen window made her jump. She looked up. Miss Oliphant! Around her grinning, ghostly face hung five or six brown, shriveled spheres with squinty eyes and crooked smiles.

A chill ran down Minni's spine. She stood to run, but Miss Oliphant was already at the door. "It's hotter than a grease-poppin' griddle out here. Too hot to be weeding flower beds, if you ask me. I bet you could use some lemonade."

Minni's muscles were taut. Her throat constricted. She glanced toward the front yard and steps, but Keira was out of sight.

"What's wrong, child? Cat got your tongue?"

No, my grandmother's glove, Minni thought, but she didn't say anything—just stood there frozen between this woman she wasn't sure she could trust and her best friend–sister who had never gotten as angry with her as she had been back there in the flower bed. Minni's eyes welled with tears. She looked quickly toward the old apple tree, blinking and hoping the woman hadn't noticed.

"Come on in and give those arms a rest. You can fetch your sister if you want."

Minni glanced toward the front again. Miss Oliphant knew Keira was her sister? Had Grandmother Johnson told her about them? Or could she actually tell? And when had she seen them together? Probably that day on her front porch . . .

Minni shook her head. "That's okay." Then she thought of the MLK monument—the smooth, calm water flowing over Miss Oliphant's name. The woman continued to gaze at her. "Well, maybe—for a minute." Minni felt pulled forward, as if she were the ocean and the woman were the moon.

The kitchen was bright and cheery, with light blue walls, gleaming chrome on the appliances, and white cabinets. A shiny silver toaster sat on the counter. Everything was spotless and well ordered. "May I use your sink?" Minni asked.

"Of course."

Minni washed her hands, then joined the woman at the table in the breakfast nook, trying not to stare at her cloudy eye or look at the heads hanging from the light fixture overhead. A stack of gingerbread squares sat on a plate on the table.

"So, Minerva has you out there weeding her flowers," Miss Oliphant said, setting a glass of lemonade in front of Minni. Minni's belly was already full from the soda, but it wouldn't be polite to refuse the lady's generosity. "It's kind of you to help your grandmother like that."

Was Miss Oliphant aware of other ways they had "helped" their grandmother, such as with the bag of poop?

"Just so you know, I don't hold you responsible for the shenanigan she pulled the other day."

Minni looked up. Could the woman read minds, too? "You don't?"

"Of course not. I saw you on my porch, of course, but as soon as I took down that bag I knew who was really behind it. That grandmother of yours is one feisty woman. When she thinks she's right about something, *no* one can stop her."

The description actually sounded a lot like Keira.

Keira. Minni looked into her lap again, not wanting Miss Oliphant to see the hurt in her eyes. Her sister had accused her of not speaking out, not standing up for her, and she was right—Minni had failed her. Her face grew warm with shame.

"Is something the matter?" Miss Oliphant asked. "If you don't mind me saying so, you seem a bit downcast."

Minni shook her head.

Miss Oliphant pushed the plate toward her. Minni raised her eyes just enough to see the thick, moist-looking squares. The bread's warm, gingery smell made her mouth water. "It's a few days old now, but it's still delicious, if I do say so myself. And I do."

Minni reached out and took a piece. She licked her lips, then bit into the soft bread. The spicy, sweet taste spread across her tongue. She couldn't not smile.

Miss Oliphant put a piece of gingerbread on a napkin and set it in front of her. "For your sister."

Minni set the rest of her piece on the napkin. The sweet treat was incredibly delicious, but it was hard to enjoy it fully knowing how things were with Keira. "She's mad at me." Minni looked out the window. That bird with the yellow head was at the feeder again.

"Oh?" Miss Oliphant sat quietly. Minni appreciated the silence. She watched the bird peck at the seeds and then fly away. "And why is that?" Miss Oliphant asked.

The question stopped Minni. She didn't know exactly. Or maybe she was just too ashamed to say. But somehow, sitting there in Miss Oliphant's presence, she felt it was okay to try. "I didn't tell our grandmother she was wrong about something."

"Mmmm. That can be a hard thing to do, standing up and speaking out for what's right. Especially when you're up against something—or someone—much bigger than yourself."

"*You* did it," Minni said. "We read on the MLK monument that you were a . . . a 'champion' civil rights leader."

"Oh, that. I suppose I've done some standing up and speaking out over the years."

"How did you—I mean, where did you find the courage?" Minni looked her straight in the eye.

"Honey child, when a wrong in the world gets inside the people you love most and starts making them think there's something wrong with *them*, well, you have to act."

Minni chewed on the woman's words as she savored the taste of cinnamon and ginger on her tongue.

Starts making them think there's something wrong with them . . .

Keira had said she felt wrong at their school sometimes. But what was the wrong that was getting inside her exactly, and how could Minni speak out about it?

She picked up the napkin and stood. "Thank you."

"Any time." Miss Oliphant smiled. Her eye wasn't so spooky, really.

"Oh! Billie Holiday took one of my grandmother's gloves."

Miss Oliphant laughed. "It's her hunting instinct. I suppose I should try to break her of the habit, but it's just so amusing!"

Minni grinned. "I won't tell." She walked back to Grandmother Johnson's yard, finishing her square of gingerbread. Keira and the soda were gone from the steps, so she slipped inside and up to the attic.

Keira sat on her bed, sketching and listening to her mp3 player. Minni set the dessert next to Keira's leg and lay down on her own bed. Keira glanced at the food but kept drawing. A while later, she picked it up, sniffed it and took a bite. Minni smiled, knowing what her sister was experiencing.

Keira obviously was trying not to show how much she liked the gingerbread, but she couldn't fool Minni. The corners of her mouth twitched and her cheeks rose up a little, and Minni felt happy knowing she'd given her sister a reason to smile again.

Chapter Twenty-two

☀ ♡ ☾

Keira barely said two words to Minni all the next day. Minni didn't even try to tell her about sitting in Laverna Oliphant's kitchen or the conversation she'd had with their new neighbor. Anyway, she wasn't sure she wanted to. It seemed like something to keep to herself, at least for now.

She sat on the porch swing reading a book from their grandmother's shelf, *Up from Slavery*, by Booker T. Washington. She thought it was interesting that Washington had a black mom and a white dad, just like her and Keira, although his mother had been a slave and his father a slave owner. Minni was *so* glad she didn't live back then.

Between her bum knee and an upset stomach, Grandmother Johnson wasn't feeling too well. She mostly stayed in her room with the AC unit running. Keira practiced her tumbling routine in the side yard (Grandmother Johnson didn't know she was outside without sunscreen); then she disappeared inside.

A while later, Miss Oliphant stepped onto her porch with a bag of cat food. "Good afternoon," she called. "It's a beauty of a day, isn't it?"

"Yes, ma'am, it is." The air felt soft on Minni's bare arms and legs, as if she were soaking in a tub of warm water scented with flowers heated by the sun. Summer air in the South was different than summer air back home, with its smells of pine, pulp and salt water, and the cool breeze coming off the ocean, but she liked it all right. It was nice, actually.

"Got yourself a good book?"

Minni glanced at the cover. "*Up from Slavery*, by Booker T. Washington," she said.

"An important work," Miss Oliphant replied. She stooped to pour cat food into a dish. "Mr. Washington worked tirelessly for the education of black people at a crucial time in our history." She stood again. "When you're done with that one, make sure you read Dr. W.E.B. DuBois."

"Doo Boyz?" Minni squinted.

"That's right. DuBois. *The Souls of Black Folk*. That man put down in words what it is to be black in America, better than anyone I've ever read. He burned with a passion to rid this country of racism—devoted his whole life to the struggle."

Minni was intrigued. "Thanks," she said.

Miss Oliphant gave a nod and went back inside.

$\mathcal{L}$ater, when Minni went to see what Keira was doing, she found her holed up in the bathroom. Minni stood outside the door. She started to knock, then stopped. She rested her head on the door frame. "Are you okay in there?" she asked softly. Every few moments, something clinked against the porcelain sink. Keira must be doing her hair.

"I'm fine."

"You want to play hearts or something?"

"No, thanks."

"Speed?"

"No."

"Two-person solitaire?"

Silence. "I just want to be alone, all right?"

"We should really do some more reading. You haven't done any since Monday."

"Leave me *alone*, Minni!"

Minni swallowed. It felt as if someone with an ice cream scooper had dug out half her heart. "All right," she whispered, and went to the porch again, where she sat on the steps and watched ants come and go from a crack in the cement. Two ants approached each other, stopped and touched antennae.

Together, Keira had said. They would get through this together.

So why was she insisting on going it alone?

* * *

That night, after they were both upstairs, Minni pulled out the tape recorder she had hidden under her pillow earlier in the day. She had also gone looking for Dr. DuBois's book on Grandmother Johnson's shelves, but she hadn't found it.

Keira sat on her bed filing her toenails. She had washed and blow-dried her hair that afternoon, then pressed it straight with her ceramic flatiron. Keira still wasn't talking, but Minni had to at least try. "I've got another idea," Minni said. "An idea for how we can get back at her again . . . for the stupid thing she said to you yesterday."

Keira lowered her eyelids. "What?"

"You're really going to like this one."

"Great. What is it?" Keira leaned back against the wall and crossed her arms.

"But we've got to do it together."

"Okay, okay! Tell me already!" Keira shook the emery board impatiently.

Minni lowered her voice and held up the tape recorder. "We'll record her snoring."

Keira's face broke into a smile for the first time that day.

"I'm nervous, though," Minni said. "What if she wakes up while we're in her room?"

"You know she sleeps like a cow in a coma." Keira slapped her bed, laughing. "Ooo, just think what she'll do when she hears how she shakes the walls of this house!"

Minni grinned. For once, she couldn't wait for Grandmother Johnson to start her log sawing.

When the snuffling and snorting began, they went into action. Minni stood and saluted. "Operation Silence the Saw—now in progress."

Keira threw her pillow at her. "You're such a goof."

Minni smiled, glad that everything was finally back to normal between them.

"We'll just get in and get out, okay?" Keira's voice had turned serious, as if they were about to engage in a life-threatening mission and could end up prisoners of war or something.

"Okay." Minni went first. She took the stairs slowly, trying to remember the spots that creaked and step around them. At the bottom, she let her eyes adjust to the darkness. Fortunately, the moon was putting off a nice glow that night. In the living room, light frosted the tops of the furniture. The light spilled into the hallway, helping her see where to put her feet. The end of the hall, however, where Grandmother Johnson slept, was pitch black. She'd have to let the sound guide her.

She walked toward the snoring with an outstretched hand. Keira followed close on her heels.

Get in and get out.

Bang! She ran right into Grandmother Johnson's closed door. Keira bumped into her.

Grandmother Johnson slept with her door closed? Minni had been sure she must sleep with it open, the way they could hear her sawing two-by-fours all night long.

Keira giggled.

Minni put a hand over her mouth and pinched her nose to keep herself from laughing.

Fortunately, Grandmother Johnson's snoring didn't miss a beat. She really did sleep like a cow in a coma.

Minni groped for the doorknob. She twisted it carefully, holding her breath until she could feel her heart galloping between her lungs. The knob gave and she moved into the room, grateful for the moonlight oozing around the pulled shades.

Grandmother Johnson's large body looked like a mountain range under her crumpled blankets and rumbled like a volcano about to blow.

"Phhhhht!"

Minni clamped her hand over her mouth and nose again and strained against the tsunami of laughter that swelled inside her. Grandmother Johnson was letting out air from both ends! She must have taken her antigas pills earlier that night.

Keira apparently couldn't control herself any longer. She rushed out. Minni heard muffled laughter in the other room. She imagined her sister with her face buried in a throw pillow.

Minni tiptoed toward the bed, grateful that their grandmother was the kind of person who would never leave her clothes or shoes on the floor, as Minni was prone to do. She held her finger over the Record button, getting closer, closer . . .

The mattress creaked as the giant mountain rolled.

She dove for the end of the bed and crouched behind the footboard, ready to ditch the recorder if she needed to. *I had a bad dream . . . I had a bad dream,* she rehearsed. It would be her excuse for being in the room.

Any moment, their grandmother's sharp voice would be

demanding to know who was there. But the voice never came—just a heavy exhale—and within two breaths, she was back at it again, snoring just as loudly, if not more loudly than before.

Minni didn't wait. She pushed the Record button firmly (thankfully, the machine ran on batteries), then hurried back to the side of the bed. She held the recorder near Grandmother Johnson's head. She stayed put as long as she could—until the fear of getting caught became greater than the enjoyment of gathering this evidence that would force Grandmother Johnson to face the cold, hard truth that she was indeed a *snorer*.

She slunk from the room and shut the door quietly, leaving Grandmother Johnson to her rest.

"Mission accomplished," she whispered to Keira, and they crept back up the stairs.

Later, while Keira slept peacefully on the other side of the room, Minni tossed and turned, wishing that tomorrow—the first day of the dreaded pageant—would never come.

Chapter Twenty-three

☀ ♡ ☾

Keira primped longer than usual before they left for the orientation, and though Grandmother Johnson fumed at her, she still took her own sweet time.

Once Grandmother Johnson finally got into the bathroom, Minni returned the tape recorder to the desk. She and Keira had listened to a little to make sure it had worked and then rewound it to the beginning. They would leave the tape in the machine for now so as not to raise any suspicions. Later, they would hide the recorder in a cabinet or the clothes hamper and push Play. The snoring was so loud and awful, their grandmother would probably think a rabid raccoon had found its way into her house.

They showed up at the Hotel Lamont later than Grandmother Johnson wanted, which of course she blamed on

Keira, although she had at least told her that her hair looked nice. Keira had given her pressed hair a zigzag part. Four small bear-claw clips held two flat twists in place in the front. She'd curled the ends under with her curling iron. As soon as they got inside, Keira ran to a bathroom to make sure her clips were still in place.

Minni gazed around the large lobby, awed by the huge crystal chandelier and the fancy red velvet furniture. A shiny black grand piano sat in a corner. Minni suddenly wished she knew how to play the instrument. A beauty like that shouldn't be left standing quiet and alone.

"Let's go. Your sister will catch up." Grandmother Johnson pulled her down a red-carpeted corridor into the ballroom where the competition would be held. Long tables were set up at the back and a large stage stood at the front. Rows of chairs filled the rest of the space.

Brown-skinned girls with their brown-skinned mothers chatted in groups around the room. There were at least eighty people there. The range of hues was broad, but no one had skin as pale as Minni's, or hair as molten-lava red. She felt like Pippi Longstocking.

And she stood out.

She had told Mama last year how much she hated standing out.

"Why do you think you stand out?"

"I'm taller than all the boys. I've got hair the color of a pumpkin. And my shoe size is the same as my age, which is not good when you're ten."

"Your life sounds hard." Mama was being sarcastic.

Minni had wanted to knock the palette from her hand and watch the colors go flying. She raised her voice instead. "Can't you try to understand—even for one minute—what it's like to be me?"

Mama tucked her lips around her teeth and looked at Minni through squinted eyes. She looked and looked, quiet, serious, the way she looked at a flower when she was getting ready to paint it. She blinked—once, twice, three times—and Minni was starting to think Mama might just sit there staring at her forever, when she said, "You're right. I didn't like standing out when I was your age, either."

She put down the palette and wrapped her fingers around Minni's wrist, which stuck out from her too-short sleeves because she was always growing faster than they could get to the store to buy her new clothes. Minni felt her pulse beating against Mama's fingertips. "But you know what I've learned as I've gotten older?"

Minni shook her head.

"It's not a bad thing to stand out. It can actually be quite good—so long as you're being yourself."

Being yourself, Minni had thought at the time. Even if she *was* good with animals and a good speller and she cared about the environment, if being Minni King meant being the things she'd listed to Mama, she wasn't so sure she wanted to be herself.

Grandmother Johnson tugged on Minni's elbow, pulling her forward in the registration line. "Quit your daydreaming, child. It's time to get serious now."

Two girls called out and ran to hug each other. Minni

noticed the woman from church who had said her grand-daughter was coming for the competition. Next to her stood a tall, ballerina-like girl—slender, not skinny—wearing a crisp white sleeveless shirt tied at the waist and a black A-line skirt. She wore black slip-on sandals with a slight heel. Very stylish. Even Keira would have to agree. The girl surveyed the room as if she were taking stock of the competition, which she probably was. Her gaze turned in their direction. Minni became suddenly interested in the nubby carpet.

Soon after this, they reached the front of the line. The "meddlesome" lady was checking girls in.

"King," Grandmother Johnson said, as if she were announcing royalty. "Minerva and Keira."

Minni glanced around, wondering how many people had heard The Name.

"Of course," the woman said. "Sisters like you would be hard to forget."

Minni's cheeks got warm.

The woman started to hand two folders to Minni. "Here you go."

Grandmother Johnson intervened. "Thank you." She waved the folders toward the center of the room. "Go start meeting other girls. It's good to mingle." She nudged Minni forward, then went and found a seat in the front row.

Minni felt vulnerable and exposed without Keira, like a turtle without its shell. The church lady's granddaughter sauntered up. She was as tall as Minni. Her hair was straight, pulled into a high ponytail that flipped up at the ends.

Her eyelashes were as long and dark as spider legs. She was almost as pretty as Keira.

"You know this is a pageant for black girls, right?"

"Yes."

"So what are you doing here?"

Minni swallowed. "My grandma entered me."

"But you have to be black."

Minni wanted to run, but her feet felt glued to the floor. "I know."

"You're not black."

It was happening exactly as she had feared.

Keira walked up just in time. "Who are you? The president of the Who Can Be Black Club?"

"I'm Alisha Walker from Kansas City. Who are *you*?"

"Keira King from Washington State."

"They got black people out there?"

"A few." Keira linked arms with Minni. "And this is my sister, Minni."

Minni fought to keep the girl's words outside her heart, but she was losing the battle quickly. She began to tremble, starting from her stomach, then outward to her arms, legs and knees.

Alisha looked them over. "Too bad. Judges don't look favorably on sisters with different daddies. I would know— I've been competing in pageants since I was five."

"We don't have different daddies," Keira said. "We're twins."

The girl's jaw dropped. "Uh-*uhhh*. You came out of the *same* mama at the same time?"

"Not exactly the same time. Minni went first and I came out seven minutes later." Keira's mouth stretched into a thin, close-lipped smile.

"Hey!" Alisha motioned to a girl walking by. "Check this out. These girls are twins!"

Minni wished she could make herself disappear.

"So?" The girl clasped her arms in front of her slightly rounded middle and stared at Alisha, looking very unimpressed. She had dimples the size of sinkholes.

"One's black and the other's white."

"One's dark and the other's light," the girl corrected. She had a slight accent—sort of Southern, but not deep-down South.

"We're both black," Keira said. "Like *President* Barack Obama, except our dad is white instead of our mom."

"How you gonna try and be black when you got white skin?" Alisha cocked her head and crossed her arms.

Minni's thick tongue felt stuck. She swallowed, trying desperately to think of some defense for herself and her skin.

"How you gonna compete in this pageant with a broken arm?" Keira squared herself in front of the girl. Alisha towered over her.

The girl with dimples put her hands on her hips. "Y'all need to chill. Or you're both gonna get yourselves kicked out."

Alisha's eyes narrowed at Keira. "If you think you've got a chance at winning this competition, you can forget it. The best thing you can do for yourself is to stay on my good side, so you can be my friend when I'm crowned Miss Black Pearl."

Keira took Minni by the hand and led her away. When they were out of hearing distance, Keira stopped. "Ignore her. And anyone else who tries to tell you you're not black."

"But—"

"But what?"

Minni searched Keira's face, desperately wanting her to understand. People went by what they saw on the outside. Didn't she know this from her own experience?

Maybe so, but that didn't mean she could understand Minni's experience. Being dark-skinned might at times be difficult in Port Townsend, Washington, but at least no one would ever question whether Keira was black.

"Nothing."

They went and sat next to Grandmother Johnson. Minni fidgeted in her seat, unable to quiet Alisha's voice in her head. *How you gonna try and be black when you got white skin?*

Keira didn't seem to have any questions about what Minni was. If only Minni were as sure.

Chapter Twenty-four

☀ ♡ ☾

They waited for the orientation to begin. Minni tried to calm herself after the run-in with Alisha by reciting her personal introduction in her head, but she kept getting stuck at the first line. She didn't realize she was pulling on the skin of her neck until Grandmother Johnson reached across Keira and prodded her. "Stop your fidgeting, child. You're making me nervous."

The dimpled girl and a woman who looked just like her but bigger sat next to Minni. The girl introduced herself as Donyelle from "Lua-vull." Minni asked her where that was.

Donyelle looked shocked. "You've never heard of Lua-vull, Kentucky?"

"Oh, you mean *Louisville*," Minni said.

"Right. Lua-vull." Donyelle grabbed Minni's forearm.

"So, what's it like to be a twin? Is it great? I've always thought it would be so great."

"It is," Minni said.

"Can you, like, read each other's minds?"

"All the time," Keira said, peering around Minni.

"Really?" Donyelle was wide-eyed.

"No. Not really." Keira laughed. "I'm just playing."

Donyelle smiled at them. A real smile. She was nice. Minni let her shoulders relax. Donyelle had called her light, not white. Apparently she could see that Minni was black, too. Just a different shade of black.

A minute later, Dr. Billie Hogg-Graff appeared onstage. She tapped the microphone on the podium and cleared her throat. "Good afternoon, ladies—and gentlemen." She nodded her head toward a man sitting behind them. "It's always good to see the fathers. We are so glad all of you are here."

She went on to describe the rehearsal and performance schedule. The more she said, the heavier Minni's chest felt, until she could barely breathe from the weight of all she would be expected to do over the next two days, especially the number of things she would have to do in front of others: performing a choreographed group dance, reciting their personal introductions, doing their talents, and walking across the stage in their silly, frilly, long gowns.

Minni looked around at the other girls, their faces glowing with excitement about what they had to look forward to, smiling up at Dr. Hogg-Graff as if they were already being judged—the more teeth, the higher their score. Keira smiled just as big as the rest of them. How was it that Keira, her *twin* sister, was so excited about this, while she sat there shaking inside like a washing machine on the spin cycle?

"Now I have the pleasure of introducing you to the program judges. These three ladies and two gentlemen are outstanding individuals who serve as tremendous role models for our young people."

Dr. Hogg-Graff introduced the judges one at a time, describing their work and their community involvements. "Our last judge has made a difference for black people not only in this city and state but throughout the South—although she would never say that about herself." She glanced toward the side of the room, where each of the judges had stood after being introduced. "She is a poet, a prophet, a pillar of the black community . . ."

The woman rose to her feet. Her face was thin and pale. Gray braids sat atop her head like a crown.

Minni sucked in her breath.

"Dr. Laverna Oliphant," Dr. Hogg-Graff announced.

Grandmother Johnson gasped so loudly that people around them turned and looked.

Minni glanced at Keira, and in that moment she was pretty sure they actually *were* reading each other's minds.

Grandmother Johnson is going to have a fit!

"A judge! They made *her* a judge? She's practically blind in one eye!" Grandmother Johnson fumed.

Minni and Keira sat in the backseat of the car holding the participation certificates they'd received at the orientation.

Minni would be discarding hers as soon as she got a chance. They had filled it out with The Name.

"Which social organizations does she belong to? Which charitable clubs? I've been involved with the Historic Oakwood Preservation Society from the day I moved in; she's never attended even *one* public meeting. They've obviously never been to her house. I've peered inside—only once, mind you—making an attempt to be civil the week she arrived."

Civil? She had probably been snooping.

"Her house is full of *junk*."

Minni and Keira cut their eyes at each other. She was one to talk! She had junky stuff all over her house, like the bag of wigs they had found in her closet the afternoon she went to her garden club meeting. And the bin of dusty pantyhose in her bathroom. And the kitchen cabinet stuffed full of hundreds of plastic grocery bags.

"And do they know she dabbles in the dark arts? Not that I believe in any of that hocus-pocus, but still . . ."

Was Grandmother Johnson mad they had chosen Miss Oliphant and not her?

"I just can't believe they would ask that woman, and they've never *once* asked me."

Bin-go.

"I've got half a mind to challenge her credentials. How can she judge effectively if she can't see?"

For all Grandmother Johnson's recent emphasis on character, she sure seemed caught up in appearances.

* * *

That night, Grandmother Johnson insisted on reading with Keira. They stayed downstairs while Minni went to the attic.

As soon as Minni rolled into bed, her phone rang. Mama. Minni answered.

"How'd the orientation go?" Mama asked.

"Grandmother Johnson's neighbor is one of the judges."

"Mr. Henry?" Mama practically yelled. Minni pulled the phone away before her eardrum burst.

They'd seen Mr. Henry on his porch several times. He wore a straw hat like the men in those barbershop quartets, and he constantly snorted and spit into his grass. It was such a disgusting sound that as soon as they saw him out there they'd turn around and go back inside. He'd lived next door to Grandmother Johnson since before Mama was born.

"No! Why would they have a phlegmy old white man judge Miss Black Pearl Preteen?"

"Oh, of course. The new arrival. Good ol' Miss Oliphant. Mother must be thrilled."

"Why does she dislike her so much?"

"As far as I can tell, plain old-fashioned jealousy. Dr. Oliphant has always gotten a lot of attention for her civil rights activism. The whole 'neighborhood wrecker' thing is just a cover-up for Mother's true feelings."

Minni stared up at the ceiling. Alisha's words still rang in her ears. She wished again she weren't doing this pageant.

"Still there?"

"Yeah."

"You've gone serious on me. What're you working out now?"

"Mama?"

"Yes, daughter."

"Do I count?"

"Do you *count*?"

"Yeah. Do I count?"

"Last time I checked you could count just fine. In fact, you've been counting since you were two and I can't say I've heard you miss a number yet."

"You know that's not what I mean!"

"What do you mean, then?"

"Do I count as a black person?"

"Do you want to?"

"Yes!"

"Well, then, you do." Mama paused. "Although even if you said you didn't want to, I'd still tell you you did."

Minni sat quietly, thinking about what Mama was saying.

"Daughter of mine, you need to remember something. Especially as you participate in this whole pageant thing."

"It's a *program*, remember?" Minni had told Mama about the lady in the office correcting Grandmother Johnson.

"Right. This program. You need to remember that these bodies we're in are just vehicles. They're part of who we are, sure. An important part. But what's riding around inside is a whole lot more important."

Mama had told them this before. Keira liked to say that

if their bodies were vehicles, then hers was most definitely a Jaguar. Minni had decided on a hybrid—because she was mixed, of course, but also because hybrids were environmentally friendly.

"Many ways to be black, Min. Remember?"

"Okay."

"Good night, Little Moon."

"Good night."

Chapter Twenty-five

☼ ♡ ☾

The next morning, they headed back to the hotel for rehearsal. Grandmother Johnson delivered her piano recording and Keira's dance music to the man in charge of sound, then exited the ballroom as instructed. To Minni's great relief, all parents—and grandparents—were prohibited from watching them practice.

Minni stuck to Keira like a fly on flypaper—being extra careful to avoid Alisha—until Miss Jackie, a petite lady in pink and gray nylon sweats, arrived to teach them the group dance number. She pulled Minni to the back row, right next to Alisha. Keira was put in front.

"We want the tall girls in the back to start, but don't worry, you'll all get your chance to be front and center." Minni was happy to be safely in back, but she didn't like being separated from her sister. She felt like that naked turtle again.

They went through the routine a few times. Keira was awesome. She had it down after the first go-round. She was clearly a standout in the group.

Alisha was also a natural. She had long legs to match her long lashes. Minni found herself watching Alisha to make sure she was getting the moves right. Unlike Minni, Alisha was graceful and coordinated. She didn't look as though she was constantly about to trip over her own feet.

"Watch out!" she said under her breath when Minni got a little too close. "You're crowding me."

Kick on one. Spin on two. Reach to the side on three. Head tilt on "and." Slide on four. As long as they were doing it at half speed, Minni could follow, but as soon as the music started and everyone was kicking and spinning and sliding around her, she got totally thrown off.

Miss Jackie stopped the music—a remix of "We Are Family"—and asked Keira to demonstrate the kick, spin, reach and slide, which Keira did so well she could have been practicing it for weeks. Alisha stood with her arms folded and her hip pushed out. She frowned as she watched Keira perform the moves flawlessly.

Minni's heart swelled with pride. Keira was really good.

"Okay, all together now. Let's do that sequence again." Miss Jackie turned on the music.

Minni felt herself slipping behind. She was spinning when she should be kicking. Zigging when she should be zagging.

"One, two, three, and—"

Minni jabbed to the side. Something squished under her finger.

"Ow!" Alisha stumbled backward. Her hand flew to her face.

The music stopped again. Miss Jackie swished over. "What's wrong? What happened?"

"Albino girl poked me in the eye!" Alisha pointed to Minni. Her eyelashes fluttered.

Minni's arms dangled at her side. All eighty-some eyes bored holes into her until she half expected to look down and find that her body looked like Swiss cheese.

"There'll be no name-calling," Miss Jackie said. "It's not in the spirit of Miss Black Pearl."

"I'm really, *really* sorry." Minni reached out to touch Alisha's arm, but the girl jerked away. "It was an accident. Really." She looked at Miss Jackie, hoping the woman would decide it was better for everyone's safety that she sit out the opening number. According to the materials in her orientation folder, the group dance wasn't even a part of the official scoring.

Minni glanced at Keira, who stood in her place up front. She couldn't tell if her sister looked concerned or just embarrassed. Between having their names announced at the orientation and Alisha spreading the word about "that girl and her white twin sister," everyone knew they were related.

Miss Jackie put her hand on Alisha's shoulder and peered into her watering eyes. "I don't see any broken vessels. You should be fine." She turned to Minni. "Be more careful next time, and try to keep up, okay?"

Minni nodded, wishing she could melt on the spot and become floor wax.

Miss Jackie returned to the front.

"If you think your light skin's going to make up for your lack of coordination, it's not," Alisha hissed.

Minni stood stiffly, frozen in shock at Alisha's suggestion. The music started up again and Miss Jackie counted off. Minni kept her legs and arms close to her body, working hard to keep *her* eyes from watering.

At lunch, several girls circled Keira, wanting her to show them moves from the dance routine. Minni sat nearby, eating the soggy ham sandwich out of the boxed lunch they'd been given. She hadn't told Keira about Alisha's mean remark. Keira would just get angry—maybe even fight the girl—and Minni didn't want her sister to get kicked out on her account.

She was thankful for Donyelle with the dimpled cheeks, who came and sat next to her—even though she talked the whole time about her one hundred and fifty-seven Barbies.

"They're all still in their boxes," she drawled. "It makes them more valuable."

Minni thought it just made them sound creepy—peering out from their clear plastic windows with their stiff arms and legs and their painted-on smiles. Donyelle's father had built shelves around her entire room to house the dolls, which was even creepier. How did she sleep with all those dolls watching her? Minni had never gotten into Barbies, but she was genuinely interested to learn that Barbie had been both a marine biologist and a jet pilot, and that they made every version of Barbie in both white and brown. All Donyelle's Barbies were brown.

Learning this reminded Minni of the time she and Keira went to the house of a third-grade classmate who had Barbies. The girl had all white Barbies and one brown one and she kept insisting that Keira had to be the brown one because she and the doll had the same color skin. Keira had gotten up and stomped out.

When Minni caught up to Keira on the sidewalk, she was surprised to see tears on her sister's cheeks. She had felt bad with Keira, even if she hadn't understood completely what they were feeling bad about. They stopped talking to the girl at school and boycotted her house after that. If the girl noticed, they couldn't tell. She never invited them back.

After lunch, the girls were told it was time to change into their interview outfits. They would be called on five at a time to meet with one judge each while the rest of the group stayed in the ballroom and practiced the walk across the stage for the formal-wear portion of the competition.

Minni's stomach flipped. Even though they didn't have to do the interview in front of a large audience, the thought of being interviewed by a stranger made her feel like she might lose her oatmeal. Maybe she would get Miss Oliphant. That calmed her a little.

When Minni saw that the dressing room was just an open space with a few chairs scattered about, she pulled Keira aside and told her she was headed to the bathroom.

"Why?"

"I don't want anyone staring at me."

"Your chest isn't *that* flat, Skinny."

"Shhh!" Minni glanced around, hoping no one had heard, even though that wasn't the reason she wanted to leave. "It's not that."

"Then what?"

"I feel like everyone's staring at me—wondering what I'm doing here. They're just not saying it like Alisha did." She glanced around at the girls filling the room. "I don't look like I belong."

Keira's lips twitched. "I guess now you know what it's like to be me."

Everything around them—the chattering girls, the four walls, the hotel itself—fell away. There was nothing but her and Keira and the words Keira had just spoken.

Minni's brain got so quiet, she thought for a moment that it had stopped working. Then she heard her own voice pleading with Mama, *Can't you try to understand—even for one minute—what it's like to be me?*

"Remember that 'wrong' feeling I told you about?" Keira searched Minni's eyes. "I don't think it's something you can really feel or understand . . . until you experience it yourself. Maybe now you can get it."

Minni felt as though she were being yanked away, as if by a cosmic-sized rope and pulley. She was already halfway into outer space.

She clambered toward her sister—reaching for words that would fill the chasm growing between them. She started to say that she stood out at Crawford Elementary, too. She had red hair and big feet and the boys called her Ronald McDonald.

But she couldn't say it, because in spite of all that—when it came down to it—her skin still allowed her to fit in.

Here she was being given an opportunity to feel what Keira felt—in a sense, to be inside her sister's skin—to get even closer to her . . . and she didn't want to. She wanted to go back to the place where her skin didn't matter. Where she wasn't preferred or excluded because of it. Where she could just *be*.

Did a place like that even exist? Had it ever?

And what about for her sister? Would Keira ever be able just to *be* where they lived?

An ocean suddenly separated them. It didn't matter that they were twins or best friends. Even their closeness couldn't bridge the distance their different colors had created. Minni wanted to grab her sister and hold her close. Instead, she picked up her clothes, slipped behind a rack full of gowns and changed quickly, alone.

Chapter Twenty-six

Minni sat in a chair against the wall of the red-carpeted hallway. The four girls waiting alongside her talked in pairs, leaving Minni alone with her thoughts. Soon they'd enter the room where they'd each have a private interview with a judge and be evaluated on their ability to communicate—twenty percent of their final score.

If Minni couldn't get her teeth to stop chattering—whether from the air-conditioning or her nervousness she couldn't tell—she'd get a big, fat zero for this part. She wished she had time to call Mama for words of advice or Gigi for a pep talk.

She also couldn't stop thinking about Keira. She hadn't known how much looking different bothered her sister. She supposed she *had* heard Keira say things to Mama now and then, but she'd never *really* understood it—Keira's frustration—especially when she was the popular one, the outgoing one, the one who made friends so easily. Keira was the sun. People were drawn to her—orbited around her, even. Everyone liked Keira. Or at least lots of people did. Why was she complaining?

That was when Minni started remembering.

The girl with the Barbies.

And that kid in kindergarten who asked Keira why she was so dirty.

Even their teacher this year, who had told Keira she should be the most grateful one in their class for Martin Luther King, Jr., because if he hadn't done what he did, white and black people might still not go to school together.

And that dumb boy who, after that, told Minni he wished he'd lived in the days when black and white people *didn't* go to school together so he wouldn't have to be in the same class with her sister.

Minni sucked in her breath. She had pushed the boy's hurtful remark so far out of her mind that letting it back in made her heart race.

She slowly recalled her response. She had stood there, stunned. Completely frozen in disbelief.

And *angry*.

How could someone say something so horrible about the person she loved more than anyone in the whole world?

But she hadn't said a word.

A hot wave of shame washed over her. Why hadn't she put that boy in his place—told him he was wrong to say that about her sister?

And why hadn't she confronted that dress shop lady with her two-faced treatment?

And why hadn't she stood up to Grandmother Johnson when she said Keira didn't need to be getting any darker, as if being dark was a bad thing? Keira's skin was as gorgeous as her naturally curly hair. Couldn't their grandmother see that? Keira was beautiful, not in spite of her color, but *because* of it.

Why didn't Minni *ever* speak up?

Because she was scared. Plain and simple. Grandmother Johnson was right. She needed more character.

She rubbed her damp palms against her skirt. Admitting this terrible truth was probably one of the hardest things she'd ever had to do. Harder than finding her gerbil dead in its cage. Harder than telling her parents she'd helped Keira cheat on a test. Maybe even harder than singing in front of a bunch of strangers—she wasn't sure. But thinking about how cowardly she had been created an even bigger pit in the bottom of her stomach than the thought of performing onstage.

The conference room door opened. "Are you ready, girls?" A smiling lady stepped into the hallway.

Minni shook from head to foot, the same way she had the day that boy said that awful thing.

The other girls rose from their seats and filed into the room.

"Are you all right, dear?" the woman asked.

Minni didn't move.

"Child, you look terrified."

Minni looked up into the woman's smiling face. "Don't you worry none," the woman said. "It'll be easy as pie. The judges are all very friendly people. You'll see."

Finally, Minni stood, not entirely sure her trembling legs would hold her. The woman took her by the elbow and led her into the room.

Five tables stood around the room. The other girls had already taken their seats—one per table—and had begun to chat with the judge sitting across from them. One judge sat alone. *Miss Oliphant!* Thank goodness.

Minni sat, careful to keep her back straight, her knees together and her hands in her lap, just as Grandmother Johnson had instructed.

"You can relax, baby," Miss Oliphant said. "We're neighbors, remember."

Minni smiled then, and the interview began, although it really just felt like a chat with an old friend. The anxiety and remorse she'd been feeling in the hallway ebbed.

Miss Oliphant asked her what subjects she enjoyed in school, what she thought she might want to do when she got older, what concerns she had about the world today and if she had any pets. Minni loved telling her about Bessie Coleman and all the smart things she could do and say.

Then Miss Oliphant asked who her best friend was and why.

"Definitely my sister. Because she's fun to be with."

Miss Oliphant nodded. "The best kinds of friends to have." She eyed Minni thoughtfully. "Is it ever hard . . . being a twin?"

"Oh no!" Minni said quickly. "It's wonderful!"

Miss Oliphant squinted and let out a little hum.

"I mean, most of the time. I guess it's a little annoying when people wonder why we're never dressed alike—or why we don't look alike."

Miss Oliphant nodded again.

"And I suppose sometimes I compare myself to her . . . but all siblings do that, not just twins."

"If you don't mind me asking, what do you think when you compare yourself to her?"

Minni glanced at her watch. Wasn't it almost time for them to be done?

"We still have five minutes," Miss Oliphant said, again seeming able to read her mind.

The woman's opal eye mesmerized Minni. She felt an urge to be completely honest. "Well, I guess . . . I wonder sometimes why I couldn't have been born with browner skin so people would know we're sisters." She paused, waiting for Miss Oliphant to say something, but the woman just nodded as if she understood. "Sometimes I think about how much more confident she is than me, and I wonder, will I ever shine like Keira?"

Miss Oliphant cocked her head. "Why do you need to shine like your sister? Why can't you shine like yourself?"

"I don't shine." Minni looked at her pale, freckled arms. "Unless you count glowing in the dark."

Miss Oliphant blew out her breath. "Child, everyone shines—just in different ways. Look at the sun and moon. One was made to light the night, the other to light the day."

"The moon doesn't shine, either. It just reflects the sun's light."

"Now, don't go getting all scientific and edu-ma-cated on me. Can you see better by the light of a full moon or can't you?"

Minni nodded grudgingly.

"So one burns hot and the other glows cool. The sun may keep us from freezing to death, but the moon keeps the earth itself from spinning out of orbit. If it weren't for the moon, the oceans would stop their going in and coming out. Do you know how important those tides are?"

Minni nodded slowly. "Without the tides, all life would eventually come to an end."

"Exactly. Both bodies are critical for our survival, and they work *together* to fulfill their joint purpose. Neither one would be able to do what it does without the other. Do you hear what I'm saying?"

She did. She and Keira needed each other.

It was easy to see how she needed Keira, who was always making her laugh or helping her meet new friends or standing up to the boys who made fun of her freckles or big feet or hair. But how did Keira need her? If the moon was just as important as the sun—just in a different way—how was she important?

"Our mama named us for the sun and the moon," she said.

"I wondered about that. In Ireland, the name Keira means 'dark' or 'dark-haired,' but in Persian it also means 'sun,' and I saw on your application that your middle name is Lunette—'little moon.'"

"The day we were born the sun and moon were up at the same time. Mama saw it as good luck."

"Sounds like your mama has grown into one wise woman. I remember her as a teenager, before she left Raleigh to pursue her fame and fortune as an artist." Miss Oliphant smiled, then reached across the table and patted Minni's hand. "Well, then, my moon child, go on and do your job. Your sister relies on you more than you know. You'll see."

Chapter Twenty-seven

☀ ♡ ☾

Minni approached the rows of chairs where everyone sat watching the girl onstage parade around while a lady read from a card about her awards, school and volunteer activities and hobbies.

Why was Keira sitting next to Alisha? Was she actually trying to buddy up to that stuck-up girl? Alisha had told them she'd been doing pageants since she was five years old. Could Keira possibly think she had something to learn from her?

Minni sat in the first empty chair she saw, a couple rows behind her sister. Keira glanced in her direction, then went back to watching the girl onstage. No smile or "How'd it go?" or anything.

Minni crossed her arms. She tried not to let Keira's brush-off bother her, but it did.

The rehearsal wore on. Every time Minni tried to talk to

her sister, she was at the center of a circle of girls, and soon Minni understood.

The ocean she'd felt in the dressing room was still there. And she was floating out in it, in a boat all by herself.

In the car, Grandmother Johnson wanted all the details, but Minni didn't feel like talking. She only spoke one or two words at a time.

Did they have the opening number down?

Yes.

Had they rehearsed their talents in front of everyone?

No, because the talent portion was optional.

Was the girl Alisha good?

She was okay.

Keira's mouth was padlocked.

At home, Keira went straight to the attic. Minni went to the bathroom to wash her face and brush her teeth. She stared at her big blue eyes in the mirror, then scrutinized her face, trying to decide which of her features were "black" and which were "white." So she had Mama's round eyes and fuller lips than Keira. Why couldn't she have been born with darker skin, brown eyes and dark, curly hair as well?

Yes, that would make her stand out back home— probably even more than she felt she did already—but at least then she and Keira could stand out in the same way . . . *together*. At least then no one would question whether she was really black.

She looked in the mirror again, taking in the overall effect. If she had been alive when schools were segregated, she would have insisted she go to a black school, even if people tried to make her go to a white one because of how she looked. She had a black mama and a black sister and lots of black relatives. Eight silly little genes weren't going to keep her from being black, too.

Why did people have to be so obsessed with this color stuff anyway? It all made her so mad.

She said good night to Grandmother Johnson and slowly climbed the creaky stairs. Keira lay on her bed, quietly talking on her phone to Mama and Daddy. "Do you want to talk to Minni?" she asked them.

Minni shook her head. She just didn't feel like it.

"She's too tired," Keira said. "I love you, too. Bye." She hung up the phone, got into bed and stuffed her earbuds into her ears.

Minni put on her pajamas and turned out the light. She slipped under her covers and looked out the window. A full moon shone in the dark night sky. "Keira?" She looked toward her sister.

Keira took out an earbud. "What?" The sound of her tumbling routine music spilled out.

"I'm really sorry for all the stupid things you've had to deal with . . . back home. I get it now, I think. How hard it is to look different."

Keira turned off the music and rolled toward her. "Do you think you're better than me?"

Minni's heart dropped. She pushed up to her elbow.

"*What?* How could you even—? Why would I think I'm better than you?"

"Don't play dumb, Minni." Keira sat up. "You know, to a lot of people lighter is considered better."

"Not to me!"

"Our grandmother sure seems to think so. And you don't know how many times I defended you today to girls I heard saying you probably thought you were 'all that' because you're light-skinned. They think you're stuck up because you didn't try to talk to anyone. Why didn't you try to talk to anyone?"

Girls had been talking behind her back? Panic rose in Minni's chest. She pushed herself all the way up and looked across the darkness that separated them. "I don't think I'm better than you."

"Maybe you do."

"But I *want* to be darker." Minni reached out her hands as if Keira could touch them with a magic wand and make them as brown as her own.

"Not that I have a problem with my color," Keira said, "but you don't know what you're asking for. And it doesn't mean you couldn't still think you're better."

"I don't!"

"You could. Deep down in your heart. So deep that you don't even know about it." Keira leaned against the wall.

"How can I think it if I don't even know about it?"

"Remember what Mom says? People keep secrets—even from themselves. Like Dad and his fear of getting old."

That made Minni stop and look at her chest. Buried

below the blackness Mama said was hidden in the soil of her soul, could there be something hidden even deeper—something that told her her skin was somehow better than Keira's? Just *thinking* about thinking she was better than Keira made her want to cry.

She rushed to Keira's side and, in the glowing light of the moon, begged her with her eyes to take her hand, touch her skin. "You *know* I don't think I'm better. Tell me you know."

Keira kept her hands clasped around her legs and looked out her window.

Minni collapsed against the wall. The thought that there could be something like that lurking in a shadowy corner of her heart, prowling like a tiger, just waiting to pounce and tear everything apart . . .

Keira put her earbuds back in and lay down.

Minni rose. Her body had never felt so heavy. She lay on top of her blankets, still as a log washed up on the beach, but roiling inside like the ocean during a storm.

When Keira's breathing got deep and steady, Minni rose again. She crept across the room to the dormer windows and sat in the window seat. Her heart throbbed with pain. How could her sister doubt her?

The ceiling suddenly felt low. The air seemed hard to breathe. She needed wide-open space. She wanted so badly to be on the beach hurling stones—and with them, all her worries—into the bottomless sea. The sky was kind of like the sea, inky and mysterious and vast. Maybe she could get closer to *it*.

She pulled on one of the dormer windows until it

released. She glanced toward Keira's bed. Her sister hadn't moved. She stood on the bench seat, then hoisted herself out and shut the window quietly behind her.

The roof wasn't too sloped. If she sat still and was careful she'd be fine. She crouched and looked up at the moon, feeling like a wolf. . . . She wanted to howl out all her sadness—to yell at someone for making her look the way she did. But who? If there really was a God, then wouldn't he be the one responsible? Was it okay to yell at God?

She had never really talked to God on her own. Mama had taught them one prayer, and until they were about seven they'd said it every night before they went to bed. "Now I lay me down to sleep. I pray thee, Lord, my soul to keep. If I should die before I wake, I pray thee, Lord, my soul to take . . ." Minni would always add silently, "But please don't let me die in my sleep, God, unless Keira does—then I'll go, too."

So God was someone you recited a prayer to before you went to sleep at night, someone you asked not to let you die, but that was it. She didn't know anything about being angry with God, but if God really was the one who made people, then it was his fault she had this glow-in-the-dark skin— not to mention her five-alarm-fire red hair and circus-grade size-ten feet.

She didn't know where to look when talking to someone she couldn't see, so she focused on the Man in the Moon. "Couldn't you think of anything more original?"

She felt funny talking to the sky. She looked down to make sure no one was walking by.

Then a little louder: "Did you have to go and copy Bozo the Clown?"

She glanced up and down the street again. Still no one. Keira had her music in her ears. Grandmother Johnson had already started snoring. No one was going to hear.

Minni opened her mouth and let God have it.

She yelled at him about her skin, her hair, and her eyes. She moved on to the dress shop lady, the boy at school, the man at the airfield with the cigar. Then to the pageant, Dr. Hogg-Graff, Alisha. How she stood out among the other black girls. How she didn't look like she belonged with her own mama and sister. Yes, she shared Gigi's hair color and Daddy's blue eyes, but would anyone ever see her as black, too?

If she had come out looking more black, she and Keira would experience the same things, right alongside each other. Neither of them would have to feel as if she were going through this stuff alone. Minni could tell her sister she understood and Keira would believe her.

And would there be people who thought *she* thought she was better than them, all because of her light skin, for the rest of her life?

The complaints rolled out like thunder, getting louder and louder, as the storm that had been brewing inside her moved in and took over.

Grandmother Johnson would have a heart attack and die on the spot if she heard Minni yelling. Maybe that was why Minni kept on. Maybe she wanted Grandmother Johnson to hear. Not so she would drop dead on the spot, but so she would hear Minni saying loud and clear that she didn't agree that dark skin was bad, or that her hair was "good" because it wasn't kinky-curly like Keira's.

But Grandmother Johnson was deep asleep. She wasn't hearing any of this. *Was God?*

Minni had no idea, but she had one last thing to say. "You think you're so perfect? You're not! Look at me!" She threw her head back and her hands into the air. "Look at the big mistake you made!"

Silence.

There was no one there.

Her chest heaved with the effort her ranting had taken.

"So, you'll take on the Lord of the Universe but not prickly old Minerva Johnson-Payne?"

Minni looked across the inky darkness to the lavender house. Miss Oliphant stood on her balcony, wrapped in a shawl.

"I . . . I was just . . ." Minni shut her mouth. She was embarrassed, and yet not. She felt cleansed, like the air after a good, hard rain.

"No need to explain to *me* what you were doing. You were calling the Creator to account. There's not a person on this planet—at least not an honest one—who hasn't done the same in one fashion or another."

Miss Oliphant pointed to the sky. "You see that star up there? The brightest one, just down to the right from the moon?"

Minni found the star and nodded.

"That star could have burned out twenty minutes ago,

but we wouldn't know it because what we're seeing is what that star looked like *twenty years* ago. Things are not always what they appear, Miss King."

Minni continued gazing at the sky.

"Would you care to join me for some hot chocolate?"

Minni looked across the darkness again. Grandmother Johnson would be mad if she knew how friendly she and Miss Oliphant were becoming, but then again, who cared? "Yes, ma'am."

"I'll meet you at the front." Miss Oliphant disappeared. The darkness was so solid and undisturbed that for a moment Minni wondered if she had imagined the whole conversation.

A glow came from the downstairs windows.

It dawned on her that she would be drinking cocoa with one of the judges the night before the competition. If Alisha or Alisha's grandmother or anyone else found out, they might accuse her of trying to gain an unfair advantage.

She could be disqualified. . . .

Perhaps she had finally found a way out of this whole thing.

Keira's participation, on the other hand, couldn't be put in jeopardy. Minni dropped her legs over the edge of the roof, searched with her toes for the porch railing and climbed down to solid ground.

Chapter Twenty-eight
☀ ♡ ☾

Bright light scattered the darkness around Miss Oliphant's porch. The bowls of pet food and water sat here and there, filled and waiting. The heavy purple door opened.

"Welcome." Miss Oliphant wore a long cotton gown of red, black and green that reminded Minni of the African fabrics Mama sometimes worked into her art. The woman wrapped her winged sleeve around Minni and pulled her inside. The cloth smelled gingery and warm.

Minni stepped into a living room glowing from at least a dozen candles.

"I hope you don't mind the unconventional lighting. Candlelight is easier on my bad eye than electric."

"It reminds me of my dad's bonfires on our beach."

"Your beach?"

"There's a beach near our town." Minni felt a pang of

homesickness, but something new as well. It was a feeling—no . . . more than a feeling, it was a knowing—a knowing that Keira would leave Port Townsend as soon as she could, and when she did, Minni would leave, too, and she would never live there again.

"My grandmother thinks you do séances or something."

Miss Oliphant chuckled. "What other mess has she put in your heads?"

Grandmother Johnson's charge of voodoo suddenly seemed ridiculous. "Just that you're bringing down the property values in the neighborhood."

"Quite possibly guilty as charged. But then, I've always felt money is somewhat overrated. Having what we need is crucial, but always striving to have more than the next person . . . Greed will do you in."

Minni glanced around. There were piles of books and magazines here and there, and a few boxes sitting around. Whether they were filled with junk, as Grandmother Johnson claimed, Minni thought it was hard to say. She sidled up to a box and peered in.

Fabric scraps. White, woolly stuff. Trinkets, beads and other bric-a-brac.

"For my dolls," Miss Oliphant said.

"Your dolls?" Minni looked up quickly. Had Grandmother Johnson been right after all?

Miss Oliphant pulled down a doll from the top of a cabinet and held it out to her. Minni saw the wrinkled face and pulled back. This was one of those heads she'd seen hanging in the kitchen! Did Miss Oliphant have a doll in one of these boxes that looked like Grandmother Johnson? "Is it for voodoo?" Minni glanced at Miss Oliphant, then back at the doll.

"*Voo*-doo? No!" Miss Oliphant laughed—a hearty belly laugh. "What in the world would make you think I practice voodoo? Oh. Of course. Your grandmother."

Minni knew it had been ridiculous. She giggled nervously.

"It's a dried apple," Miss Oliphant said, pointing to the face. She held out the doll again and this time Minni took it.

"*Oh.*" The doll wore wire-rimmed glasses and an African-print dress. Her hair was made of white wool. It was parted in a way that made Minni think of Frederick Douglass, and smelled thick and oily, like Mama's lanolin conditioner. The more Minni looked at the doll's face, the more real it became. The doll looked as if she knew everything there was to know.

"They're my wisdom dolls. I sell them at local boutiques and give them to friends. Her name is Sophie. 'Sophia' means 'wisdom' in Greek."

Minni thought of her own name, Minerva: goddess of wisdom. The meaning had never meant much to her because, although she'd looked up the definition of "wisdom" in her Webster's dictionary, she didn't see how having "accumulated philosophic learning" or even "good sense" was all that desirable. She'd much rather have Keira's outgoingness or MLK's courage. And she certainly didn't feel like any kind of goddess.

"What is wisdom, exactly?" she asked. Miss Oliphant seemed like the kind of person who would know. The kind of person who had a lot of it herself.

Miss Oliphant led her to the living room and they sat, Minni on the couch, still holding the doll, and Miss Oliphant in an upholstered chair with claw-shaped arms. A deck of large cards sat on the coffee table. Were those the cards Keira had seen her looking at the other night? Minni had to work hard to refocus on what Miss Oliphant was saying.

"Well, it's certainly not something you can pick up at the grocery store or in a fast-food drive-through." Her opal-fogged eye glowed in the candlelight. "It's not something you gain without a struggle. It's not going to just drop out of the sky and into your lap." She sighed. "You might get lucky and have wise parents who help you find the way to wisdom, but even then, it's not like an inheritance that gets handed down from one generation to the next. Just because you have wise parents doesn't mean you will end up wise. You've got to go down the wisdom path yourself."

"How do you find the wisdom path?"

"Everyone's wisdom path is different. You've got to find your own."

"What if I can't find it?"

"If you really want to find it and seek it with all your heart, you will."

Minni thought about her recent realization that she had been a coward at the worst times—times when she'd had a chance to fight the wrong in the world that threatened to get inside her sister, but she had chickened out instead. "I'd rather have courage."

"You need both. Being foolishly bold will get you nowhere but in trouble. Wise people know that 'what's essential is invisible to the eye.' They don't make rash judgments based only on what they can see.

"I need to check on the milk heating on the stove. Be back in a moment." Miss Oliphant went to the kitchen. Minni glanced over her shoulder, then peeked underneath one of the cards. The queen of hearts.

Playing cards. Minni flushed. How silly they had been to think she was reading fortunes. She probably used bigger cards to be able to see them more easily, like large-print books.

Miss Oliphant returned. She handed Minni a mug, then picked two cards off the deck and used the one closest to her as a coaster. "I love these big cards—useful for so many things. Do you play?"

"We play hearts in my family."

"I'm a sucker for solitaire. Can't tell you how much sleep I've lost trying to beat the deck. A friend even told me I needed to look into Solitaire Players Anonymous. Can you believe such a thing exists?"

Minni raised her eyebrows.

"Sadly, it does." Miss Oliphant sat in her chair, picked up her hot chocolate and blew on the surface. "Made with whole milk and real dark chocolate. Heavenly."

Minni lifted her mug slowly, considering the old woman. Her skin was almost as pale as Minni's. But at the orientation she had been called a "pillar of the black community." So was she black, or white? Or what?

"Miss Oliphant?"

"Please, call me Laverna." The old woman set down her mug again.

"Miss Laverna . . . do you consider yourself more black or white?"

The woman was still. "I contain multitudes." The corners of her mouth turned up in a small smile like the *Mona Lisa* painting in one of Mama's art books. "But I consider myself black."

"You do? Why?"

"Because that's what fits my soul." She rested her hands on the chair's arms. "What about you?" She gazed at Minni intently.

Was this some kind of trap? Would Miss Oliphant tell Dr. Hogg-Graff Minni's answer? Not that Minni cared . . . or did she?

"If I was hearing you correctly on the balcony—and I'm pretty sure I was because it's my eyesight that's going, not my ears—you're not too crazy about the color of your skin."

Minni looked at the white swirls on the surface of her cocoa. "No, ma'am. I guess I'm not."

"Miss King, do you know what the body's largest organ is?"

"Please call me Minni."

"Okay, then, Miss Minni, do you know what your largest organ is?"

Minni had a book at home that talked about the human body. She could see the colorful diagrams in her mind's eye, exactly as they appeared in the book. "The liver," she said confidently.

"Your *skin*," Miss Oliphant said.

Minni stared into her drink.

"That's an awful lot of yourself not to like, don't you think?" Miss Oliphant watched Minni carefully and slurped her hot chocolate.

Minni took a sip. Maybe so, she thought, but that was how she felt, and she didn't see how knowing her outer layer was her largest organ would change that. It wasn't just her largest organ—it was the part of her that people saw before anything else and decided who she was . . . how to treat her . . . whether she belonged.

"Man looks on the outward appearance, but the Lord looks on the heart," Miss Oliphant said.

Her heart. *What was hidden in her heart?* "I'm scared," Minni said.

"Of what, child?"

"Of getting treated better than my sister." She looked up at Miss Oliphant. "And that it will come between us."

"Hmmm. That's a tough one. Your color *will* get you treated differently than your sister, sometimes better. The question is how will you use this to help make the world a more equitable place?"

Minni gripped her mug. Miss Oliphant hadn't given her any assurances about what effect all this might have on her and Keira.

"So, back to my original question. What fits *your* soul?" Miss Oliphant asked.

Minni closed her eyes and tried to let herself be. How did she feel, deep inside? What did she believe? For some reason, she thought about sitting in Grandmother Johnson's church, swaying to the choir's voices. Something had stirred inside her. She was not an outsider peering in, a spectator. She was connected to the people there—maybe not by outer appearance, but by something deeper. Something in all their hearts. These were her people. This music, this feeling, this longing to be seen as a person and not just a color—it was hers, too.

But then there was Daddy, with his desire to be alone—in the sky or in the woods—and she could relate to that, too. She was connected to him, by their skin color and by something in their hearts as well. He would always be her daddy. She was about to say "I'm not sure" when she felt Miss Laverna's hand on her arm.

"You don't have to know right now. You've got time."

Minni set down her mug. "Thanks for the hot chocolate. It *was* heavenly." She took one last look at Sophie, the wisdom doll, and headed for the door.

Miss Oliphant followed her. "Good luck tomorrow."

"Thank you."

"And, Minni, if you think your skin is going to keep you from belonging, it will. But it doesn't have to."

Minni cocked her head, considering Miss Oliphant—Miss Laverna—once more. Then she turned and walked down the steps. She might not have known what label best fit her soul, but she was confident of at least one thing: She didn't think she was better than Keira. She knew this as surely as she knew they came from the same mama.

Chapter Twenty-nine

☀ ♡ ☾

The next day, first Gigi and then Mama and Daddy called
to wish them good luck. Minni used her speakerphone so
she and Keira could talk at the same time. Keira was still
acting kind of distant after last night's conversation, but she
jabbered with excitement during the calls.

"You'll be great!" Daddy said.

"Be *yourselves*," Mama added.

They promised to do their best, then hung up and gathered their things to leave.

Grandmother Johnson had gone completely overboard
with her dress—a full-length black gown with curlicue ap-
pliqués and a surprisingly low neckline. Instead of her gold
locket, she wore a blindingly bright diamond necklace and

teardrop earrings to match. A sheer black wrap lay on the car seat beside her.

She talked nonstop all the way to the Hotel Lamont. "We remembered everything, right? Opening-number outfits—leotards, tights, skirts . . . gowns, heels, nylons . . . talent outfits . . ."

She glanced in the rearview mirror. "Are those flowers holding up all right?"

Keira had asked Grandmother Johnson if she would cut her a couple of yellow roses to accessorize her hair, which was still straight from the flatiron, but which she'd gathered into a bun behind one ear, opposite her side part. The flowers rested on her lap in a plastic baggie, their stems wrapped in wet paper towels. "They're good," Keira said.

"Fine. Let's see . . . what else? Hair spray, makeup—keep it modest, remember . . ." Grandmother Johnson glanced at Keira again. "You're sure you have everything you need to do your sister's hair?" They'd run out of time at the house.

Keira nodded.

"Good. And don't forget to smile at all times. Not forced, never forced—natural smiles. And when you're walking across the stage in your gowns, keep your chins up and your shoulders back, but don't let your chests protrude too much. And drink a little water before you go onstage, but sip, don't gulp, lest you trap air in your stomach. And . . ."

Minni tuned her out.

At the hotel, Grandmother Johnson pulled into the circular drive and around the spouting fountain to the gold-framed front doors. She got out, handed the keys to the valet and ordered a bellboy to bring a luggage cart for her grand-daughters' things, all at the same time.

That was when Minni noticed. She nudged Keira with one hand and used the other to point. "Her shoes," Minni whispered.

Keira gasped.

Their grandmother wore her sturdy pumps, but only one was black. The other was clearly navy blue! "Should we tell her?" Minni asked.

"Nah." Keira snickered and her eyes sparkled with a familiar light.

Minni's insides were a mess—between her nerves and the awful fear that Keira was still questioning whether Minni thought she was better than her—but at that moment she reveled in Keira's smile. There was no greater feeling in the world than sharing a secret with her sister.

Inside, Alisha's grandmother, Alisha and a middle-aged woman who Minni guessed was Alisha's mom stood in the corridor talking. Grandmother Johnson and Mrs. Russell gave each other once-overs.

"Ernestine," Grandmother Johnson said coolly as they passed. Mrs. Russell nodded in response. Fortunately for Grandmother Johnson, she didn't notice the mismatched shoes.

"This is *it*, Alisha," the middle-aged woman said. Minni felt Alisha's eyes following them. "Stay focused. No stupid mistakes. All right?"

"All *right*." Alisha sounded aggravated.

When they reached the dressing room door, Grandmother Johnson pulled Minni and Keira aside. "I know you will compete with the utmost decorum . . ." They started to leave but she grabbed them by their shoulders. "But one of you needs to beat that girl, Alisha. Got it?"

They glanced at each other, then headed for the door.

Grandmother Johnson called out. "Take no prisoners!"

They got into their opening-number outfits—black tights and ballet slippers, sparkly leotards and silver skirts—and then Minni sat in front of a mirror so Keira could do her hair. Girls dressed and twittered excitedly around them.

Keira worked silently and was a little rougher than usual. She never looked Minni in the eye. The chill coming off her made Minni feel cold. Why was Keira still mad? Minni had *told* her she didn't think she was better. Didn't Keira believe her? Didn't her sister know her better than that?

Keira used her curling iron to make ringlets around Minni's face, put in the two rhinestone flower clips, then sprayed the hair spray. Minni would have to make sure no one lit a match within ten feet of her head or they would all go up in flames.

Minni stood to let Keira take her chair. "Would you please talk to me?" she pleaded.

Keira opened her makeup pouch and applied some sparkly blush. She glanced at Minni in the mirror. Her lips scrunched to one side. She rose and pulled Minni behind a clothing rack. "*Why* didn't you talk to any of the girls yesterday?" she whispered.

"Why did you ignore me all day?" Minni asked, still feeling the sting of what seemed like her sister's abandonment.

"Because you need to learn how to make friends on your own!"

"I never go up to new people and start talking. That's what *you* do."

Keira huffed. "You could, too, if you tried."

Minni's neck and ears got hot. "You know I'm not stuck-up, Keira. I'm shy!"

"Of course I know that, but I'm not always going to be there to help you out . . . or to defend you."

Minni's eyes stung with tears. She grabbed Keira's hand. "Please don't be mad at me. I can't go through with this if I feel like you're mad at me. I *won't*. You said we'd get through this *together*."

Keira exhaled again. Her eyes looked sorry, but her jaw was still firm and her arm was stiff and tense.

Minni let go of Keira's hand and put her fists on her hips. She spoke loudly. "I officially withdraw from the Miss Black Pearl Preteen of America pageant—"

Alisha rounded the rack, nearly bumping into Keira. "Thank goodness," Alisha said. "Now I don't have to worry about getting a black eye."

"Bug off," Keira said.

Alisha looked aghast. "What did you say?"

"Bug off!"

"After I chose to sit next to you and be nice to you yesterday?"

"We all know you're just trying to win Miss Congeniality along with the title. You're as see-through as Saran Wrap, Alisha."

The girl's eyes narrowed. "You better watch yourself, Keira King. My mama's been preparing me for this since the day I was born, and I *will* win." Alisha opened a canister of Vaseline, scooped out a glob and ran it over her teeth.

Minni shuddered at the thought of the thick stuff in her mouth, but she did something else as well. Something that surprised her, but she did it. She stepped forward and looked Alisha right in the eye. "Well, Alisha Walker, I hope your mama's ready for a big disappointment, because my sister's going to beat you."

Alisha gave her an evil eye, then spun, whipping her ponytail in Minni's face. She stalked away.

Keira took Minni's hands in her own. "You *have* to do this, Min—not for Grandmother Johnson or our parents, not even for me. For your *own* sake." She looked straight into Minni's eyes. "You have to believe it's your right to be out there."

Minni's heart felt like an egg being pecked on from the inside. With each moment she gazed into her sister's deep brown eyes, her heart cracked a little more. She was overcome by a sudden need to tell her sister about the lady at the dress shop. "She treated me kindly, Keira."

The skin between Keira's eyes crinkled.

"The lady at the gown shop. Before you and Gigi came

in, she was totally friendly and full of compliments. I put my hands all over a bunch of dresses and she didn't say a thing." Minni hadn't realized how heavy the secret had become. She suddenly felt fifty pounds lighter.

Keira looked at the floor.

"I didn't mean to pass for white—really, I didn't."

Keira looked into her eyes again.

Minni knew her sister's eyes better than any others, even better than her own. She'd been staring into them since before she was born. "And I *don't* think I'm better than you." She squeezed Keira's hands. "You're the other half of my heart."

Keira squeezed back. The hairs on Minni's arms prickled.

Miss Jackie opened the door from the stage. "Let's go, everyone! In your places!"

Minni and Keira jumped to finish getting ready. Keira gave Minni a coat of lip gloss and a little of Gigi's Marla Ray blush. They pinned each other's numbers to their hips. Then they stood at the stage door, the last ones in the room. Keira messed with Minni's hair, repositioning her bobby pins. "Ready?" she asked.

"I don't know," Minni said. "I guess I'm about to find out." She took her sister's hand. "Shine, Keira. Brighter than ever. *Shine.*"

Chapter Thirty

As soon as they stepped through the door, Miss Jackie grabbed them and pulled them toward the stage. The other girls were already in position behind the closed curtains. "Where have you been? You're late!"

"Sorry, Miss Jackie," Keira said. She squeezed Minni's hand, then smiled her brilliant smile. "Break a leg!" She paused. "Wait. Scratch that. Have fun!" She ran to her place in front.

Minni stood frozen. She couldn't remember a single dance step. What were they supposed to do first? Step left or right? Or was it forward? A spin?

And her personal introduction—how did it start? She couldn't even remember the first line. What was she doing out there? *I can't do this! Help, someone . . . anyone, help!*

Miss Jackie pushed her toward her spot in back. "You'll be fine. Just do the best you can."

"Ladies and gentlemen," a man's voice announced. The girls around Minni murmured with excitement—everyone except Alisha. She stood in position, eyes straight ahead, like a hunting dog on point.

"Welcome to the ninth annual Miss Black Pearl Preteen National Achievement Program!" Lots of applause.

"And now, let's meet our girls as they dance to a song that reminds us all—'We . . . Are . . . Fami-leeeee'!" More applause. The music started. The curtains parted.

The spotlights were so bright, Minni couldn't see a single face in the audience. Looking at the crowd was like looking at the ocean on a dark, moonless night. She fixed her eyes on Keira's back, and though she was a little late with the first step, she took it. Suddenly she was off and dancing with the rest of them.

She spun one direction: one, two, three, and clap! And the other direction: one, two, three, and clap! Time for the back row's chance to show their stuff. They sashayed forward.

Here in front, she could see the table of judges. Miss Laverna looked dazzling in a sparkling lavender jacket. She winked at Minni, and Minni almost lost her place in the routine, but then the girls around her stooped to the ground, and even though she was a beat behind, Minni did the same, and she was back in the swing of things.

She had half a mind to reach when she was supposed to slide so she could get Alisha in the eye again, but while that might be bold, it wouldn't be very wise. She did the sequence correctly . . . *kick, spin, reach and slide.* Her row returned to the back.

They ended with their arms in the air, waving their hands. Minni could smell her melony sweat, but she smiled anyway. The only other people who could smell it back here would be the girls to either side of her, and if the stink caused Alisha to make a sour face, that would be all the better for Keira. Minni waved even harder to get the odor to waft toward the snooty girl's nostrils.

Now it was time for the girls to run forward one at a time for their thirty-seconds-or-less personal introductions. They clasped hands and swayed back and forth while they waited their turns. Alisha held Minni's hand as stiffly as a Ping-Pong paddle, as if in protest at having to touch her.

Minni frantically searched her mind for the words she had rehearsed at Grandmother Johnson's so many times. Keira, one of the first to go, did beautifully, of course.

Too quickly, girls in the back row were pulling away to take their turns at the microphone. Suddenly Alisha was at the front of the stage, bragging to everyone how she'd been competing in pageants since she was five.

Minni silently repeated the one line she could recall. Hopefully the rest would follow once she got up there.

Alisha was returning to her place. Minni's shoes felt as if they'd been nailed to the floor. "*Go!*" the girl to her right whispered. She gave Minni a little shove.

Minni jumped, then started her jog forward. She avoided looking at Alisha as they crossed paths. She rounded the

261

front row. Keira gave her another big smile. She stepped up to the mike, took a breath and enunciated every word as loudly and clearly as she could. "My name is *Minni* King. I'm eleven years old and I'm from Port Townsend, Washington. My best friend and twin sister, Keira, and I were born in our daddy's airplane . . ." She thought she heard Grandmother Johnson cry out. "And I plan to learn to fly one day. I love animals, reading and spending time with my family. Most of all, I want to be like Dr. Martin Luther King, Jr., and do something to make the world a"—she looked at Miss Laverna—"a more *equitable* place for everyone. Thank you."

People applauded, and she ran back to her place. Alisha smirked. "An *airplane?*"

Minni ignored her and smiled out at the audience. She had done it.

After a few more introductions, the curtains closed and everyone hurried offstage.

Keira grabbed Minni. "You were great!"

"You too."

"How'd you do on the dance routine?"

"I tried to throw off Alisha with my stinky pits." They ran into the dressing room, laughing.

While Keira changed into her tumbling outfit, Minni read the lyrics to "His Eye Is on the Sparrow" from the sheet music. Over and over, until it was as good as branded on her brain. Then she sat in the corner with her eyes closed and breathed deeply, in and out, just like Mama had taught Keira to do before she took a test.

Breathing reminded you you were alive, Mama said, and that was the most important thing to be.

Minni wasn't sure if God watched her the way the song talked about or not, but there *was* someone who would always be aware of her existence. Always care that she was alive. Always know who she was.

Keira.

The deep breathing got her so relaxed, she drifted into a dream. She and Keira were climbing the Sisters, hand in hand. They had just reached the summit of the tallest peak when someone shook her. "I'm going on soon," she heard.

Minni jerked awake. Keira crouched next to her. Minni remembered where she was and scrambled to her feet. She changed into her blouse and skirt, then hurried with her sister to the wings and watched as Keira took flight. Keira soared through her routine, tumbling, twirling and flipping to the raucous remixed symphony music. She was awesome. The applause was deafening.

Just like that, it was Minni's turn. No way through it except to do it.

Keira ran up, breathing hard. "I love you." The words spilled from her mouth. "Just . . . the . . . way . . . you are."

Minni took another deep breath. Someone shoved a cordless microphone into her hand.

"And now," the emcee announced, "Minerva Lunette King will perform 'His Eye Is on the Sparrow'!"

It felt as if someone were using Minni's stomach as a trampoline. She shuffled to center stage and waited for the recorded music. Her head floated a few inches above her neck. Dizziness caused her to sway. Would she topple in front of everyone?

She glanced at the judges. Miss Laverna winked again. Her parting words from last night came back: *If you think your skin is going to keep you from belonging, it will. But it doesn't have to.*

Minni inhaled and exhaled. *Keira knows who I am.*

I contain multitudes . . .

She heard the soft static that signaled that the tape was rolling.

Minni swallowed, trying to moisten her dry tongue. She clutched the microphone, waiting for the piano intro, but instead of Grandmother Johnson's so-so playing, an awful grating sound filled the room—a loud, low rumble followed by a high-pitched whistle. Waves of cold dread washed over her.

Grandmother Johnson's snoring.

Minni had recorded over Grandmother Johnson's accompaniment! She had never gone back to take the tape out of the machine.

People shifted in their seats, glancing around. The snoring went on and on, and then stopped suddenly. The room was dead silent.

Minni stood frozen, nervous laughter welling at the base of her throat. Someone coughed. What was Grandmother Johnson doing? Had she fainted in her seat? Or rushed to the sound guy and ripped the tape from the deck? Whatever she was doing, she would be livid.

Keira stood offstage with her hands clamped over her mouth. She waved frantically and whispered, "Sing! *Sing!*"

Minni wanted to flee, but something deep inside wouldn't let her. She had to do this and she knew it. She took a breath. *"Why should I feel discouraged?"* Her voice shook, soft and airy. *"Why should the shadows come?"*

Her eyes slid to Keira, who gave her a thumbs-up. Minni closed her eyes and imagined she was on the beach, singing to the ocean and the sky . . . to the sun and the moon. No one was there except her and her sister.

That was when it happened. Someone yelled out. "Go on, girl!"

If she hadn't been to Grandmother Johnson's church, she might have thought the person was impatiently telling her to get on with it already. But she'd heard people shouting things like this all over the church that day, and it clearly meant one thing: *We like what we're hearing. Give us some more!*

She took a deeper breath and let her voice ring. More people called out encouragement. She even heard a woman who sounded like Mama. She smiled.

"I sing because I'm happy. I sing because I'm free!" Her voice soared and floated like the sparrow she sang about. *"His eye is on the sparrow. And I know . . ."* She made her voice loop up and down and around, just like that girl at the church.

Sort of.

"I know . . ."

Not as confidently or as beautifully, but she tried. *"I know . . . he watches . . . me."* She held out the last note as long as she could, just like the choir had done.

For a moment, the room was silent again. And then . . . applause! And it was loud! Not as thunderous as Keira's had been, but it was loud. They thought she'd done a good job. More importantly, she realized, *she* thought she'd done a good job.

She rushed offstage and into Keira's arms.

Chapter Thirty-one

Keira and Minni helped each other into their gowns, giggling hysterically about the tape snafu.

"Do you think she left the building in humiliation?" Minni asked.

"Never. She'll blame it on the sound guy or the tape player or something."

Donyelle, who hadn't performed a talent, came up and told them how much she liked their performances. Alisha, who had twirled a baton—quite well, Minni had to admit—stood at a distance and scowled.

Keira decorated her side bun with the roses. Then she touched up their lip gloss, and it was time to get in line.

Minni was feeling good, in spite of how uncomfortable she was in her long dress. She'd done the hardest part. She'd sung in front of a whole crowd of strangers! They'd even shouted for her!

"Remember, chin up and shoulders back," Keira said as the girl ahead of them walked around the stage to the emcee's reciting of her awards, activities and achievements. "But don't let your chest protrude!"

Minni stifled a giggle with her hand.

Alisha sauntered over. "Good luck, Keira. May the most deserving girl win." A huge grin spread across her face as she held out her hand.

Keira shook Alisha's hand just as the emcee called her name—her cue to start walking. "Keira Sol King is the daughter of Gordon and Lizette King . . ."

Keira turned and stepped, but her foot caught on something. Minni sucked in her breath as Keira lurched onto the stage and tumbled to the ground. She lay spread-eagled, just past the curtain. The audience gasped as if they were one giant person. The emcee stood by dumbly.

Minni rushed to her sister's side and helped her to her feet, brushing dust from her bright yellow dress. "Chin up, Keira," she whispered. The audience applauded and Keira started again. Just like that, she was floating around the stage, as beautiful and graceful as ever. Her smile looked a little more forced than usual, but in a way that only a twin sister could tell.

Minni stood in the wings, fuming. That brat, Alisha! She had tripped Keira, no doubt about it. No way would Keira trip on her own. That was Minni's department. Minni wanted to go find the cheater and tell her she knew what she'd done, but it was her turn next. She had to stay put— for now.

Keira's list of activities and awards was impressive, even to Minni, who already knew them all so well. The national fashion design contest. All her gymnastics awards. Her Girl Scout badges. Volunteering at the senior citizens' center. Her plan to own her own fashion design business. Her desire to start a foundation to assist AIDS orphans in Africa and to bring attention to the struggles of kids with learning disabilities.

"Keira Sol King, ladies and gentlemen," the emcee finished. Keira exited on the other side.

"Minerva Lunette King . . ."

Minni stepped back onstage, still distracted by what had happened to her sister. She wound around on her way to the other side, barely paying attention to what the emcee was saying. She was walking faster than Miss Jackie wanted them to, but she didn't care. She needed to find Keira and make sure she was okay.

Finally done with her turn, Minni rushed toward the dressing room. Alisha was in the wings again, waiting to be called. She should shove the girl onto the stage—give her a dose of her own medicine. No, she wouldn't sink to her level. Instead she walked straight up and stomped on her foot.

"Ow!" Alisha screeched. "How dare you!"

"No, how dare you!" Minni growled, and kept walking. She pushed through the dressing room door. Keira wasn't there.

"Have you seen my sister?" she asked Donyelle.

Donyelle shook her head. "Is she going to be okay? What happened?"

Minni didn't stop to answer. She clutched the skirt of her dress and hurried from the room.

After checking the hallway bathroom and the lobby, she decided to try outside. Keira sat on a bench, watching the spraying fountain in the turnaround. The setting sun still lit the night air. The almost perfectly round moon shone opposite in the sky, making its way up.

Minni sat next to her sister. "Are you all right?"

Keira nodded, gazing at the sky.

"She tripped you, didn't she?"

"It doesn't matter."

"Of course it matters! That's cheating! She should be disqualified."

"I feel sorry for her—all the pressure she must be under. If she has to win *that* badly, let her have it. There's always next year." Keira smiled.

"But Grandmother Johnson said there might not be a competition next year."

"You know she only said that to get Mom to go along. You've seen the way she and Alisha's grandmother look at each other. She wants to show that woman up. That's probably why she insisted we had to come this summer instead of waiting until next."

"You could still win."

Keira shrugged. "I've realized there are more important things."

Minni looked into her sister's eyes. "Like not letting anything come between us?"

Keira grabbed Minni's hand and held it tight. "Or any*one*."

270

Minni looked at the sun and moon hanging in the summer sky. They had always been together. They would always be together. "Whatever happens, I'm with you."

 $\mathcal{F}$ inally it was time to return to the stage. Standing next to Alisha on the risers, Minni wanted to throw up. Not just a little pea-sized throw-up. Buckets. Gallons. Bushels.

She wasn't nervous for herself anymore. She was nervous for Keira. She so badly wanted her to win, or at least for Alisha not to.

The emcee came to the podium. "All of our girls are winners already—" The crowd applauded, with a few whistles and hoots thrown in. "But now it is time to acknowledge a handful of them for their outstanding merit in particular areas. First, because achievement and success mean little without a kind heart and a friendly spirit, the Miss Congeniality award goes to *Donyelle Dyer!*"

With a rush of excitement, Minni threw her hands together and clapped long and hard. Donyelle, grinning from ear to ear, stepped away from the first row to receive her trophy. She jiggled with excitement as she posed for a photo with last year's Miss Black Pearl Preteen of America, her dimples deeper than ever. Minni waved at her and gave her a big thumbs-up. Donyelle totally deserved that award. She had made Minni feel welcomed from the very start.

The category awards continued, with girls receiving trophies for school activities, leadership, athletics and the arts.

Minni was not disappointed a bit when her name wasn't called for academic excellence, although she was sort of surprised Keira didn't win the arts award.

"The humanitarian award goes to a girl who has exhibited an exceptional commitment to making our world a better place. For her work in her school library helping children to read, her environmental cleanup efforts, her involvement with Girl Scouts and her volunteer service with a local animal shelter, this year's award goes to Minerva King!"

A tremor ran through Minni's body. Her face turned hot.

Alisha leaned over. "Are you just going to stand there with your mouth open?"

Minni took a breath, then gathered her dress in her hands and descended the risers carefully. Other girls' hands patted her back and arms as she passed. At the bottom, Keira rushed over and hugged her neck.

Minni received the trophy from last year's Miss Black Pearl Preteen, thanked her and posed for the photo. The bright flash made her see stars, but she still managed to locate Miss Laverna at the judges' table and give her a little wave. She went back to her place next to Alisha, who stood straight and tall, looking smug. "Congratulations."

Somehow Minni didn't think she meant it.

"The talent award will be next," Alisha said.

"Now on to the talent award," the emcee announced.

"See?" Alisha said, never once losing her pasted-on smile. "In most pageants, the girl who wins talent wins the title." She couldn't seem to help herself. She just had to be a show-off.

"This isn't a pageant. It's a program," Minni said dryly.

Alisha sneered, then quickly put on her smile again.

"The judges had a very difficult time with this one, as there were so many fine performances."

Alisha's smile held steady.

"And so, for the first time in the history of Miss Black Pearl Preteen, we have a *tie* for talent. The co-winners are Miss Alisha Walker"—Alisha squealed and started for the stage—"and Miss Keira King!"

Alisha stopped in her tracks. Minni didn't need to see the girl's face to know the smile had been knocked clean off.

Minni cupped her hands around her mouth and shouted, "Yeah, Keira!" Then she clapped as hard as she could for her sister, who posed for a photo along with the clearly still-in-shock Alisha.

The emcee waited for the girls to return to their spots. "And now, ladies and gentlemen, the moment we've all been waiting for . . ."

The crowd was completely silent, but the room was not quiet. It crackled with the excitement of everyone waiting to hear who would be crowned the next Miss Black Pearl Preteen of America.

Last year's first and second runners-up joined Miss Black Pearl Preteen onstage, waiting to give this year's court their crowns, sashes and large pretend checks representing the U.S. savings bonds that the winners received.

"The second runner-up, and first princess in the Black Pearl court, is Miss Shauntay Daniels!" The audience erupted in shouts and applause. Shauntay put her hands over her mouth when she heard her name and then hugged the girls next to her. She lifted the hem of her dress and hurried to receive her regalia and check.

"The first runner-up, and second princess in the Black Pearl court, is . . . Miss Alisha Walker!"

Minni bit the side of her mouth to keep from smiling and turned toward Alisha. She could at least give the girl a pat on the back.

Alisha stood with her arms straight down, her fists and jaw clenched. She wasn't even trying to fake looking happy. She stalked to the front of the stage and forced a smile for the camera. She looked as if someone were pulling her fingernails off one by one.

"And now, to the winner." The emcee held up a card. "Ladies and gentlemen, boys and girls, the ninth Miss Black Pearl Preteen of America is . . ."

Minni smiled, knowing what was coming.

"Miss KEIRA KING!"

The audience roared. Minni's heart soared. There were cheers, whistles and the most applause of the whole program. People rose to their feet.

Some cheesy instrumental music started to play. Keira hugged the girls around her, then walked forward proudly to receive her foam-board check for one thousand dollars in U.S. savings bonds and stand next to the huge trophy, which was almost as tall as she was.

Minni beamed as last year's Miss Black Pearl Preteen put a crown on Keira's head and a sash around her middle. Then she handed Keira some flowers and kissed her cheek.

Keira walked across the stage, waving at the audience, her eyes shining brightly. Flashing cameras lit up the room.

Minni smiled so hard her cheeks ached. She looked out at the audience again. Grandmother Johnson plowed down the aisle, leading the charge on her way to the stage.

She wasn't alone.

Mama, Daddy and Gigi were with her!

Chapter Thirty-two

☀ ♡ ☾

Daddy blew kisses. Gigi snapped pictures. Mama beamed at Keira, then at Minni. She gave Minni a big thumbs-up.

Grandmother Johnson had apparently forgotten about decorum. She cheered wildly, bouncing up and down. Hopefully, in her ecstatic state, she had also forgotten about the earlier broadcasting of her "heavy breathing" habit.

When all official photo-taking was over, Miss Jackie signaled to the girls that they were free to leave their places and mingle with each other and family members waiting to greet them. Alisha fled from the stage, wailing.

Donyelle grabbed Minni before she could reach Keira, who was surrounded by a hundred people anyway. It would be a while before Minni had her sister to herself again.

"Congratulations on your award!" Donyelle said.

"You too! You totally deserved it."

"Thanks. Hey, you wanna trade e-mails?" Donyelle held out a pen and a piece of paper with her address already written on it: Iluvbarbies157@chatter.com.

"Sure," Minni said, grinning. She ripped the paper in half, wrote down her address and handed it back to Donyelle. They hugged.

"It was fun to meet you," Donyelle said.

"You too."

"Don't forget to write."

"I won't."

"I'll send you a picture of my Barbie collection."

"Okay. I'll send you a picture of me and Bessie Coleman."

"Great!" Donyelle headed off to exchange addresses with someone else.

Minni scanned the judges' area, looking for Miss Laverna, but all the judges were gone. She headed for the stairs at the end of the stage and made her way to her family.

She sank into Mama's embrace, breathing in her lovely scent. She was home again.

It turned out Daddy had flown Mama and Gigi out in one of his friend's charter planes in exchange for a favor. They had decided to keep it a surprise and had actually called that morning from Raleigh. Grandmother Johnson had known all about it. "I'm an excellent secret keeper," she said with a grin when the truth came out. They stood around Keira in the emptying ballroom, admiring her gargantuan trophy, the bouquet of stargazer lilies and the big check.

Minni and Keira retrieved their things from the dressing room—Alisha was nowhere to be seen—received a final word of congratulation from Dr. Hogg-Graff, and then joined their family in the lobby. They begged to go with Mama and Daddy in the rental car.

"I'll keep you company, Minerva," Gigi said. Her dangling earrings and dental-strip-whitened teeth sparkled in the lobby's light. "How is it that in all these years, we've never had any one-on-one time?" She tweaked Grandmother Johnson's arm. Grandmother Johnson looked at her sharply, but Gigi didn't seem to notice. "On our way, you can point out places to go for a hot night out on the town. I wouldn't mind meeting myself a good old-fashioned Southern gentleman while I'm here."

Daddy rolled his eyes. He put his arms around Minni and Keira, and they all went out into the warm evening air.

Back at Grandmother Johnson's, another surprise awaited.

"Ruff! Ruff-ruff!"

"Banjo!" Minni ran to the dog and knelt. Banjo put his paws on her shoulders and licked her face. She untied the dog's leash from the railing along the back steps and scooped him up.

Gigi came along next.

"I can't believe she let you leave him in her yard!" Minni looked around the grass for any "dirty deeds."

"Only after practically making me sign a contract," Gigi

muttered, then raised the pitch of her voice to sound like Grandmother Johnson, "'to remove any and all ill effects of his messes from the premises.'"

Grandmother Johnson clip-clopped down the walkway from the garage. She harrumphed and raised The Eyebrow at the sight of Banjo but didn't stop to comment. She clomped up the steps and unlocked the back door.

Finally, Mama, Daddy and Keira came. Keira still wore the crown and sash. She talked a mile a minute. "I just can't believe it! I actually won! Can you believe it?"

"Absolutely," Daddy said, squeezing her shoulders from behind.

Seeing Banjo's food and water dishes in the grass, Minni thought of her parakeet. "Who's taking care of Bessie Coleman?" she asked Daddy.

"Mrs. Anderson will check on her tomorrow." Mrs. Anderson was their neighbor in Port Townsend. "And we should be home by tomorrow night."

Home. She loved the sound of that word. Although she wondered what it would be like to be there again, now that she understood better what it was like for Keira. Now that she knew it wasn't always so easy for her.

Mama, Keira and Gigi went inside. Daddy came over and put his arm around her. "I'm really proud of you." She rested her head against his side. "And Bessie will be able to tell you the same. We worked hard on that while you were gone."

Minni nuzzled Banjo's scruffy face, then tucked him under her arm and followed Daddy inside.

"What is *that* doing in here?" Grandmother Johnson asked, eyeing the dog. She was setting dishes of pudding on the dining room table, still in her long black gown.

"He's a wonderful indoor dog—completely potty trained," Gigi replied. "A lapdog, really."

"I'll hold on to him," Minni said. "Promise." She clutched Banjo to her side.

Grandmother Johnson's eyebrows pinched together tightly, but, amazingly, she didn't protest. Instead she grabbed a handful of spoons from the hutch in the corner, mumbling under her breath.

Everyone sat at the table, Grandmother Johnson at one end and Mama at the other. Keira and Daddy sat across from Minni and Gigi.

Minni couldn't believe it was possible for her to feel this way about something Grandmother Johnson had cooked, but she was pretty sure this banana pudding with vanilla wafers was the best thing she had ever tasted. She finished hers quickly, then held the dish under the table so Banjo could lick it clean. The ferns in the window seat caught her eye. They looked much healthier than when they'd arrived. Maybe buttermilk was good for something after all.

They talked and laughed about the pageant, Keira and Minni filling the others in on all the behind-the-scenes drama. Gigi and Grandmother Johnson wanted to know *every* detail. Grandmother Johnson even seemed to forget that Banjo was there. Minni was dying to tell them what a terrible person Alisha was—how she had tripped Keira and the mean things she'd said—but Keira never uttered a negative word about her, so Minni didn't, either.

Grandmother Johnson sighed. "I am just so *proud* of you!" She squeezed Keira's hand, which rested on the table.

Keira smiled. "Thank you." She slipped her hand out from under their grandmother's and put it in her lap.

Something bothered Minni about Grandmother Johnson's praise of Keira. And it wasn't jealousy. It was the fact that she hadn't seemed so proud before—before she won Miss Black Pearl Preteen of America.

"You *both* were something else," Daddy said, shaking his head.

"You sang beautifully, Minni," Mama said.

"Exquisite!" Gigi agreed. Her spoon clanged against the glass dish as she scraped every last bit of pudding from its sides. Grandmother Johnson frowned at Gigi's behavior.

Minni looked at Keira. Was this when Grandmother Johnson would finally ask about what had happened to her piano accompaniment?

Gigi's scoured dish thudded on the table. She wiped her mouth with her napkin. "Minerva, that was the best darned banana pudding that has ever passed my lips! If I cooked, I would ask for the recipe. But, as I say, why slave over a hot stove when there's a Country Kitchen Buffet just ten minutes away?"

Grandmother Johnson's prune lips twitched, then curved into a small smile. "I appreciate the compliment, Gretchen." Her eyebrows pulled together sharply as she turned to Minni.

Uh-oh, Minni thought, *here it comes.*

"I *told* you you could sing. But what on God's green earth was that horrible racket on my tape?"

Minni looked to Keira for help.

"How did those people botch up my recording? They only had it in their possession for a short time, for heaven's sake."

Keira's eyes popped open.

Minni choked back a laugh and accidentally sucked some saliva into her windpipe. Grandmother Johnson really didn't *know?* Minni coughed so much, she had to hand Banjo to Gigi and excuse herself from the table. She hid in the bathroom with a pink towel pressed against her face until all her coughing and laughter were gone.

She wiped her watering eyes with the towel. How could their grandmother not know the source of the tape's sound? Was she *that* blind to herself?

When Minni returned, Grandmother Johnson was going on about Alisha's grandma. "That Ernestine Russell thinks she's so high and mighty—she and all her progeny. She's always putting on airs, bragging about her talented and beautiful granddaughter. We shut her up good tonight, didn't we?" She smiled at Keira. "I have to say, child, you really surprised me with your superior performance—so articulate, vivacious and well put-together. Stunning, really. You came across *so* intelligently, Keira!"

What? Surprised? She really hadn't thought Keira was capable of it!

"That's because she *is* intelligent, Mother," Mama said, not sounding very pleased.

Keira's mouth scrunched to one side. She didn't seem too happy about Grandmother Johnson's "affirmations," either.

Minni's fingers throbbed. She looked down. She hadn't realized how hard she was squeezing her hands together.

Yes, Grandmother Johnson was proud of Keira now that she had made her look good in front of Ernestine Russell and others. But what about when she had a fit about her grades? Or when she thought Keira's hair wasn't good enough the way it was? Or when she told her she didn't need to be getting any darker? Had she been proud then?

The need to speak pressed against Minni's voice box. *Speak up, Minni. Now or never. Tell her she was wrong.*

She had sung before hundreds of strangers. And she had promised her sister that whatever happened, she was with her.

She swallowed. "Have you always been proud of Keira?" she asked quietly. She lifted her chin and raised her voice. "Or is it only now, because she won?"

The room fell silent.

Chapter Thirty-three

☀ ♡ ☾

"What?" Grandmother Johnson's stare bore down on her. "How could you—?"

Mama interrupted. "Perhaps you should consider your response before going further, Mother. Frankly, I'm interested to hear what you have to say." Mama turned to Minni. "Why do you ask, daughter?"

Keira gazed across the table. The light in her eyes encouraged Minni to continue.

"Well, because sometimes, well, sometimes it doesn't seem like you *are* proud of Keira"—she looked into their grandmother's eyes—"just the way she is."

Grandmother Johnson's face turned hard. "I—I don't know what you're talking about. Of course I'm proud of her. I'm proud of both of you."

Daddy's arm rested on the back of Keira's chair. Minni

wanted to run around the table into his safe embrace, but there was no hiding now. Daddy nodded just a little—enough to embolden her to press on.

"Then why do you think my hair is perfectly good, while Keira's needs to be straightened to be pretty?"

Mama cleared her throat.

"And why did you say Keira didn't need to be getting any darker? What's wrong with having dark skin?"

Mama drew in a sharp breath. "I swear, Mother—"

Daddy put a hand on Mama's arm. Keira's lips stretched into a satisfied, closed-mouth smile.

Grandmother Johnson sat straight, gripping her armrests. Everyone stared, waiting to hear what she had to say for herself. "There's nothing *wrong*. . . . It's just, there are certain realities . . ." Her eyes bounced around the table. "It's—it's hard to explain," she faltered.

"Try," Mama said, her voice more forceful than usual.

"They're too young."

"Not too young to have noticed."

Their grandmother looked defenseless, almost small, as if she had shrunk in her chair. She even looked a little scared. "Grandmother Johnson," Minni began, "your skin is just as dark—darker—"

Grandmother Johnson cut Minni a look that stopped her from saying more.

Gigi's chair creaked as she shifted in her seat.

Grandmother Johnson fidgeted with her cloth napkin, rubbing it between her fingers. It took a long time for her to speak. The silent tension was growing unbearable.

Grandmother Johnson's cheeks and shoulders sagged. She took a deep breath. "I will never forget the first time I came into Raleigh with my grandmother. I was seven—I had only been living with her a few weeks. Uncle Booker took ill and for one reason or another, no one else was available to watch me. . . ." She trailed off, as if trying to remember where everyone had been. "So Grandma brought me along with her to Old Man Buchanan's.

"When we transferred to the city bus in Raleigh, the driver was cordial and polite. He even addressed my grandmother as Missus Harris. It stood out to me because white people *never* called black people missus or mister. And then he saw me—hiding behind her dress folds, clinging to her skirt, and the expression on his face . . . well, it was clear as day."

Grandmother Johnson's eye twitched and her cheek trembled.

"All the times she had ridden his bus on her way to work, he had thought my grandmother was a white woman. The white people on the bus stared as we walked by, headed toward the back. They glared at my grandmother as if she were a murderer. And I realized—she had sat next to some of these people. They had likely rubbed shoulders. And now, because of me and my dark skin, she had been exposed. There'd be no more sitting in the front of the bus, or on the ground floor of the theater, or walking through front doors, or drinking from the fountains with the cold, clean water." Grandmother Johnson hadn't stopped fiddling with her napkin.

Keira watched their grandmother closely. Her eyes contained a mixture of curiosity and compassion.

Chills ran down Minni's arms. To have all those people staring at you like that. To have them think you were dirty, undeserving, less than.

Had the wrong in the world gotten inside Grandmother Johnson and caused her to think those people were right?

For the first time she could remember, Minni felt truly sorry for her grandmother. "Isn't it possible your grandmother *wanted* those people to know she was black?"

"Most certainly." Grandmother Johnson finally unclenched her napkin. She set it on the table and sat up straight. "As I told you before, she was a black woman all her life—and proud of it. But she admitted to me when I was older that she had periodically used her looks to enjoy some of the privileges whites enjoyed all the time. She liked feeling as if she were putting one over on people—subverting the system, so to speak, in her own private way. Her employer knew her race all along, of course." Grandmother Johnson gazed into her lap. "She assured me she didn't mind one bit relinquishing those occasional comforts, but still, it was hard to accept—the reality that your skin color could determine your material well-being and others' treatment of you."

She looked at Keira. "You know I don't believe in playing the victim, but people still make those judgments to this day. Life *is* harder for darker-skinned women. We need to work harder to prove them wrong."

Minni wanted to protest—things were totally different

287

from when Grandmother Johnson was a girl. America had elected a black president, even! Yet Keira had said herself that she felt her skin color had affected how their teachers perceived her intelligence. And of course there was the dress shop. Minni could never forget that.

Nor could she be silent any longer.

She'd come this far—she might as well go all the way. "Wouldn't it be better to try to change people's wrong views, instead of trying to change Keira?"

Grandmother Johnson shook her head. "These views have been in place for hundreds of years. They are not going to change in your lifetime. Keira is not too dark, but there is no reason for her to get any darker. That was all I meant by my comment." She looked at Keira again. "In all I've ever said or done, I was only looking out for your best interests."

"Well, I think brown skin is beautiful," Minni said. "No matter how dark." She almost added that she wished she were brown, too, but stopped herself, thinking of what Miss Laverna had said about loving one's skin, the body's largest organ.

"Me too," Daddy said.

"Me three," Gigi said.

"Make that four," Mama added.

Banjo barked as if agreeing with them all.

Grandmother Johnson pressed her lips together, then rose and began to clear the table. She walked into the kitchen.

Keira came over to Minni and held out her fist. Minni smiled and pressed her knuckles against her sister's. "Together," Minni whispered.

Gigi offered to help Grandmother Johnson in the kitchen while Mama went upstairs with Minni and Keira to pack their things and Daddy took Banjo for a walk.

Minni asked Mama if she could run next door to say goodbye to Miss Laverna. "Of course," Mama said, "but quickly. It's getting late."

Minni slipped out the front door and across the yard. She climbed Miss Laverna's front steps. Billie Holiday meowed in greeting. "Hi, kitty." Minni stooped to pet the cat. She glanced up at the big purple door. The nail was still there. Miss Laverna had hung a beautiful wreath of dried lavender.

Minni stood and knocked. A few moments later, Miss Laverna opened the door. She was wearing plain clothes this time—a lime-green T-shirt and tan pants, not the fancy lavender jacket from the pageant or an African-printed gown. "Well, hello. I've been thinking about you. You and your sister did a wonderful job tonight." She stepped back and beckoned Minni with her hand. "Come in, come in."

"I can't stay. I just came to say goodbye. And to thank you." She gazed into the woman's face. When it came to standing up for what was right—or having a beautiful heart—it didn't matter what color your skin was.

"Whatever for, child?"

"For showing me how to be myself."

Miss Laverna's good eye twinkled. "I've got something for you." She walked to the cabinet in the living room, took Sophie down and pulled another wisdom doll out of a drawer. She came back and held out Sophie. "Something to remember me by."

Minni took the doll in her hands and stroked the wrinkled brown face. "I'd never forget you, with or without the doll."

"Well, then, may she always remind you that things are not always what they appear." She smiled and held out the other doll. "For your grandmother. Tell her her name is Akilah—Arabic for 'wise, bright or smart.' Just like my neighbor."

Minni nodded. She started to turn, then stopped. "Miss Laverna?"

"Yes, child."

"I know now."

"Know what?"

"What fits my soul."

Miss Laverna waited.

"I'm a mixture. Of black and white, Mama and Daddy, and all the people who came before me. Even if Keira decides she feels differently about herself, we'll always be sisters."

Miss Laverna smiled a big smile. She wrapped her arms around Minni and they hugged. "That's right, baby. No matter what, you'll always be sisters."

"See you next time," Minni said.

"I'll see you, too."

Minni started to pull away, but Miss Laverna held her by the shoulders. She peered into her eyes. "You make sure to see *yourself*, Minerva-Goddess-of-Wisdom. See yourself rightly, you hear?"

"Yes, ma'am," Minni said, thinking The Name suddenly didn't sound so bad.

Chapter Thirty-four

When they were ready to leave the house, Minni held out the wisdom doll to Grandmother Johnson, who finally had changed into slacks and a blouse. "It's from Dr. Oliphant," she said.

The Eyebrow lifted.

"She makes them to sell at local shops . . . and gives them to friends."

Grandmother Johnson took the doll slowly.

"Her name is Akilah, which means 'wise, bright or smart.' Like you, she said."

Grandmother Johnson's lips remained tight, but her eyes widened with pleasure. She sniffed and pulled herself a little straighter. "Thank you." She walked to the fireplace and set the doll on the mantel, next to a vase full of pink roses.

Daddy said goodbye first. He gave Grandmother Johnson a peck on the cheek. Then Gigi came forward, holding

Banjo. She clutched Grandmother Johnson's arm. "Come back and visit us real soon, Minerva. I'll treat you to a massage at my favorite spa." She winked and moved in for a hug.

Banjo stretched his neck and planted a juicy kiss right on Grandmother Johnson's chin. *Lick!*

Grandmother Johnson yelled and jumped back as if she'd stepped on a tack. She grabbed the disinfectant by the door and sprayed it at the dog.

Minni giggled. Keira laughed. Mama worked hard to hide her smile.

"Whoops!" Gigi said. "Got ya! But, believe me, he doesn't kiss just anyone. By any chance, do you wear Marla Ray?"

Grandmother Johnson glared at the dog. She shook her head, breathing heavily.

"I'm going to send you a jar. You'll *love* it. Don't be a stranger now, you hear?" Gigi stepped outside.

"Goodbye, Mama." Mama hugged her mother. "You going to be all right?"

"I think I'll survive." Grandmother Johnson smoothed her hair with her hand.

Mama backed away, and Minni and Keira stepped up.

Their grandmother hugged each of them tightly—real hugs, not awkward ones with too much space between their bodies.

At the motel, Minni and Keira convinced their parents to let them get in the pool, since the night air was still warm and humid. They splashed around, cooling off after the day's events. Keira didn't wear her swim cap. She wanted her hair to curl up again.

Minni squatted underwater and Keira climbed on. A shoulder stand was much easier in a pool. They shot from the water and Keira did a backflip. Just like the days in Mama's womb. Mama and Gigi clapped. Daddy looked up from *Around the World in Eighty Days* and whistled.

Minni felt for the pendant around her neck to make sure it was still there. Mama had given her and Keira matching necklaces for doing her proud in the Miss Black Pearl Pre-teen National Achievement Program. The charm she'd given them was a Chinese character that meant "change." The character was made of the moon and sun—the moon on bottom and the sun on top.

Some sisters might fight to be the one on top, but Minni would always be happy to be the "under-stander." Minni knew this didn't make her less important, just different. She was the one whose shoulders provided support. The one Keira could count on to be there. And, when push came to shove, Minni knew, too, that she could always count on Keira to be there for her as well.

Minni clasped her sister's hands in the water. They intertwined their fingers and circled round and round. Sun and moon.

Pearls of different shades.

Two halves of the same heart.

Acknowledgments

As I type these words of gratitude, our second child could be born any day and our first is a two-year-old who has lived her entire life hearing about two girls named Minni and Keira. I am extremely aware that I never could have written this book without a lot of help.

Thank you to the people who so willingly gave their assistance: my editor, Michelle Poploff, for the seed of the idea that bloomed into this story, and for giving me space and time to let it grow; editorial assistant Rebecca Short, for insightful feedback and a perfect last line; my agent, Regina Brooks, for the pep talks along the way, and for helping me realize that this was a story not of sisters against each other but of sisters against the world; my readers, Fina Arnold (my ofttimes muse), Bethany Hegedus, John Weber, Holly Huckeba, Carla Saulter, J. J. Hansen and especially Anastasia Hansen, an intelligent and generous young lady with a bright future (and maybe some novels of her own ahead); and Courtenay Edelhart, for sharing her personal experience as a biracial twin. Thanks also to Trish Parcell, cover designer extraordinaire, and to the girls at Forest Ridge School in Bellevue, Washington, whose votes and feedback moved the book's title from a barely considered option to front-runner.

Finally, thank you to my parents, for their unflagging enthusiasm and support (Mom, I truly could not have done this without your babysitting help); to Aunt Kathy, for the dried-apple doll and for telling me there are many ways to be black; and to my husband, Matt, for knowing what I look like deep down, seeing the whole of me and loving so sacrificially. With you, I can truly be myself.

About the Author

SUNDEE T. FRAZIER is the author of *Brendan Buckley's Universe and Everything in It,* for which she received the Coretta Scott King/John Steptoe New Talent award. About her sister characters, she says, "They reflect twin sides of my own heart—the unsure and the bold—or self-doubt and self-acceptance."

Sundee lives with her husband and two daughters in Washington State, where, as a teen, she was crowned Miss Palouse Empire and first runner-up in the Washington State Junior Miss Program (*not* pageant). Learn more about her and her books at www.sundeefrazier.com.